The Changeling's Daughter

R. Chris Reeder

Black Rose Writing | Texas

The author grants the final approval for this literary material.

First printing

This is a work of fiction. Names, characters, businesses, places, events, and incidents are either the products of the author's imagination or used in a fictitious manner. Any resemblance to actual persons, living or dead, or actual events is purely coincidental.

ISBN: 978-1-68433-181-9
PUBLISHED BY BLACK ROSE WRITING
www.blackrosewriting.com

Printed in the United States of America
Suggested Retail Price (SRP) $20.95

The Changeling's Daughter is printed in Calibri

Poem in Chapter Six is from "A Midsummer Night's Dream" by William Shakespeare.
Lyrics in Chapter Twelve are from "The Stolen Child" by William Butler Yeats.
Lyrics in Chapter Twenty-Four are from "Down By The Water" by Polly Jean Harvey. Permission sought from Kobalt Music Group.
Author photo by Jen Doser

For Lisa, who read it first

The Changeling's Daughter

No, I've made up my mind about it:
if I'm Mabel, I'll stay down here!
It'll be no use their putting their heads down and saying
'Come up again, dear!'
I shall only look up and say 'Who am I, then?
Tell me that first, and then,
if I like being that person, I'll come up:
if not, I'll stay down here till I'm somebody else.'

—*Lewis Carroll, Alice's Adventures in Wonderland*

Prologue

The strange little man came to the door again today. He stood there at the threshold, his rumpled little hat on his rumpled little head, with his wizened face and his beady eyes and his tweed vest buttoned tight over his fat little belly.

Brynn watched from the top of the staircase and refused to move, no matter how many times her mother tried to shoo her back to her room. She watched the strange little man pull a crisp manila envelope out of his briefcase. She saw her father take the envelope, open it, and lift out the black-and-white pictures that nestled within. She couldn't see what was on the pictures, but whatever it was, her father didn't like it. He grimaced and shook his head.

"Please," he said, "I told you. I don't want to do this anymore. Can't you find someone else?"

The man at the door just shook his head, grinned, and tapped a long, knobby finger on the outside of the envelope.

"You can't run from who you are," he wheezed. "Good neighbors we are, good neighbors we were, and good neighbors we shall always be."

Then Brynn blinked, and somehow the stranger was gone. Her father closed the door and retreated to his office. He didn't come out again for the rest of the night.

"Who is that man?" she asked her mother, who stood with hands clutched protectively over her swollen belly. "And why does he always call us his good neighbors? He doesn't live nearby, does he?"

"No," her mother answered, "nowhere nearby. And who

he is doesn't matter. Now come downstairs and get ready for bed."

The first time Brynn saw the strange little man, he came to their old house, out in California, where the sun was bright, and it never snowed, and the nearest neighbor was five miles away. When her father opened the door that night and found the man standing there, she saw him crumble inside. He stood there for minutes, silently, while the man at the door did nothing but stare at him. When her father finally invited him in, they retreated to the kitchen for what seemed like hours. After they emerged, the strange little man bid them good day with a twinkle in his eye, and her father said that they were moving.

"But why was he here again?" Brynn asked. "Papa said he wasn't coming back."

"Your father hoped he wouldn't. So did I. Apparently, our luck ran out."

The second time she saw the strange little man, he came here, to their new house, and afterwards, her father packed a bag and was gone for a month. They hadn't seen the strange little man after that for almost a year. They hadn't seen him again until now.

"What does he want Papa to do? Will Papa have to leave like he did last time?"

"Never you mind. Papa will be fine. I'm sure it's just...I am sure it's just another job. There's nothing to worry about."

"But what if—"

"No more. I told you. There's nothing to worry about."

One thing Brynn knew about her mother: she was a terrible liar.

"Now come on, both of you. It's time for bed."

Once teeth were brushed, and clothes were changed, and her brother Conn was settled, and Brynn was snuggled deep in the blankets, her mother waddled in, on feet she said were already intolerably sore after five months of pregnancy. She brought in a bowl of thick, tarnished metal and set it down on Brynn's nightstand.

"Do we have to tonight?" Brynn asked.

"Of course we do. I don't want the goblins to steal you away from me."

"Mama. Still with the goblins? I'm fourteen now."

"I know you are. Indulge your poor mother in her irrational, antiquated fears about goblins who will steal my darling girl away and leave a changeling in her place."

"Oh, Mama, come on—"

"I love you," the older woman said, effortlessly ignoring her daughter. "No changeling children for me. I want this Brynn, and no other Brynn at all. You don't have to believe. I believe enough for both of us, I promise. Here we go. Are you ready?"

Brynn rolled her eyes and nodded. Her mother lifted a small brown egg from the pocket of her robe and cracked it into the metal bowl, then set the fragments of the shell carefully atop the liquid within. She picked up a long, stiff ribbon that had once been white, but was now frayed at the edges and yellowed with age. An unbroken string of writing, in characters that Brynn had never been able to decipher, ran the entire length on both sides. Her mother wound the ribbon around Brynn's wrist three times and tied a delicate, looping knot to hold it in place. Then she placed her hand on Brynn's chest, just over her heart, while she chanted these words:

> *Egg and Iron encircle this heart,*
> *Fire and Clay crumble apart,*
> *We need no gold,*
> *We need no luck,*
> *There is no child here, nothing but dust.*

"There we go. All done. Good night, Brynn."

"Good night, Mama. I love you."

Her mother kissed her on the forehead, flipped the light off, and closed the door. It was the same thing her parents had done every night, for as long as Brynn could remember. Only that night was different. That was the first night she disappeared.

Chapter One

It was 3 a.m. in Jeffersonville, Indiana, and Brynn McAwber couldn't see her hands. She was also in the yard for some reason and couldn't remember why. But the strangest thing was her hands. She held them up in front of her face, and nothing was there but the full moon, shining in the sky.

She clasped her hands over her eyes, but she could still see the moon. She could feel her palms pressing against her cheeks, could feel the tears running down her wrists, but there were the stars.

She felt groggy and dizzy, and her mouth tasted like cotton and a little bit like metal. Something tickled the back of her brain. There was somewhere she was supposed to go. The tickle in her brain told her so. There was something she needed to do. She looked around. The world began to move. She didn't know where she was supposed to be going, but her feet apparently did.

She ran down the sidewalk. She could hear her bare feet slapping against the concrete, but she didn't have the courage to look down and see if they had disappeared as well. She ran one block, as if she was in a dream, running beneath streetlights casting their pearly glow on the misty world beneath. Her feet told her to turn left, and she did. She ran down a narrow street, and then her feet took her into an alley between two brick buildings.

A figure lurched out of the shadows, dark and hunched. There was something long and narrow in its hand, something which glinted in the moonlight. Brynn insisted that her feet come to a halt and they did. As the shadows cleared, she saw a disheveled man in a grungy overcoat, who readjusted his grip on the knife he held shakily in his hand. She screamed, and the man in front of her snapped his head around, but his eyes were wild and they saw nothing. His eyes were looking past her, beyond her and into the night, as if she wasn't even there.

She couldn't remember why she was running anymore. The tickle in her brain was gone. She couldn't remember where she had been going. She did, however, remember that she wasn't supposed to be out alone at night. She remembered that she needed to stay away from grungy, knife-wielding figures in alleys.

She started to run again, back down the alley, back down the street, the concrete cold and hard underneath her. Her feet hurt, and she realized they were ice-cold. She wondered how long she had been outside, standing in the yard, before she came to her senses. She was back to their street, could see their house just down the block. She ran across the yard, felt the dew on the grass, felt the blades slice wetly across her soles. She threw open the door and staggered inside and collapsed on the carpet in the living room. Her body was shaking, her breath came in shallow gasps, and there was cold sweat covering every inch of her.

Her hands were grasping at the carpet as she tried to

stifle the panic, and it was then that she realized she could see them. Her hands, there they were, right in front of her, and then there was another pair of hands, and they were her father's, and they were pulling her to her feet.

"Brynn," he gasped in a voice choked with fear. "Brynn, what happened? Where were you?"

"Something was wrong, Papa. I was out in the yard, I don't know why, and I couldn't...I couldn't see my hands. Why couldn't I see my hands?"

She could feel her father's hands picking her up, carrying her down the hall, up the stairs, and placing her back in her bed.

"Hush," her father said. "Hush. You were just dreaming. That's all it was. Time to go back to bed now. You mustn't leave the house at night. You know that. Never leave the house at night, especially during a full moon. Never during a full moon. Back to bed."

He held her close against his chest, like he had when she was a child.

"I swear to you. It was nothing but a dream."

Chapter Two

"I had a weird night last night," Brynn said to Makayla as they were walking home from school the next day. Makayla was her best friend, practically her only friend since they'd moved to Jeffersonville.

"Yeah?"

"I don't know. I think I was sleepwalking or something."

"Oh, man, my Ma does that sometimes. Creeps me out."

They walked their usual route, past the Asian market, past the vacant lot, past the dingy seafood restaurant with its dingy, foam rubber fish mascot standing out front, which they assumed was worn by an exceptionally sad man who could barely muster the enthusiasm to wave his grubby sign.

They paused, as they often did, to peer in the windows of the appliance store on the corner. The windows were grimy. The lights were out. The handwritten sign on the door shouted 'CLOSED' in faded Sharpie, as it always did. The stoves in the window (proudly proclaiming 'NEW MODELS!') looked as if they had arrived decades ago. The carpet inside was worn bare, and the wood paneling on the walls was cracked and dark. No one was inside, and neither of them had ever seen anyone inside. The reflections of the two girls on the plate glass windows were the only movements to be found.

"This place is so weird," Brynn drawled.

"I know. I mean, have you ever seen it open?"

Brynn shook her head.

"It's just this time capsule of all the terrible life choices our grandparents made," Makayla said. "Wood paneling, shag carpeting, and obsolete technology. I mean, I think that's a dot matrix printer, and that might even be a fax machine over there."

"Like something out of a museum."

"Yeah."

They stared again in silence.

"How do you think they keep this place?" Brynn wondered. "I mean, they've got to pay rent on it or taxes or something."

"Maybe it's a front."

"What, like money laundering? Wouldn't they need to bring in money to launder? I think to do that, you'd at least have to open the doors every once in a while."

"I don't know," Makayla shrugged, "maybe it's some kind of secret headquarters for a gang."

"Or the Mafia."

"Or the CIA."

"Or aliens."

Makayla shook her head in mock disgust.

"Man," she said, "you'd think any of those people could find somewhere better than Jeff to hang out in."

"Maybe that's why it's always empty. They set up a secret base and then they died of boredom. There are alien bodies rotting in the basement."

"There is literally no other rational explanation."

As they left the abandoned appliance store behind, Brynn saw a woman standing on the opposite corner. She was motionless, her blond hair hanging in a thick braid down her back, all the way to her waist. Her eyes were hidden behind mirrored aviator sunglasses, but her head turned slightly as the two girls walked by, and Brynn felt icicles on her neck. She increased her pace and gave a quick look back. The woman had something strapped to her back, something long and leather, with a metal crosspiece at the top.

"Did you see that?" Brynn hissed.

"What?"

"That woman back there, on the corner. She was staring at me."

"She had sunglasses on. You couldn't even see her eyes."

"But you saw her, right?"

"Yeah. Blond hair, leather boots?"

"Yeah. Did she...was she carrying a...a sword on her back?"

Makayla arched her eyebrows.

"You think that blond lady back there with the sunglasses had a sword?"

Brynn just pursed her lips and shrugged.

"Yeah," Makayla said, "I'm really not sure you got enough sleep last night. I think you're seeing things." She looked behind them as they walked. "Well, whatever was going on with that lady, you don't need to worry about her anymore. She disappeared."

"Yeah, that's kind of what happened to me last night, too."

Makayla cocked her head and stared at her friend.

"What's wrong with you?"

"I don't know." Brynn paused and then whispered, "Maybe I'm a changeling."

"That's a weird thing to say."

"Well—"

"And it's not the first time you've said it."

Brynn just looked away, past the other girl, back to the corner where the woman had been standing.

"Maybe you could stop saying it," Makayla suggested.

"Yeah. Maybe."

Chapter Three

Brynn disappeared again three days later. This time, though, she could tell it wasn't just her hands. Her feet were gone, and her legs too. She found this out when she reached down to steady herself, which she did because she was standing on the roof of their house.

She clung to the shingles as best she could, confused to find herself there, worried she would fall, unsure how to navigate the steep pitch when she couldn't see her hands or her feet in the black of the night, and then she heard the voices. It was her parents, and they were talking, and the subject of the conversation was her.

"It wasn't supposed to happen like this," her mother said, her voice shaking.

"But it did," her father responded.

"I'm worried about her."

"Of course you are. I am too. But she...she'll be fine."

"You saw what happened," her mother insisted.

"I...we don't know for sure what happened."

"Gaf!"

"We don't," her father said.

"We have to tell her."

"It's not time yet."

"When, then?"

"I don't know. Soon."

"What if something happens?" her mother asked, suddenly and curiously calm. "What if she...what if she does something? Gaf, we have to consider...I mean, what about the baby?"

A raven let loose a dark chortle in the night. Brynn's parents broke off their conversation and the window was thrown wide. Brynn sat perfectly still, not daring even to breathe. Although she couldn't see it, she could hear the long ribbon, still tied to her wrist, rustling in the wind, the only sound in the silent sky.

When the window was finally closed and locked up tight again, Brynn clambered across the roof, to the balcony on the far side, and let herself into the house, thankful to see that she was now, once again, fully visible. She slunk back to her room, back to her bed, and tried to sleep, but she couldn't shake the feeling that something was wrong, desperately wrong.

She stared at her hands, and there they were, even though they hadn't been, just minutes before. This couldn't be real, she thought. People didn't just disappear and wake up on rooftops. Invisibility wasn't a thing that just happened to a person. But then again, she realized, maybe she wasn't a person. Maybe her mother was right. Maybe children really did get stolen away and replaced by changelings.

Brynn repeated the rhyme over and over to herself, hoping that, whatever was happening, she could stop it somehow, she could make it go away.

Egg and Iron encircle this heart,

Fire and Clay crumble apart,
We need no gold,
We need no luck,
There is no child here, nothing but dust.
Nothing but dust.
Nothing but dust.
Nothing but dust.

That would do it, she thought. That had to do it. If she just believed in it, like her mother did, the rhyme would keep her safe, keep her here at home, keep her from disappearing.

But three days after that, it happened again. This time, she was standing on a porch she'd never seen before, miles from home. She had no idea how she got there, and she had no idea why she would have come to this house, to this street, to this porch. She slipped away, luckily without attracting any attention, and managed to find her way back.

When she got home, her feet were practically numb, and her father's suitcase was in the front hall. The next morning, he was gone.

Chapter Four

"I've been feeling really weird lately," Brynn said on the walk home a few days later.

"Yeah, you've been acting really weird lately," Makayla responded.

"No, I'm serious.

"I know you are. So am I."

"I mean, it's like...I heard my parents talking the other night. They were kind of freaked out. About me. They've been worried my whole life that I was going to be stolen by goblins and replaced, and we have to do the stupid thing every night with the egg and the bowl and the rhyme, and until a couple weeks ago, I thought it was just my parents being totally nuts, with these weird old superstitions they got from their grandparents or something. But maybe it's not just some weird story they tell my brother and me to get us to do what they want. Maybe it's real. Maybe it already happened. Maybe it happened years ago. Maybe their real kid is long gone. Maybe I'm a changeling after all."

"Well, I mean, you don't actually look that much like your parents," Makayla said dryly. "Your mom has that super-dark skin, and you're practically translucent. Your dad's hair is wicked curly, right, and yours is like flat as a board. And speaking of that..." She gestured to Brynn's chest. "I mean, you...your mom..."

Brynn's eyes went wide.

"Oh my god, you're right," she said, her voice far shriller than she'd expected. "I never thought about that. I don't look anything like them!"

"Oh, come on!" Makayla rolled her eyes. "I was just messing with you. Of course you do. You're everything like them. You guys are freaking peas in a pod."

"No, you're absolutely right, how did I never see this before—"

"Dude. B. Stop. No way that's true. Worst case scenario is you're adopted and your parents just never told you. And even that is super unlikely. Your parents are awesome. Gavin and Louise. Gav and Lou. You guys do all kinds of stuff together. You go on and on about it. The level of your family bonding is nearly sickening. They are great. And you," she said, poking Brynn on the arm, "are just like them."

"I do believe it," Brynn said. "I think I'm a changeling. I think I was stolen away, and I never knew my real family. I have a...a fairy family or something out there. That has to be the truth. It would explain...it would explain a bunch of things."

She pursed her lips in stubborn defiance until Makayla sighed and nudged her toward home.

"Seriously, man, you need to get some sleep."

They walked on in silence. They passed the market, and the vacant lot, and the woman with the sword strapped to her back, standing at the corner, as she was almost every day now.

When they passed the dingy seafood restaurant, the sullen man in the stained, foam rubber fish costume wasn't even moving. He was just standing there, his head hung low, his sign dangling from his fingers and dragging on the ground. As Brynn glanced over at him, he turned his head slightly, and a felt eyelid snapped down over one of the costume's plastic eyeballs and flapped back up again. Brynn stopped in her tracks and cocked her head at him. He did it again.

"Oh my god." Brynn pulled at Makayla's arm. "Come on. We have to go."

"What? Why?"

"The fish guy just winked at me."

"As if this day could get any weirder."

Chapter Five

Her father came home the day after that, but he locked himself in his office again and wouldn't come out. Her mother was unusually quiet, pacing around, singing to the baby inside her, and Conn was in a sullen mood and wouldn't even tell her what he was reading.

Brynn stayed up late in her room, hiding under the covers with a flashlight. She held her hand out in front of her, concentrating, trying to make it disappear. If it was real, she thought, it had to happen when she was awake too. Otherwise, maybe she really was just dreaming it all.

She looked at her hand and thought about windows, about the air, about a clear, flowing brook, about saran wrap and milk bottles and her father's glasses and jellyfish and tap water. But nothing happened. Her hand just sat there, like a hand usually does.

She tried again and again, but still, nothing happened. Her hand was a hand and nothing but a hand.

"If it isn't real, I'm not a changeling," she muttered to herself. "If I don't disappear, I'm just a kid with a bad sleepwalking problem and I'll go and get some pills or some therapy or something and everything will go back to normal."

She put her hand on the book she had under the covers with her, her English homework.

"One last try."

She pressed her hand into the pages of the book and concentrated. She thought about fire and clay and iron and gold and tried to conjure up the hazy hollowness she felt when she woke up on the nights she disappeared. She concentrated on the nothingness that sang within her on those nights and all of a sudden, there it was. She could see through her hand to the book beneath. She could see the words, plain as day.

> *Up and down, up and down,*
> *I will lead them up and down:*
> *I am fear'd in field and town:*
> *Goblin, lead them up and down.*

"Oh, crap."

Chapter Six

Brynn was walking home with Makayla, and even though they followed the same route, and saw the same things they did every day, it was all beginning to feel unreal. There was the market, there was the vacant lot, there was the seafood restaurant, there was the sad man in the sad fish costume, there was the woman with the massive sword strapped to her back, and there was the empty appliance store. But none of it felt real. All of it felt to Brynn as if it might disappear at any moment, just like her.

"Did you see the news last night?" Makayla asked her as they pressed their faces to the glass at the appliance store, where nothing moved within but motes of dust floating in the sun.

"You know we don't have TV," Brynn answered.

"Yeah, but you didn't even hear about it? This kid went nuts."

"Wait, what?"

"Remember last year, when there was that one kid, that baby, who did all that crazy stuff?"

Brynn nodded.

"It happened again," Makayla continued. "This kid yesterday broke into a freaking bank. Bypassed the security systems, picked the locks, was just about to get into the vault when he tripped an alarm or something. So, he scoots out of there and steals this beer truck across the street. Led the cops on this high-speed chase, lost them out in the 'burbs, then MacGyvered the truck so it would crash itself into that old paint factory out on the edge of town. When the cops got there, they said he was standing in the middle of this mountain of empty beer bottles, dancing in the middle of these flames from the explosion. He finishes another six pack while the cops're driving up, and then when they advanced on him? They swear he breathed fire at them and ran to the river. The news crews caught just the very end of it, this kid sprinting away, jumping into the water, and disappearing. Someone else says they saw him climb out of the river, three miles away, and run into the woods. They're already blaming the whole thing on mass hallucination or a gas leak or both, but I don't know. The parents were freaked, like catatonic, pulling their hair out, rocking back and forth, freaked."

"What, was this like a teenager or something?"

"No. This kid was five."

"You said he was driving a truck," Brynn said slowly, after a long pause. "And drinking beer."

"Yeah. Crazy."

Brynn thought again, and then spoke very faintly.

"Maybe it's a changeling," she said. "Maybe the goblins came and stole that kid and put an evil kid in his place."

"Why are you always talking about that?" Makayla shouted, throwing her hands up. "It's weird! Kids don't get stolen and replaced by elves or whatever!"

"Kids don't drive beer trucks and break into banks."

Makayla only shook her head and stared in the window of the empty appliance store.

"You know, this stuff never used to happen before you moved to town."

Chapter Seven

That night, Brynn woke up as she was walking down the sidewalk by the coffee shop. There was no denying it now, she realized. It was happening, it was happening all the time, and there didn't seem to be anything she could do to stop it. This night was just like the other nights. She woke up in a strange place, and her body had disappeared.

This night was just like the others, only this time it was raining.

She looked up into the sky, and she could see the raindrops falling, slicing through the streetlight's glow. She held out her hands, and she could see the raindrops falling and then splashing in midair, a collision, an explosion, as they collided with an unseen impediment.

She cupped her hands and the rain collected between them, a pool of water from the sky in the middle of the air, a pool without a shore, a pearl without a shell, a soul without a body.

Chapter Eight

The next day, the day after Brynn disappeared in the rain, there was a new boy at school. Nobody saw him arrive, but he was sitting in the front row in first period English, and by lunchtime, he was the most popular kid in the building.

A week later, nobody even seemed to remember that he hadn't always been there. The students who circled in his orbit followed his every command, and even the teachers began deferring to him, allowing him to copy from the answer books, letting him skip whenever he wanted, halting class in the middle of a lecture if he felt like having a nap.

He was very pale, with jet black hair and the darkest eyes imaginable, and he said his name was Finian.

Brynn and Makayla did their best to steer clear of him and his cloud of underlings, but sometimes he could not be avoided.

"Buy me a Coke?" he said to them in the lunchroom one day, as he approached through the path cleared for him by the bruisers who constantly flanked him.

"Sure," Makayla said, trotting over to the bank of machines that lined the wall.

"Why did you do that?" Brynn hissed when her friend returned, as Finian sipped the soda and stared at them both with eyes blacker than the night sky. "You don't even know him."

"I don't know," Makayla shrugged. "He asked me to. I felt like it. He's really cute, though, isn't he?"

"No!"

"How about you?" Finian said to Brynn, after finishing the Coke and throwing the can over his shoulder, which was promptly caught by a waifish girl trailing in his wake. "Let me have your seat?"

"I don't think so," Brynn scoffed, trying to sound more confident than she felt.

"Huh," Finian said with an impish smile, "feisty."

He carefully looked her over, his eyes boring so deep and scanning every inch of her so thoroughly that when he was done, Brynn's flesh felt as if it had been peeled away.

"You know what," he said finally, "if you lost a few pounds, I would totally ask you out."

"Take off, jerk."

He ignored her, but threw a wicked smile at Makayla as he departed. She responded by sighing and fluttering her eyes, both of which were very un-Makayla-like things to do.

"You should do that," she said to Brynn, once Finian and his cohort had left the lunchroom.

"What?"

"Lose a few pounds."

"Are you serious?" Brynn practically shouted. "No! What is wrong with you?"

Brynn didn't speak to Makayla for the rest of the day, which wasn't much of a problem, as Makayla seemed to be lost in a haze of newfound admiration for the new boy. But finally, as they were walking home, she seemed to shake it off.

"Did I...at lunch today, did I tell you that you needed to lose weight?" Makayla asked with a grimace.

"Yeah. You suck."

"I didn't mean it. I'm sorry. I...I'm not sure why I said that." Makayla knit her brow. "The new kid...he makes me feel funny. Like he talked to me and my brain shorted out and everything went fuzzy. I don't know. You don't need to change anything. You're great just like you are. You know that, right? There's nothing wrong with you."

Brynn paused.

"You like me like I am?" she asked.

"Of course I do."

"Okay. What do you like about me?"

"Seriously?" Makayla groaned.

"Yeah. Seriously," Brynn insisted. "What do you like about me?"

"Come on."

"You're the one who said the crappy thing."

"Oh, god. Okay...umm...you're smart," Makayla said, rolling her eyes. "You're ballsy as hell. You don't care what anyone thinks about you, especially dudes like Finian. I don't know, man. I mean, we can walk home and even if we don't say anything, it doesn't matter. I mean, I always have something to say, but even when I don't, and I'm with you, it's okay. It's enough."

Brynn just stared at her shoes and refused to show her friend her smile.

"What else?" she asked.

"Seriously?" Makayla groaned dramatically. "Uhh...I like your hair."

Brynn raised her eyebrows.

"You like my hair?"

"You have great hair," Makayla intoned robotically, "I love your hair."

Brynn thought about it for a moment, and decided there was nothing to do but let it go.

"Well, I like *your* hair," she responded dryly to Makayla. "It's so...big."

"Shut up."

"No, seriously, you do have amazing hair. It's so...big."

"Shut up."

They walked on.

"Are we good?" Makayla asked.

"We're good."

Chapter Nine

Brynn was disappearing almost every night now. And the episodes were lasting longer. Even once she came to her senses and found her way back home, it wouldn't end. The disappearing wouldn't end. She'd lie awake, invisible in her bed, talking to herself, singing, chanting, fearful that if she fell asleep while her body was gone, the rest of her would disappear as well.

She wondered if there would come a day when she never came back at all. She wondered what she would be then, if a person without a body is even a person at all.

But even more than that, what haunted her was the possibility, the very real possibility, that none of this was actually happening. She could be dreaming, or hallucinating, just like the people who said they saw a five-year-old steal a beer truck and breathe fire. Or it was entirely possible that she was simply losing her grip on reality, and this thought she had that she was disappearing in the night was nothing more than an outward manifestation of an inward terror.

But if that was true, how could she tell? She turned the questions over and over in her mind. How could she figure out what was real and what was not? How do you tell someone that you woke up in the rain in the middle of the night and stared through your hand at the moon?

There were only two choices, she realized: either she was breaking down, or the rules of reality were, and neither choice seemed to offer a better solution than screaming into the night. And she knew that if she opened her mouth, if she breathed even a word of this to another soul, they would be left with the exact same choices.

She walked to the window of her room and placed her hand on the glass. There was no difference. Her hand was like the window, and the window was like her hand, and the moon shone through both.

Chapter Ten

"I have to show you something," Brynn said to Makayla while they walked. She'd tried to say the words a dozen times, and she'd failed a dozen times. But she couldn't wait any longer. She couldn't hold it all in anymore. It was too much for her. "There's something that's been going on, and I need to show you. And then maybe if you can see it, I can decide if it's real, or if it's not real, or if I'm losing it, or what."

"Whoa, okay, what do you mean you need to show me something?"

Brynn gulped and looked nervously at the ground. Makayla's eyes went wide.

"Do we need to be in private?" she said slowly.

"No," Brynn answered, her nerves so taut she could pluck out a melody on them. "Right here. Right now. I should have done this before."

"Just tell me what's going on."

"I just...no, I can't explain it," Brynn said, fighting the panic, fighting the tears. "It's doing or nothing, no more thinking about it. Is anyone watching?"

Makayla shook her head.

"No. No one's around."

"Okay," Brynn said. "Okay."

She pressed her hand against the plate glass window of the appliance store. She closed her eyes and concentrated. She thought of clay and fire and nothingness. She focused on the hollow haze that filled her on the nights she woke up far from home. She opened her eyes, and she saw dancing motes of dust and obsolete home furnishings where a hand should be. She looked to her friend, whose face was ashen, and whose lips were trembling.

"Holy crap," said Makayla. "What the hell is that?"

"I disappear."

"Yeah, I can see that. Just your hand?"

"No," Brynn said, her voice as ashen as her friend's face, "all of me. It happens to all of me. Usually at night."

Makayla stepped up to the window and peered closely at the spot where a hand should be. She placed her own over it, and felt the hand she could not see, warm and firm but there, definitely there, despite its apparent absence.

"Oh my god," she said, "you really are a changeling."

"Do you think so?"

"I don't know! I don't even know what a changeling is, but I know it's something you're always going on about, and they're involved in mystical crap or something, so when you come up to me and make your freaking hand freaking disappear, I'm thinking, sure, what the hell, changeling."

The two girls slumped down together, their backs against the cold glass which harbored the world out of time that lingered on the other side.

"That's really weird," Makayla said, after a long, morose silence. "I don't know what else to say. It's really weird and there's a ton of weird stuff going on. That kid who stole the beer truck, and stupid, hot Finian showing up at school and now practically running the place, and a woman with a sword wandering around. And now this thing with you."

"Plus, that fish guy winked at me."

"Yeah. That too, I guess."

"I'm sorry," Brynn offered sincerely. "Maybe I shouldn't have shown you. I just...I didn't know what else to do."

Makayla shook her head.

"Nothing to be sorry about."

"Are you okay?"

"I don't know," Makayla answered with a shrug. "I really don't know. I'm kind of scared."

"Me too. And not just kind of."

"Maybe we should ask someone about it."

"Really?" Brynn said flatly. "We should ask someone about the fact that I was maybe stolen away from my fairy family when I was a baby and now I have superpowers? Like who do we ask, maybe a police officer? The President? The aliens who live in the basement here?"

"Yeah, I started saying it and it already sounded dumb."

They sat again in silence, not looking at each other. They stared out at the dingy streets, at the cracked curb, at the buildings of dull brick, at the rain which had just started to fall. Brynn leaned her head over and rested it on the shoulder of her only friend, who did not object, despite Brynn's fears that she would.

"What does it mean?" Makayla asked her.

"I don't know."

"Who would know?"

"I don't know," Brynn said quietly. "Where do you find the answer to a question you don't even know how to ask?"

Chapter Eleven

The strange little man showed up again that night. This time, Brynn's mother ushered both children immediately off to bed while her father talked to the man in the kitchen. As soon as the egg was cracked and the ribbon was tied and the verse was chanted and her mother had turned out the lights, Brynn crept over to the door. She could hear the voices still, very faintly, but soon she heard a chair scrape across the floor, and then she heard footsteps in the hall downstairs. She ran over to the window. A spray of light streamed through the front door. The strange little man was leaving.

Her parents had never told her just who he was, despite her repeated entreaties, but the last time he showed up was the first night she disappeared. Maybe he had answers, she thought. Or if he didn't have answers, maybe he could lead her to them. She was a mystery now, and he was a mystery too, and maybe the mysteries were unrelated, but she couldn't stand not knowing anything.

She concentrated. She thought about fire and she thought about clay. She closed her eyes and focused on nothing. She opened her eyes and looked in the mirror and the mirror was empty. She gave an inward cheer of relief at this outward victory. Her body immediately flickered back into visibility as her concentration faltered. She took a deep breath and closed her eyes again. She focused in on the nothingness and the hazy hollowness of waking up in the rain and she was gone.

She eased her window open and clambered out. The strange little man was walking down their driveway. She pulled herself over the edge of the eaves and dropped to the ground. The strange little man didn't seem to notice.

She followed him for one block and then another. His gait was slow, and his path seemingly aimless. He muttered to himself as he walked and then, after a few blocks, as Brynn listened more closely, she realized that he was singing under his breath, in a kind of warbling wheeze.

> *Come away, O human child!*
> *To the waters and the wild,*
> *With a fairy, hand in hand,*
> *For the world's more full of weeping*
> *than you can understand.*
>
>> *Where the wandering water gushes,*
>> *From the hills above Glen-Car,*
>> *In pools among the rushes,*
>> *That scarce could bathe a star,*
>
> *We seek for slumbering trout,*
> *And whispering in their ears,*
> *Give them unquiet dreams;*
> *Leaning softly out,*
> *From ferns that drop their tears,*
> *Over the young streams.*
>
>> *Come away, O human child!*
>> *To the waters and the wild,*

With a fairy, hand in hand,
For the world's more full of weeping
than you can understand.

She followed the little man, as he muttered and as he sang, as he wandered between houses and through yards, across parking lots and into alleys, until she realized that he was following a winding path back into town, back toward her school. And just as she realized that, she thought of the woman with the sword who often stood on the exact corner they were about to pass. And just as Brynn thought of the woman, she saw her. There she was, wearing the same sunglasses, with the same thick braid, with the same sword strapped to her back. Brynn's concentration faltered, she let out a gasp, and she flickered back into view.

The woman with the sword ripped her sunglasses off, and it was the first time that Brynn had ever seen her eyes, which were blue as ice and just as cold. The eyes bored into Brynn's soul as a voice called to her.

"I do command thee to halt!" the woman cried, in a voice that was velvet wrapped in steel. "Gwyll! I have thee at the last!"

The strange little man looked back over his shoulder for the briefest of moments, and then Brynn heard a loud pop, and suddenly he was gone.

The woman, however, was not gone. She unzipped her jacket, and beneath it, Brynn saw a coat of burnished iron rings. From her back she drew the sword, which she now held in front of her as she walked slowly across the street, the moonlight cascading over her, seeming almost to follow her as she moved.

"There thou art," the woman cried, "yet another of the loathsome Tylwyth Teg, mine avowed enemies. Yet another to quench the never-slaked blood-thirst of my blade. Long have I waited. But now, I do see thee. No more evasions. No more skullduggery. I see thee."

"What did you call me?" Brynn asked, her voice shaking.

"Tylwyth Teg," the woman spat, as if the words were poison in her mouth. "Gwyllion. Bendith y Mamau. The fair folk. The underground people. The good neighbors. I do know all your names. And not a one of them will save thee now. I have slain untold hordes of thy kith and kin. Their wretched souls have fallen from my hands like sand, but still I rest not."

Brynn tried to concentrate, tried to think, tried to breathe. Almost reflexively, she began to whisper the chant her parents recited to her every night, but before the first word had even escaped her lips, she was stopped short.

"And do not think to use thy charms against me!" the woman commanded, in a voice of melodious hatred. "Thy hexes can do naught but provoke me. For I am here, I am my mother's daughter, and I am bent on thy destruction!"

"Who...who are you?"

"I am thy soul's antagonist, and that is all thou needst to know."

"I don't...why are you doing this?"

The woman spat again in disbelief.

"Dost thou really know not?" she asked incredulously. "Have thy misbegotten progenitors sent thee into the night as ignorant as this? The full moon is here, and thou, thou foul wretch, hast come into it, unarmed of both weaponry and knowledge."

Brynn tried to form a response to this, but found nothing within herself but confusion, fear and a burgeoning sense of nausea.

"Very well," the woman continued, "I shall grant thee the boon of my name before I send thee screaming into the netherworld. The arm that shall take thy life from thee belongs to Gwenllian ferch Gruffydd, daughter of Angharad, princess and battle-maiden, vengeance and steel."

The woman paused again, as if she expected Brynn to say something, but all that escaped Brynn's mouth was a confused whine.

"But now, wretch, the time for words hath ended," the woman cried, ignoring Brynn's inability to contribute to the repartee. "The time hath come for thou to return from whence thou comest. The deepest pits, the blackest night, they wait for thee. And I mean to hasten thy reunion!"

She assumed a fighting stance, her blade held lightly in her hands. Brynn saw a dragon's head carved upon the pommel of the sword. The crosspieces were its wings, and its long, sinewy body was engraved upon the blade. The sword looked heavy, and it looked sharp.

"Oh my god," Brynn said, coming to a realization, "that's actually a real sword, isn't it?"

The woman squinted her eyes and paused.

"Mayhaps thou seekst to beguile me with a feigned dimness," she said unsurely, "but thy ruse shall not succeed. Have at thee, fiend!"

The point of the sword sang through the air, directly in a path to engage Brynn's heart, and she barely managed to throw herself to the ground to avoid it. The woman recovered gracefully, and held the blade over her head, preparing for a downward thrust. Brynn somehow managed to avoid this as well and somehow managed to scramble to her feet.

"Thou art quick," the woman said, "like all thy kind. But thy deviltry shall not save thee, netherspawn! I shall take thy quickness from thee, and with it, thy life. Face me. There is no escape. 'Tis time to die!"

The woman stood, her eyes sparkling, her golden hair shimmering in the moonlight, her chest heaving with the thrill of the fight. She waited for Brynn to engage. Brynn did not. Instead, she turned on her heel and ran.

"Coward!" the woman bellowed. "Stand and face me!"

Brynn ignored this clearly insane request. She ran down the street, begging her feet to move faster than they had ever moved before. She looked back. The woman was right behind her.

Brynn ran past the seafood restaurant. She ran past the vacant lot. The woman was still only seconds behind her, shouting all the while. Brynn wondered why no one was hearing this. There was a woman in armor, carrying a sword, chasing a teenager down the street. Where were the random passersby with their cellphones when you needed them?

She was approaching the empty appliance store. She glanced over her shoulder. The tip of the sword seemed to be mere inches from her ear. She knew she needed to do something other than simply try to outrun this woman, who almost certainly could run faster and longer.

She passed the corner of the building, and cut into the alley behind the store, the woman just on her heels. She turned sharply in the parking lot beyond, and then again at the front of the appliance store, and then into the alley.

"Running in circles will not preserve thy life!" the woman shouted, following closely behind. "'Tis a confusing tactic, to be sure, but it shall *not* save thee!"

Brynn hadn't realized that she was simply running a circle around the store, but of course, yes, that's what she was doing. However, as she had no other ideas, she kept doing it. She seemed to be pulling incrementally away, but even encumbered as the armored woman was, it was clear that, in the long run, Brynn had no chance of outrunning her. There was only one hope. She needed to disappear.

She tried to calm herself, tried to focus. She thought about the rain and the fire and the clay and almost immediately she began to feel it, the transparency, as it diffused through her body. She cut around the corner into the alley again, but this time she pulled herself flat against the wall and focused on nothing. Either this would work, she thought, or she was about to die.

The armored woman careened around the corner and skidded to a stop. She looked up and down the alley and into the sky above it. She knelt on the ground, scanning the length of the alley, and threw open the lid of a nearby dumpster. Brynn focused on nothing.

"You Tylwyth Teg have your tricks, do you not?" the woman hissed. "Tricks will not save thee forever, little fiend."

The woman scrutinized the alley once again but clearly could see nothing. She sniffed around for a bit, as if she could locate her prey by smell alone, but Brynn thought it was just for show.

"Thou dost nothing but delay the inevitable!" the woman called impatiently. "If it be not now, thy death will come, and it shall be at my hand, and it shall be soon. Should we not just have it done with this night? It would be a truer death for you. A mote of honor at the end of an otherwise execrable existence!"

The woman stood and listened, her long, golden braid wafting in a gentle breeze that had somehow arisen out of nowhere. Sensing nothing, she walked to the end of the alley and turned the corner. Lost from Brynn's sight, the woman shouted, "Ffwrch!" Then there was a flash of light, and the night was still.

Brynn was almost certain the woman was gone, but just to be on the safe side, she counted to a hundred, and then just to be on the even safer side, she counted to a thousand, before she relaxed, allowed herself to flicker back to visibility and slink toward home.

Chapter Twelve

Brynn's mother and father were awake in the living room, sitting on the couch and waiting for her. She didn't try to sneak back in this time, didn't try to hide the mess she obviously was. She walked right up and planted her feet to say what she now knew she needed to say.

"You should sit down," she said to them, still trying to compose herself. She took a deep breath. "You already are sitting down, which I knew," she continued, "but I'm just a little nervous. Great. I have something to say. Something important to say. And please, just hear me out. There have been some strange things going on, and I've thought a lot about it, and I really think there is only one explanation. Okay, here goes. I have come to the conclusion that I...your daughter, standing right here...I am a changeling."

Her parents both nodded, still sitting calmly on the couch.

"Okay," her father responded sagely.

Brynn paused.

"I kind of expected a bigger reaction than that," she said.

"Oh, sweetie, why would you think that?" her mother asked. "Of course you're not a changeling."

"No, you're wrong," Brynn objected, "I am. You've been

warning me about it for so long, and I think...look, I think I was put with you, years ago, and your real daughter was stolen away and is somewhere out there, frightened and alone. And I've been so scared to talk to you about it because...because you've always been so weird about changelings. I thought it was so ridiculous that you would even bring it up because things like elves and fairies and changelings don't exist. I knew it. But I was wrong. Weird stuff has been happening to me. Really...weird...stuff. I can do things a person shouldn't be able to do." She held herself and looked down at the floor. "And I'm just...I'm just scared. I don't want to leave."

Her mother stood up and enfolded Brynn in her arms.

"Oh, my darling girl," she said, "we would never let you go. I promise. We have gone to such lengths to make sure we never lose you. Taken measures that would seem unimaginable to you."

Brynn pulled away, wiping her tears with the back of her sleeve.

"What do you mean?" she asked, frantic and confused. "What does any of that mean? Something is wrong with me! Please...please just tell me what's wrong with me."

"There's nothing wrong with you," her mother told her, leading her to the couch. "Nothing at all. It's just that...Gaf?"

"Well, Brynn," her father said, pushing his glasses up on his nose, "perhaps the easiest way to put it is that you, and me, and your mother, and your brother, we...well, we are not technically human."

"What?" Brynn squeaked. "Seriously? All of us? So, what...oh my god..." She could barely breathe. She wondered what it felt like to hyperventilate. "So...what, we're actually fairies or elves or something?"

"No," her mother assured her, "you're not a fairy child. You're a goblin, and you are ours."

There was a long silence as Brynn stared into her mother's eyes, trying to process the words that had just been said, in this very room, where so many normal things were said every single day.

"Did you just say 'goblin'?" Brynn asked suspiciously.

"Well, we would...our people prefer to call themselves 'coblyn' or 'coblynau,'" her father interjected.

"So, wait, I...I'm a goblin?"

"Well, as I said, technically, we're coblyns," her father answered affably.

"I don't want to be a goblin!"

"We're coblyns."

"Goblin."

"Coblyn."

"You're saying the same word I am!"

"Gaf...," her mother said gently.

"Okay, yes, we're goblins," her father relented with a sigh.

"Your father tends to get a bit particular when it comes to the nomenclature," her mother said. "Anyone of a non-technical mindset, yes, would call us goblins."

Brynn's mouth was dry, and her brain was fuzzy.

"So what does that mean?" she asked.

"We're goblins," her father said. "We bring bad luck. Grant wishes. Steal babies. Dance in a shoemaker's kitchen when the moon is full. That kind of stuff."

Brynn fell silent. She could feel her body trembling. This

conversation had quickly veered far from the territory she thought it would reside in, far from where any reasonable conversation should reasonably reside.

"Are you okay, sweetie?" her mother asked. "Do you understand what we're saying to you?"

Brynn tried to take some deep breaths.

"So, I'm a goblin," she said to her mother, trying to regain her composure, "and you are too."

"Well...and again, this is getting technical," her father said, "but your mother is a xana."

"Which are closely related to goblins," her mother explained. "Sort of a...sub-species in the goblin genus."

"But xanas are hotter," her father winked.

Brynn's mother wiggled her hips in the direction of her father, who smiled appreciatively.

"Mama! Papa!" Brynn shouted. "Gross!"

"Sorry," her mother apologized with a giggle.

"We should have told you sooner," her father said, back on track.

"Absolutely," her mother agreed.

"That first night, when you'd been outside in the full moon, when you disappeared, we panicked."

"Speaking of which," her mother asked, "has that still been going on?"

"Has what still been going on?" Brynn responded.

"The invisibility," her father said.

"You know about it?"

"Of course."

"You know I've been disappearing and waking up in strange places?"

"Well, the onset of the abilities is different for everyone," he said, "but yes, we knew."

"So...invisibility...that's just a thing goblins can do?"

"One of the things, yes."

"Yeah," Brynn nodded, her jaw clenched, "it's still going on."

"How often?"

"Almost every night now."

"Did it happen tonight?" her mother asked. "Is that where you were?"

"I...no. Yes and no," Brynn answered, lost in the midst of this new world that seemed to be opening up all around her. "Tonight, I made it happen. I made myself disappear and I tried to follow the strange little man. But it all went wrong. It...it was really scary. There was this woman...with a sword. She was trying to kill me, I think. She was screaming about destruction and full moons and vengeance."

"Well, I mean, you are technically evil," her father said, "so it's going to stand to reason that heroes will try to slay you now and again."

"Gaf!" her mother snapped, slapping her father's arm.

"Well, it's true! She has to be prepared. We knew there would be incidents once she started presenting."

"Honey," her mother said softly, "if you see a woman with a sword watching you, that's really something you should tell us. Especially if she tries to slay you."

"Do you know who it was?" her father asked.

"She said her name was Gwen or something," Brynn muttered, as she slouched against the couch, feeling incomprehensibly exhausted and unutterably befuddled.

"Gwenllian," her mother said with a sidelong glance.

"Gwenllian ferch Gruffydd," her father nodded, his brow furrowed.

"Who is she?" Brynn asked.

"She's a hero," her father answered. "From ancient times. From an ancient land."

"And she does not like us," her mother added. "Any of us."

"She's a hero," Brynn said, piecing it together, "and I'm not. We're evil. And heroes try to slay us."

"Yeah," her father shrugged, "it happens."

"I don't feel evil," Brynn said.

"Neither do I," her mother assured her. "Your father and I...we made a decision, long before you were born. Longer than you could probably imagine. But we decided to resist that part of our natures. We decided to resist it together. It's one of the reasons we were in California. One of the reasons we're even on this continent. We had to break away from the old world, from the old ways. And we've tried to raise you and your brother to follow in our footsteps."

"But it's a new road," her father added, "one that very few goblins have trod before us. There is a bit of...well...a bit of maleficence inside of us, is the best way to put it. You will probably feel it...at some point. It will pull at you. But you don't have to give in to it."

"This is a lot to take in," Brynn said weakly.

"I know, sweetie," her mother said, putting her arm around Brynn's shoulders. "You're doing great. Really. You are."

"So all the things I thought I knew about my family and kind of about reality are sort of not true."

"Not all. The important things are still true."

"How can you say that?" Brynn shouted, lurching to her feet. "I thought I was a person! I thought I was a good person! I thought I was going to go to college and backpack around Europe and get a job and maybe get married and raise some children someday. Human children! I mean, are your names even Gavin and Louise?"

"I know this is a lot," her mother said. "This is a lot for you to try to understand, and there will be so much for you to learn. Which you will. In time. How about this? My real name is Llwynog. In the Old Language, in Welsh, it means 'fox.'"

"And she is," her father said, wiggling his eyebrows.

"Papa. Seriously," Brynn said, "I asked you before. Stop it."

"This will all make sense in time," he said, "I promise. For now, the best thing you can do is get a good night's sleep. There will be more time for talking. More time to adjust. There's so much more inside you than you imagine. But for now, no more disappearing, no more vengeful heroes. For now, for tonight, it's time for you to sleep."

"Yeah," Brynn agreed, realizing just how tired she was, "I suppose it is."

"And I know this is terrible timing. But I have to leave in the morning. I'll be back soon. Another...task."

"From the strange little man?"

"Yes. From him."

"Does he have a name?"

"He does."

"Will you tell it to me?"

"I won't. The less you know about him, the better."

Chapter Thirteen

Brynn didn't disappear that night, or the next. She slept through the night, blissfully unaware (at least for a few hours) of what she had learned. But each morning when she awoke, she remembered.

She sat with a bowl of cereal, and could not ignore the fact that she had learned there was evil inside her, which was a very strange thing to learn. She tried to read her homework, but could not forget that everything she thought she knew about reality had suddenly changed. She lay in her bed, and even though she valiantly tried to avoid the thought, she now knew that her parents had been lying to her about some very basic facts about themselves, and about her, for her entire life.

But at least she slept. There was no more waking up on strange doorsteps, no more running through the rain toward unknown destinations, no more unannounced disappearances. Now that she knew about it, knew that it was something inherent in her, that it was a part of her, a part of her family, it seemed to lose its hold over her.

And now that she knew what it was, her command over it grew. It seemed the more she learned how to control the disappearance, the less it could control her. The more she tried, the easier it became. So, she practiced almost every waking hour. If nothing else, it kept the darkness at bay, held off the uncomfortable thoughts that threatened to send her shrieking into her pillow.

Within a few days, she could turn it on and off at will, fast or slow. She could pop out of existence instantaneously, or she could fade slowly to nothingness, as if she was drifting away with the wind. And this was helpful, because with everything she had learned, she needed time to think. It was easier to think when she wasn't at home, and when she wasn't at home, it was easier to fade away, to wander through the world unobstructed, to let the world ignore her just as she was ignoring it, to slip between the people on the street and let the crowds and the traffic pass her by as if she wasn't even there.

Because she didn't think she was. She wasn't part of this world anymore. She was just an observer, an outsider, an other. She wandered, barely seeing the world around her, and the world didn't see her at all. She walked for hours, trying to make sense of what she'd learned, trying to comprehend a life that had seemingly cracked in two, right in front of her.

She sat on the roof, nothing but a piece of the sky.

She walked to the park, sat on a swing and kicked her legs, just an echo of the wind.

She wandered into town, where she was a rustle in the grass, a whisper on the bridge, a memory under the trees, a breeze whistling through an alley, a susurration on the sidewalk.

She found you could learn a lot of things when nobody knew you were there.

Their mail carrier had a flask in her hip pouch and took a pull whenever she thought no one was looking.

The nice steakhouse on the corner threw away an exorbitant amount of food.

The man in the fish costume barely ever moved. Brynn didn't understand why the restaurant owners even paid him.

The man who ran the laundromat was so lonely that he cried whenever the room was empty, the dryers' cascade muffling his sobs.

The barista at the coffee shop, the one with the pierced nose, she was skimming off the top when the manager wasn't around.

The principal at her school picked his nose. He picked it a lot.

The homeless woman downtown used spare change she found on the street to feed expired meters.

The bus drivers for the 71 and the 82 really did not like each other.

The two women who ran the comic shop were even cuter with each other when they thought the store was empty.

When Brynn finally came home, she saw her father's suitcase in the hall, saw that he must have returned while she was out, but the fact barely registered. She wandered through the house, feeling as out of place here as she did everywhere else.

Her parents' door was cracked slightly. Her father was asleep. He looked unhappy. He twitched and moaned in his sleep, and his eyes were sunken.

Her mother sat on the back deck, her head in her hands, her coffee undrunk and long grown cold. When she finally rose, she went to the kitchen, and as she began to pull ingredients together, Brynn stood and watched her cook. When the food was finally in the oven, and her mother retreated to the living room, Brynn followed her. Her mother sat silently, doing nothing, just staring straight ahead, shaking her head and trembling slightly.

Brynn stood in the living room, watching her mother's silent agony, and faded back into existence, but even before she was visible, her mother's arms were already around her, were already drying her tears, which flowed freely, her soul's utterances, as visible as she willed them to be, until they were hers no more.

Chapter Fourteen

Makayla wasn't at school the next day, which was strange, because Makayla never missed a day of school. She was the healthiest person Brynn knew, and compulsively punctual to boot.

Brynn wandered through the school day in a haze, letting her feet carry her from class to class, and at the end of the day, letting them carry her home, alone for once, without the friend who always accompanied her. Luckily, the woman with the sword was nowhere to be seen, and hadn't been seen since their encounter during the full moon, the one saving grace in an otherwise moribund week.

She passed the market and the vacant lot and the sad man in the fish costume and the empty appliance store, her eyes downcast, only idly noticing the familiar landmarks, except she realized that something wasn't right. She backtracked, slowly sidling up the block she had just walked down. The appliance store wasn't empty. The lights were on. Fluorescent lights glowed on the ceiling, and multicolored strands of Christmas lights that Brynn had never noticed before were now illuminated, draped along the top of every wall, and around the borders of the signs in the windows. There was music playing, faintly, calypso music of all things.

The ever-present 'CLOSED' sign had been flipped over, and on the other side was an elegant 'OPEN' in a bright, ornate script.

One of the glass doors was propped open, and outside the store stood an old woman with silver hair, dressed in a simple, flowered dress of white and blue. She was cleaning the glass, very methodically, every inch of each pane, and singing along with the music as she worked.

She paused and pulled an ancient-looking watch from one of the pockets of her dress and checked the time. As Brynn stood there in bewilderment, the woman closed the watch, returned it to her pocket, then turned and waved to the girl. Brynn gave a very hesitant motion with her hand, which the woman seemed to take as a return of the proffered greeting.

"Beautiful day, isn't it?" the woman called.

"Okay," Brynn mumbled.

She started to say something else, but then stopped herself.

"See you later, dear," the woman said cheerily, returning to her cleaning.

"Okay," Brynn said again as she walked away, unsure how else to respond.

Makayla wasn't at school the next day either, and she wasn't answering her phone. This was a hell of a time, Brynn thought, for her best friend to abandon her.

Chapter Fifteen

Brynn didn't recognize the face in the mirror, even though she had seen it a million times before. There were eyes looking back at her, but she wasn't sure who they belonged to. Everything she knew about herself had changed, and only her body remained the same. Except she wasn't sure she felt welcome inside it anymore.

There was a girl in the mirror. She had long hair, copper-colored and straight, that hung limply around her shoulders. She had a nose that was slightly too pointy and eyes that were slightly too large and ears that were slightly too long. (Or at least that's how Brynn felt about them in her weaker moments.) The girl's body was tall and slender, with almost no curves at all. Her lips were thin and they trembled slightly. Her eyes were clouded and betrayed a fear held deep inside. Even if Brynn didn't recognize this girl, she recognized the fear.

She scowled at herself, trying to appear menacing, trying to conjure a face that would lurk in a dark cupboard, that would bring bad luck, that could lure a hero to her doom. She tried every variation she could think of: eyebrows up, eyebrows down, teeth bared, mouth clenched. It was hopeless. She didn't seem to be able to conjure anything other than 'vague annoyance with a tinge of confusion.'

Just as Brynn gave up on scowling, her mother opened the door of the bathroom and joined her. She didn't say anything, just waited with her daughter, as they looked at each other in the silvered glass. Somehow, Brynn had never noticed how they really were mirrored images of each other. Her mother's skin was so dark, while her own was so fair. Her mother's hair was pale and soft, while Brynn's was harsh and fiery. Her mother's body curved in ways her own body had not yet begun to, and perhaps never would. They were reflections of each other, inverse copies caught in a broken glass. Their hair was fire and ice. Their skins were day and night.

Brynn had barely talked to either of her parents since they'd told her. Since they'd told her what she really was, what they really were. A million questions raced through her mind, had been racing through her mind for days, but none of them seemed as if they would shine any further light on the chaos that reigned in the forefront of her thoughts.

Her mother smiled and took her hand and Brynn tried to smile back, but wasn't entirely successful. Brynn still couldn't bring herself to look her mother in the eye, and so they stood there, hand in hand, mirror images of mirrored images, doing nothing other than being together.

They stood there in silence, neither wishing to break the moment, neither knowing how to move the moment forward. Eventually, her mother began to release her hand, began to depart, but Brynn held on. She still stared straight ahead into the mirror, not able, not willing to make eye contact. But she wanted to talk, to ask her mother something, anything.

"Tell me about the names," Brynn said finally, "the real names."

"Our names?"

"Yeah," Brynn answered, her lips clenched and jaw thrust out defiantly, "our names. Who are we, really?"

Her mother nodded, clearly trying to tread carefully, not wanting to fracture this tenuous connection.

"Well, as I told you," she said, "my real name is Llwynog. It means 'fox.' And your father's is Gafr, which means 'goat.'"

"Goat? Seriously?"

"He didn't choose it," her mother answered, a slight smile at the corner of her lips, "but it is apt, considering his eating habits."

"I suppose."

"Your brother's name is Cwningen, which means 'hare.'"

"Okay. So then, Brynn isn't my real name."

"Well...part of it."

"What does that mean?"

"Your name is Branwen. It's an old name. It means 'white raven.'"

"So," Brynn said, trying to piece it together, "our names...our names mean things."

"For you and your brother, we wanted to give you names that would protect you," her mother said softly, "that would help you escape. If you ever needed to. As your father said, we have chosen a life that very few goblins have ever chosen before. We have gone to places heretofore unknown to our kind. There are...beings...of no small import...who disagree with this choice. You're a raven. Your brother is a hare.

Should danger ever arise, you could fly away, and he could burrow deep underground."

"Wait...you mean that figuratively, though, right?"

"No. No, I don't," her mother answered. "We have different abilities, as you've learned. Goblins are shapeshifters. It's how we've kept ourselves hidden from humans for so many centuries."

"We're shapeshifters?"

"Yes."

"So, is this what I actually look like?"

"Well, it's one of your aspects."

"One of my what?"

"Aspects," her mother said. "You probably have three. Most of us do. One of which is human-looking, or nearly so, what some would call the fair folk. You also have a goblin form, and then the aspect of your namesake, the aspect in the core of your soul, which in your case is a raven. Probably. As I said, there is variation from individual to individual and from race to race. As you look at yourself now, you see your fair folk aspect. Tall, pale, slender, copper hair. Beautiful. Now, since I come from the xana, instead of the coblyn like your father, my skin is dark, but my hair is pale. You take more after your father's people than you do mine. You'll be taller than I am, most likely, and will remain willowy and slim, as you are now."

"But we can change," Brynn said.

"We can."

"Into goblins."

"Yes. Well, into our goblin aspects. Here, as we are, in our fair folk forms, we are still goblins. But your other aspect is

63

what you would more likely think of as traditionally goblinesque."

"Do I even want to know what that looks like?"

"When the time is right, you will find it. It's within you. Just as the invisibility was."

Brynn stood silently for a long time, holding tightly to her mother's hand, still not able to meet her eyes.

"I can turn invisible," she said hesitantly, after much thought. "I can change shapes. Anything else? Any other surprises waiting inside me that I need to prepare myself for?"

"Just the big one." Her mother smiled. "We can grant wishes. Under very rare circumstances."

"You have got to be kidding me."

"I'm not."

"Wishes? What does that even mean?"

"You have the ability to grant someone their fondest desire. And only their fondest desire."

Brynn felt hollow inside, and she saw herself begin to disappear. When she spoke, her voice was barely a whisper.

"Could I wish to not be a goblin?"

"I'm sorry," her mother said with a wistful smile, "but you can't grant a wish to yourself. And even if you could, I would not want you to wish that. Because then you would not be my daughter, my brave and clever girl who carries her heart with her, a heart as big as the sky."

Brynn let herself waft back to visibility again.

"You should get some rest," her mother said.

Brynn nodded.

"But whenever you have any other questions, any

questions at all, I am here for you. All you have to do is ask, my precious, darling daughter."

Brynn nodded again.

"Goodnight," her mother said, as she squeezed her daughter's hand one last time and opened the door.

"We don't have to do the thing with the egg anymore?" Brynn asked in mild surprise.

"No. Now that your powers seem to be on their way to full manifestation, there should be no need."

"Wait," Brynn said, thinking back to the conversation with her father, "Papa told me that goblins steal babies. That we steal children. That it's one of the things we do. Which is fairly horrifying, and I'm trying not to think about that part too much."

"That's correct," her mother said. "Historically speaking, when children are taken and replaced with changelings, goblins are the ones tasked with that work."

"Okay, so there's still one thing I don't understand. If we're the ones who steal the children, why did I need protecting? Why did we have to do the thing with the egg and the bowl every single night?"

"When a goblin steals a human child," her mother said, "he replaces it with one of goblin-kind. The goblin family whose child was taken is honored above all others, and receives all the gold and luck they could ever want. Your father and I didn't want any of our kind to think that you or your brother were available for relocation into a human family. Had you not been protected, one of the harvesters might have thought you were ripe for the plucking."

"So, the chant was not to keep the goblins out. It was to

keep them in."

"In a nutshell, yes." Her mother smiled. "Good night, Brynn."

"Good night, Mama."

Her mother left, leaving Brynn alone with her reflection once more. She stared at the girl in the mirror that she barely knew, at the face that was, apparently, only one of many she owned. She let her thoughts sink deep within her. She could feel the hollowness inside, and knew that if she pulled at it, she would disappear. But it wasn't what she was looking for. She pushed her thoughts even deeper, further than she'd ever dared let her mind explore. There, just at the edges of her consciousness, she felt something, something sharp and gnarled and ancient. She closed her eyes and grasped at it with her thoughts. She found the sharpness and let it pierce her. She held on to the ancientness and allowed it to consume her. When she opened her eyes again, there was a new face staring back at her, one far, far different than she had expected.

Her skin was green, not bright, crayon green, but the green of an autumn lawn before the frost. She saw the long, whip-thin nose, the pointy ears, the spindly fingers. The eyes were small but bright. Her hair was as red as fire and burst from her head like light from the sun. Her feet were longer, her toes agile and strong as they gripped the edge of the bathroom rug. She felt a curious sensation behind her, and when she looked, yes, there was a tail back there, long and sinuous, with a barbed tip.

This was her, she knew. This ugly, little, wretched creature was her. But for some reason, Brynn wasn't upset about it. It was only one part of her, she understood that now. And the more she looked, the less ugly it seemed. If this was inside her, she thought, if this was part of her, it was only ugly if she allowed it to be. This was a goblin. This was her. And somehow, she felt as if she'd known it all along. She did.

She recognized the face in the mirror, even though she had never seen it before.

Chapter Sixteen

Makayla was back at school the next day. It was the first time Brynn had seen her since she'd shared the secret of her disappearances, since she'd convinced Makayla that she must be a changeling. She'd learned so much more since then, and Brynn wondered if she could share even a piece of it. But it turned out she didn't need to worry whether she could or not, because her best friend was barely speaking to her.

She greeted Makayla before school, but the other girl just stared at the floor, and couldn't even be bothered to look up from her phone as they made their way to their first classes.

They sat together at lunch and Brynn tried to make small talk. She asked Makayla about her weekend, asked her why she'd been gone from school, asked her if she'd seen anything interesting on TV lately, but Makayla gave little more than single-syllable answers, barely made eye contact, just focused on the food in front of her, and the kids at the other tables, and anything but Brynn.

"Do you want to tell me what's going on?" Brynn asked, fighting off the tears.

Makayla just stared at her, finished her slice of pizza, and then silently stood up and walked away, never looking back.

Brynn sat at the long table, all by herself now, and wasn't sure she had ever felt so alone. She'd only had one ally since her family moved to town. There had only been one person in the whole world she felt even remotely comfortable talking to about what was happening, one sliver of solace in this whole unbearable situation, and now, it appeared, she was losing even that.

She should never have told Makayla anything, she realized that now. She shouldn't have shared anything about being different in any way. Then, even if she wasn't being fully honest about who she was, at least she wouldn't be going through it alone. Maybe she could take it back, she thought. Maybe she could tell Makayla that the whole thing had been a joke, that the disappearance had been a trick, just a stupid trick. Maybe things could go back to normal then.

It was, of course, just at this moment, when Brynn was at her lowest, that Finian appeared, striding over to her table with his usual intolerable insouciance.

"Sitting all alone today?" he asked in a voice that wound around Brynn like a snake.

"Leave me alone, Finian," she said, refusing to give him even her anger. "I'm in no mood."

"Where's your girlfriend? I thought you two were always together."

"I don't know."

"Need some company?"

"From you? I absolutely do not."

"I can be quite charming," he said, flashing his teeth. "Or so I've been told. If you're feeling glum, I'm sure I've a cure for that."

Brynn just stared daggers at him.

"Maybe next time," he smirked.

"Unlikely."

He strode off, his followers skittering behind, and she was alone once more, alone in a sea of cacophonous youth. Brynn wandered through the rest of the day in a haze, the school seeming grey and formless around her. But at the end of the day, as sullen and silent as she was, Makayla was waiting at their usual spot. They walked home together, as they always did, but it all felt uncomfortable and ill-fitting, as if someone had replaced the well-tailored suit of their friendship with a scratchy wool sweater two sizes too small.

Brynn tried to tell Makayla that the whole thing about changelings and disappearing had been a joke, but the words fell apart in her mouth even as she said them. She tried to tell Makayla about the woman she'd seen at the empty appliance store, but Makayla wasn't even listening, and besides, the place was closed today, as dull and lifeless as it had always been.

Chapter Seventeen

The next few days brought more of the same. Makayla eventually gave up even the pretense of friendship. Brynn tried to start conversations, but Makayla always put her off with a dismissive wave or simply walked away. And then she wasn't around at all. She seemed to be spending time with Finian, although every time Brynn thought she saw the two of them together, she'd look back, and they'd be gone.

She saw the two of them in the hall, standing together in intimate conversation, Finian's fingers grazing the back of Makayla's hand, and then a throng of cheerleaders passed in front of them, and the sea of students carried Brynn along through the halls, with just a whisper of this seeming betrayal carried along in its wake.

Their walks home together remained, as silent and joyless as they were now. But then finally, after a few days of the continual cold shoulder, Makayla wasn't waiting at their usual spot after school, so Brynn walked home alone.

She sulked past the market, she kicked at some dirt clods in the vacant lot, and she stared icily at the man in the fish costume, silently daring him to wink at her, or do anything at all, but he waved his sign as haphazardly as usual, before letting it fall still, dragging its battered edge along the pavement beneath.

Brynn saw the Christmas lights first, out of the corner of her eye, as she was about to turn the corner for home, and then she heard the music. She trudged up to the door of the appliance store and peered inside. The lights were on. The festive 'OPEN' sign was once again displayed. And there was the old woman, standing behind the counter, her hips swaying slightly to the calypso beat.

Brynn pushed the door open and heard airy bells tinkling gaily above her as she walked in, announcing her arrival. The old woman checked the antique watch in her pocket and then clacked it closed.

"Welcome to Avalon Appliances, dear," she said. "How can I help you?"

"I don't know," Brynn said honestly, staring in wonderment at the outdated displays she had seen through the windows so many times before. "I've just...I've never been in here before."

"Not many have."

Brynn didn't respond. She walked by the ancient refrigerators and stoves and trash compactors, running her finger over their dustless surfaces, trying to lose herself in their outmoded finery.

"Is everything okay, dear?" the old woman asked her.

"No," Brynn answered assuredly, giving all her attention to a lime green dishwasher. "Maybe. There's just a lot going on, you know? And I simply do not know how to make sense of it all."

"Is a dishwasher going to help with that, do you think?"

Brynn grinned in spite of herself.

"I suppose not."

"How about a butterscotch, then?" the old woman asked, offering an ornate glass bowl full of cellophane-wrapped delicacies.

"Maybe."

Brynn walked to the counter and leaned her elbows on it as she unwrapped the butterscotch and popped it in her mouth.

"My best friend is...well, I don't know if she's my best friend anymore," Brynn admitted slowly.

"Losing a friend is never easy."

"I suppose not. But she's also sort of my only friend. And I...I told her some stuff about myself. Really private stuff. Kind of embarrassing stuff. And ever since then, she's been super weird. I think I ruined it all."

"You know, dear," the woman said confidentially, almost under her breath, "there might be a health teacher at your school who could talk to you about that sort of thing. Or maybe even your mother. Or an aunt?"

Brynn gave the barest hint of an eye roll.

"It's not sex stuff," she said.

"It's not? Well, that makes me feel better."

"But it's still...it was really personal. And it wasn't the sort of thing I could tell just anyone. And if I couldn't even tell my best friend about it...then that means I can't talk to anyone about it, and that sucks. Because there's some stuff that's big enough...big enough that you want to feel like there's just one person on your side, you know?"

"You don't want to talk to me about it, do you?" the old woman said, stiffening up.

"I don't."

"Well, I think that shows fine judgment."

"Yeah, maybe," Brynn agreed sullenly. "I'm sorry. I don't know why I'm telling you any of this. You've got other things to deal with, I'm sure."

"You needn't worry about that. I always have plenty of time for what's important."

"I should go," Brynn said. "Thanks for the candy."

"Travel safe, dear."

The old woman checked the watch in her pocket again, and Brynn opened the glass door, tracing the roughly-Sharpied 'CLOSED' on the inside with her finger.

"Why is this place never open?" she asked, turning back to the old woman.

"Oh, it's open when it needs to be."

"Will you be open tomorrow?"

"Well, that, my dear, will depend on you."

Chapter Eighteen

Makayla was dating Finian now, as far as Brynn could tell. Not that Makayla had actually spoken to her about it. But the whispers that traveled like lightning from locker to locker spoke of nothing else, and try as she might, Brynn could not block out the titters and murmurs that announced her supposed friend's attachment to her distasteful new beau.

The fact of the matter became more than evident when, during Spanish, the one class that she and Makayla and Finian all had together, the black-eyed boy, after sighing and groaning through the lecture for a full five minutes, finally cleared his throat.

"You know," he announced loudly as he took up residence in the teacher's heavy, wooden swivel chair, "this is boring. Supremely boring. I think there are much more interesting ways I could be spending my time. Come here, pet."

Makayla was on his lap scant seconds later, and Brynn turned her head away to avoid seeing what was about to occur. The sounds were bad enough. When Finian came up for breath, he noticed the teacher still standing silently nearby.

"What are you doing?" he groaned petulantly.

"I don't know," the teacher answered, obviously

uncomfortable.

"Are you watching?" Finian chortled, squinting his eyes. "What are you, some kind of pervert? Don't watch us. I'm not putting on a show here. Not for you, anyway."

"What else am I supposed to do? Class is in session."

"Go away! Leave. Go balance your checkbook or do your taxes or some other boring thing that boring people do."

"I already filed my taxes this year."

"I don't care what you do! Just leave!"

The teacher retrieved his satchel and walked quickly to the door.

"I'll have to come back before the bell rings," he said meekly, turning back.

"Don't move," Finian insisted, his eyes flashing, in a voice commanding obedience. Then he picked up a stapler from the desk and hurled it across the room, catching the teacher on his left brow. "Now you can move," he said, as the blood began to flow down the teacher's face, "and now you can leave. And don't come back while I am still in this room."

Brynn couldn't watch what Finian and Makayla were beginning to do to each other, so she slunk out the door as well, and no one seemed to notice. With no teacher in the room, there didn't seem to be any reason to sit there and endure the uncomfortable symphony of mashing tongues.

She didn't see either of them for the rest of the morning, but Finian stared at her all through lunch, as she sat by herself, which she usually did these days. Afterwards, he cornered her in the hall, which for some reason was completely and atypically silent and empty.

"Hey there," he announced, sidling up to her.

Brynn didn't respond. She tried to walk by him, but he traipsed himself into her path. She tried to walk around him, but he stretched his arms out, trapping her in a corner between the lockers and a window.

"Where you going, sweetness and light?"

"Anywhere but here, honestly," she said, trying to sound confident and hoping her voice didn't betray her.

"I think I'm heading out," Finian said, with a sparkling smile beneath his dark eyes. "Maybe grab a burger or something. Why don't you come with me?"

"Come with you?"

"Yeah. Come with me. It'll be fun. I'm sure we can find some ways to...entertain each other."

"It's the middle of the school day."

"School is a big bore. I don't want to be here today. I want to be with you."

"Well, I have better places to be."

She ducked under his arms and walked briskly on ahead, but he sauntered by her and interjected himself into her path once more. She was again surprised by how empty the halls were at this time of day.

"Maybe I should just say what I want," he said.

"Maybe I should be going."

"Hear me out. It won't take but a second of your time, my fair princess." He lowered his voice and leaned in closer. "I think that you...should be...with me."

"Be with you?"

"Yeah. Be with me," he said, as if he was offering her a trip around the world and a box full of kittens. "You and me. Together. A thing. An item. A duo. Intertwined and interconnected and ensconced and inseparable. I think we would fit...very nicely together. I think we could make each other very happy."

"I thought you were with Makayla," Brynn scoffed, now both disgusted and confused. "Your display this morning certainly seemed to indicate that, anyway."

"I don't care about her," Finian said blithely, with a dismissive flick of his fingers.

"You don't? Then what was all that about in Spanish class today?"

"Maybe I was just trying to make you jealous," he said, raising his eyebrows suggestively.

"By mounting an assault on my best friend's tonsils right in front of me?" Brynn fairly screamed, trying to keep her emotions in check and not succeeding greatly.

"I promise you. She doesn't mean anything to me. You're the only one I want. You're the only one I've ever wanted."

"So, you're willing to put on a heavy-breathing, make-out performance in front of the whole class with someone you don't even care about? That may not be the selling point for being in a relationship with you that you think it is."

"Maybe it wasn't the best way to make my case," Finian said, his voice oozing gracious defeat. "Let me make it up to you. What do you like? Music? Movies? Fancy food? Video games? Whatever you want, let's go do it. Right now."

"I kind of have this feeling the only reason you're interested in me...is because I seem to be the only person in this entire school who can see through your crap."

"Come on," Finian breathed. "Don't be so dumb, sugarplum. It's not like that." He inched forward and Brynn crept backward until her shoulder blades were pressed against the window. "Just take a second. Think about it. You and I. The mysterious stranger and the red-haired princess—"

"I'm not a princess."

"To me you are."

She shuddered.

"Gross."

"Don't make the wrong choice here. Together, we would be unstoppable. We would rule this school."

"That...that may be the cheesiest line I've ever heard."

Finian's smile faded from his face and his dark eyes suddenly grew bright, flecks of orange catching the light, as if his anger at her denial lit a fire within him.

"Bloody hell!" he shouted, pounding the window on either side of her. "You're impossible! Fine. You should know that this is your loss." He thrust an insistent finger in her face. "I'm through with you. Hey, doll!"

Makayla stepped out from behind a nearby bank of lockers.

"Yeah, you were right," he said, backing away from Brynn, "she said no. She's a stick."

"I told you," Makayla sneered, "she's impossible."

"See you later, gumdrop," he said to Makayla as he grabbed her roughly and pulled her close to him.

She entwined herself about him for a breathless moment, and then he pushed her away and strode off, leaving Brynn alone in the hallway with the girl she had long thought of as her best friend. Once Finian was out of sight, the halls began to fill again, with students and with noise. Brynn stood with Makayla in the middle of the current, as the streams of their classmates flowed around them.

"You should have agreed," Makayla said flatly, her voice betraying no emotion. "Finian doesn't like it when people say 'no' to him."

"You were in on this? Why would you let him do this to me?"

"I don't know," Makayla sneered, "maybe I thought it would be good for you to have one actual moment of human connection in your life, one slight morsel of real physical affection. Or maybe I wanted him to lead you on, and then humiliate you in front of the whole school. Maybe I wanted him to grind you down for being the insufferable little priss you are."

"Why are you acting like this? You're supposed to be my best friend!"

"You were never my friend, Brynn!" Makayla shouted, suddenly in a rage, gesticulating wildly. "You never cared about me. Come on! You have to realize that, don't you? You just needed someone in your life to vent all your crazy fairy stories to, someone who wouldn't laugh in your face. I mean, I wanted to. I wanted to laugh so bad. I wanted to tell you just how stupid and ridiculous you sounded every time you went on and on about your stupid parents and your stupid superstitions and your stupid, stupid, stupid changelings. Well, now I can! Now that Finian has shown me that I don't need you anymore, I can leave you in the dust. So, you can take your stupid, little, pointy nose and your stupid, big, sad eyes and you can march away from here and you can leave me alone and you can go cry in a puddle. Forever!"

Brynn and Makayla stood face to face. Brynn stared at

her friend, wondering how on earth she could be like this. Makayla, as usual lately, couldn't even meet her gaze. This was so unlike the girl that had befriended her the day after she'd moved to town, Brynn thought, that had gone to such lengths to make her feel welcome, that had shared so much of her life, her hopes and her fears and her joy and her sadness. This was so unlike the Makayla she'd known for so long. The girl in front of her was cruel and cold. But the Makayla she knew was the farthest thing from those that she could imagine. And if she was going to end their friendship, Brynn thought, if Makayla was going to cut her adrift, the least she could do was look her in the eyes and tell her.

"Look at me, damn it!" Brynn screamed, her voice cutting above the din of the bustling hallway. "Why won't you look at me?"

Makayla finally flung her head up and met Brynn's gaze. Brynn looked at her friend, really looked at her, for maybe the first time since Makayla had come back from her still-unexplained absence the previous week. She was the same, just the same as always, but then, the more Brynn looked, she saw things she'd never seen in her best friend before. Her mouth was clenched in an unfamiliar way. Her shoulders were thrown back haughtily. Her hands were fidgeting oddly. But above all, Brynn thought, it was her eyes. Her eyes were wrong.

And as Brynn stared at those eyes, she suddenly knew. She wondered how she could have been so blind. There was only one answer to this riddle, and it had been staring her in the face for days. She ran home, not even stopping at her locker to pick up her things.

Chapter Nineteen

Her lungs were on fire, but Brynn knew she couldn't stop running. She had to get home, had to find out the truth. She burst through the front door and found her father and her mother in the kitchen, snacking on cheese.

"You have to tell me, and you have to tell me now," she wheezed, attempting to speak forcefully, but barely managing an inarticulate snuffle as she tried to catch her breath.

"Slow down, sweetie," her mother said softly, "take your time. What's wrong?"

Brynn tried to slow her breathing, tried to quell the panic that threatened to rise up and engulf her from within.

"I need you to tell me the truth," she said. "I need you to tell me now."

"Of course," her father said, "we'll always tell you the truth."

Brynn blinked forcefully.

"Except about the most basic facts of my existence, consistently and repeatedly over the last fourteen years?"

"I know you're upset we didn't tell you sooner about who you are, who *we* are," he said. "Maybe we didn't handle it as well as we could have. But you know now. And if there's something else you need to know, whatever it is, ask us and we will tell you."

"You promise?"

"We promise."

"You'll tell me the truth?"

"Yes. We'll tell you the truth."

"Okay," Brynn said, as calmly as she could, finally in control, "we're not human. You, me, all four of us. We're not human. We do things that humans don't do."

"That's right," her father agreed.

"And we do more than just disappear and change shape and dance in shoemakers' kitchens, don't we?"

"Yes, of course."

"I mean, you've been telling me about goblins my whole life, and all you've ever told me about them is that they steal babies. I mean, you went on and on about it. We talked about it literally every night."

"Well, yeah. That's what goblins do. Historically speaking. That's kind of our thing."

"And it's not always babies, is it?"

"Not always, no," her father said, a worried crease between his eyes, "Brynn, what are you trying to ask—"

"You stole my best friend, didn't you?" she shouted, no longer in control. "You stole her and replaced her with something else! And now, it's what, some crazy goblin cousin of yours who's pretending to be my best friend, masquerading around my school, being totally crazy and mean?"

Brynn's parents were silent. Her father looked ashen, and he was wringing his hands. Her mother linked her arm in his and rested her forehead against his shoulder.

"You have to tell her the truth, Gaf. We said we would."

Her father nodded and took a deep, shuddering breath.

"I did, sweetie. I stole Makayla. I'm sorry. You have to understand...it wasn't my choice. I couldn't...I tried to say no. They said they would...I can't even repeat what they said they would do to you, to your mother, to your brother...to the baby."

Brynn clenched her jaw. She wanted to spit, to punch the wall, to disappear and never come back.

"So...the Makayla I've been seeing at school," she grimaced, "that's not Makayla at all?"

"It's not. No."

"Is it another goblin?"

"No," her father said weakly, "no, I...I couldn't bring myself to take a goblin child. It's a...well, it's a fetch."

"A what?"

"A fetch."

"What the hell is that?" Brynn demanded.

"Brynn, language!" her mother chided, a finger outstretched.

"Seriously, Mama?"

"It's okay, Lou," her father uttered, still shaking, still weak, "I think we can let it slide this once. Brynn, it's...well, it's more technical than this, and I'd be happy to get into it with you sometime, because honestly, it's a fascinating field, but take away the complexities, and essentially...well, it's a piece of wood I enchanted to believe that it's a child."

"You did what?"

"It's an ancient method," her father nodded, clearly

engrossed by the topic. "Very few know how to do it anymore. But I recreated the methodology from some old texts I located online. The results give a being which is nearly identical to the child being replaced, but is...umm...generally significantly more evil than if I had swapped in an actual goblin child."

"Yeah," Brynn said, "that adds up." Something suddenly occurred to her. "That five-year-old a while ago, who went nuts and stole that beer truck? Was that you?"

Her father nodded nervously.

"Umm...well, yeah, it was," he mumbled.

"What about that baby last year, the one that nearly offed its mother?"

"Yeah. Yeah, that was me too."

"Were those ones goblin babies?"

"No. Both fetches. And to be honest, they were my first fetches. Much too evil, I'm afraid."

"This is insane! I can't believe you would do this. I can't believe you would even think of doing this!"

"Sweetie, I know you're upset right now, but—"

"Papa. You stole my best friend!"

"I know..."

"You replaced her with an evil stick!"

Her father had gone back to wringing his hands.

"Did you think I wouldn't notice?" Brynn asked, nearly in tears. "Were you planning on telling me?"

"I was hoping to find a solution...before things got out of hand."

"Out of hand? Before things got out of hand? The moment you abducted my best friend and replaced her with an evil piece of wood, things were already way beyond out of hand!"

"Sweetheart, I know you're not happy about this," her mother cajoled, trying to intervene, "but there are complexities that you don't understand. I promise you, your father is doing his absolute best to navigate an incredibly difficult situation. The forces at play here are much older and much more malevolent than I even want to think about. All we want to do is protect you and your brother and the baby."

Brynn gathered all the composure she could muster before she addressed her father again.

"You told me...you told me that you and Mama were choosing a different road than all the other goblins who came before you. What happened to that?"

"Well...we have been," he said meekly. "It had been...honestly, and this may shock you, it had been centuries since I'd stolen a child. But then...the good neighbor found us again. We don't know how he did, but he found us, despite all the trouble we'd gone through to hide ourselves."

"The one you call the strange little man," her mother interjected.

"Oh yeah, him," Brynn responded coldly.

"Somehow, he found us all the way out in California," she added. "We're still not sure how he did it. That house was specifically constructed to hide us from specifically him."

"But he found us," her father continued, "and I tried to put him off, and I have, for the most part. But he...he is a very insistent little fellow, and he can be very persuasive when he needs to be. I know that's hard to understand, but there really were good reasons—"

"Papa!" Brynn shouted. "It doesn't matter what the reasons were. You stole three kids!"

"Only three!" he exclaimed gleefully, as if this somehow mitigated the horror of what he'd done. "And they were the only ones for the last several centuries. As an average, that's not bad. And I did it to protect you. To protect all of us."

"First of all," Brynn said, "you seem to have tried to slip in the fact that you're both hundreds of years old without me noticing, only I did, but there are more pressing issues right now, so we'll have to come back to that later." She took a deep breath and spoke calmly and coolly, the course ahead now clear in her mind. "My best friend is missing. We have to get her back."

"You can't," her father winced, "that's impossible."

"Where is she?"

"She's gone."

"Where is she?"

"I don't know," he whimpered, throwing his hands in the air. "That's the truth."

"Okay. Well, what did you do with the children after you abducted them?"

"Could we not use the word 'abducted'?" her mother chimed in. "It's making me uncomfortable."

"Mama!" Brynn turned on her. "You are in on this! Those children were abducted. By Papa." She turned back to her father. "What did you do with them after you abducted them?"

"I delivered them."

"To who?"

"To him. The good neighbor."

"And where did he take them?"

"That's the part I don't know. They were asleep when I delivered them. In stasis. They may still be, for all I know. But where they've gone, I have no way of knowing."

Brynn shook her head in disbelief.

"Mama, Papa," she said, turning to each of them, "there are three sets of parents, right here in our town, who have been dealing with suddenly and incomprehensibly evil children. That five-year-old is still supposedly missing. Those parents are sick with worry. And I am now very worried about my only friend in the entire world, who has been delivered to the King of the Goblins, apparently—"

"Oh, honey," her mother said amiably, "no, he's not the King. Not even close, he's more like a—"

"Oh my god!" Brynn exploded. "Goblin hierarchy is not the discussion we are having right now! Absolutely not! My best friend is what...imprisoned? Enslaved? I mean, do we know if she's even still alive?"

Her father's voice was barely audible as he said, "She is." His eyes were downcast, and it was only when Brynn saw the large, liquid drops falling from them and splashing upon the floor that she noticed he no longer looked human. His skin was pale green, like dried moss, and his chin was pointy, with a thin beard a foot long jutting from the tip. His ears arched upward, with a thin tuft of hair atop them, and his curly hair was parted at the center, soaring up like wings on either side of his head. His feet were long and sinewy, and his tail twitched morosely behind him. His eyes were golden, and a jewel flowered at the hollow of his throat.

"She is alive," he said, in a voice that had grown as wistful as a fallen star, "but beyond that, I cannot say."

"Can you find her?" Brynn asked the goblin who was also her father as he wept in front of her.

"I cannot," he said, shaking his head mournfully. "It is forbidden to seek a child that you have stolen."

"But if I wanted to find her, where would I look?"

"Honey," her mother cooed, trying to calm her once more, "you can't, it would be too—"

"No! You said you would answer my questions. No talk of danger. We're past that. There are already people in danger. At least three." She turned back to her father. "Where would I look?"

"I don't know. There are so many places he could have taken her."

"Who would know?" Brynn asked, desperate. "Who could I ask?"

Her father shook his head, sobbing freely now as his wife wrapped her arms around him, his dull, green skin a sharp contrast to the darkness of hers. Brynn realized, through a haze of incomprehension, that her mother must have changed shape as well, for her skin was now so dark that it appeared to be absorbing the very light around it, and there seemed to be stars within it, as if she was cased in the night sky itself. Her hair was a halo of light, cascading in bright waves around her shoulders and around her husband's, but Brynn could barely look at either of them, her vision too clouded by fury and by fear.

"That depends," the voice of her father said, seeming to reach across an untold expanse to reach her ears. "That would depend on you, I suppose. It would depend on how badly you wanted the knowledge. But certainly, you would need to find someone much wiser than I."

Chapter Twenty

Brynn spent the day at school trying to avoid The Thing That Looked Like Makayla But Wasn't. This was fairly easy, as the faux Makayla and the real Finian spent most of their time in corners now, holding hands and glowering at everyone else around them. The Thing That Looked Like Makayla tried to pants their History teacher, but it turned out he was wearing suspenders under his jacket, so she finally gave up after several strenuous attempts and stormed out of the room, satisfying herself by kicking over a trash can on the way. As Brynn was leaving school, she heard Finian and Makayla having a loud argument about what they should set on fire to cause the most disruption, but it didn't seem as if they were really serious, and by the time she'd collected her things, they had given up on arson and returned to ostentatious make-out sessions.

She made her way home and, considering how odd the last few days had been, was unsurprised to find the appliance store open, lit even more festively than the last time, although the calypso music had been replaced by a torch singer, crooning in German. The old woman had her eyes closed, her head swaying with the music.

"Well, that is not a happy face," she said as the bells tinkled. "Will a butterscotch help this time?"

"I don't think it will."

Brynn had one anyway.

"Still having problems with your friend?" the old woman asked.

"Yeah. I guess so. I think...well, there's sort of been a development. I found out that she's missing."

"Missing?"

"Yeah."

"Now that sounds troubling. Maybe you should be getting the police involved."

"Not that kind of missing. Missing in a more...profound and unsettling way."

"I'm not sure I know what that means."

"You and me both." Brynn set her forehead down on the counter. "I tried to talk to my parents about it, but they weren't much help. My dad...he said...he said if I wanted to find her, I would need to want it really badly, and I would need to find a really wise person to help me do it. I mean, what does that even mean? Who would I ask?"

The old woman reached behind the counter and the music faded away to nothing.

"Why do you want to find this girl?" she asked very delicately.

"Because she's my friend. Because she would do the same thing for me."

"But what would you receive if you found her?"

"Nothing, I guess. Just her."

The old woman stared at Brynn, then checked her watch once again. She tapped one long finger against her chin.

"Well, dearie," she said, with an airy sigh of resignation,

"you sound like you are certainly in a pickle. I do so wish that I could help, but I'm afraid I simply don't have the answers you're looking for." The old woman looked straight into Brynn's eyes, straight down into her soul, and she said in a voice both warm and hollow, "To my mind, there is only one who could help you now. You may dismiss my utterings as the clacking of an old hen, but hearken to this, for it is the truth. You must find the Salmon of Knowledge."

Brynn stared silently at the woman for a long time, but the woman did not crack a smile, did not wink, did not say anything else that would mitigate the insurmountable absurdity of the words that had just been formed by her mouth.

"That is the craziest thing anyone has ever said to me," Brynn said in a measured tone, "and I have had some astronomic-level craziness said to me lately."

"I'm only trying to help. But really, it's just the pratterings of a daft old lady. You should probably pay me no mind," the woman said, turning the music back up and reaching for a broom.

"But it means...oh god...it means you're somehow wrapped up in all of this, too, aren't you? You're not just some batty old woman who opens her appliance store once or twice a year on a whim. You're a...a what? A goblin? A hero? A wizard? I mean, maybe wizards are real too, or what else? Elves? Fairies? Demons?"

"I'm sure I don't know what you're talking about, dear," the woman said, as she swept the spotless floor.

"Hobbits?"

"Well, now you're just being silly."

"Do you know something?" Brynn pleaded. "Seriously, if you know anything, anything at all, please just tell me what is going on."

"I'm sorry, dear, it's closing time. I'm afraid I must ask you to leave. That is all I can give you. No more is allowed. If you should wish further assistance, seek out the Salmon of Knowledge."

She ushered Brynn hastily out the door, and Brynn heard it lock behind her. She closed her eyes, the utter incomprehensibility of it all pounding away at her skull, needles of disbelief rattling her temples. When she opened her eyes and turned around, the store was dark, the sign said 'CLOSED,' there was no music, there was no old woman, there was nothing to prove that the conversation had actually happened. There was nothing, nothing but the wind.

Chapter Twenty-One

It was 3 p.m. in Jeffersonville, Indiana, and Brynn McAwber was wading in a river, trying to find the Salmon of Knowledge. It wasn't a particularly clean river, and it was cold, and she suspected there weren't any salmon in it, let alone fish of any kind, but she wasn't sure what else to do. It was the only clue she had, and her friend's life might be depending on it, so she had promised herself that she would wade through every waterway in the state of Indiana if she had to, but she really hoped she didn't.

She didn't want to ask her parents any more about this, as they seemed particularly unwilling to provide her with any useful information. So, after leaving the appliance store, she'd walked straight to the nearest river, pulled off her shoes, pulled off her socks, and waded in. And, of course, she realized it wasn't actually so much a river as a stream, and perhaps even creek would be more accurate, but she knew she had to do something.

She looked down at her feet. They were sunk several inches into the mud of the creek bed and a cloud of sickly green algae was amassing around her legs. Her hands were dripping with sludge from a variety of unsuccessful attempts to find any living thing within the fetid water. She wiped them on her pants, which left the fabric streaked and crusty. This was clearly doing no good. Her life, to this point, appeared to have left her remarkably unprepared to search for a magic fish.

Chapter Twenty-Two

The next morning, before school, Brynn rose early and dug through the garage and found her father's old fishing pole and tackle box. She carried them to the pond down the road. She fitted the pieces of the rod together, and combed through the tackle box to find the other things she thought she might need. She dug in the earth on the bank, found a thick, wriggling earthworm, and baited her hook. She cast the worm out into the pond and waited. Nothing happened. She tried again using a lure. Nothing happened. Then a thought came to her. She realized that she was going about this all wrong. If she wanted to catch a magic fish, maybe she needed more meaningful bait. She ran home, tore a page from her favorite book, and brought it back to the pond. She carefully pierced the page with a barbed hook and cast her unconventional bait as far as she was able, toward the middle of the pond. She waited for an hour, but caught nothing except curious looks from the ducks that were nesting on the shore.

Chapter Twenty-Three

The day after that, when school ended, Brynn walked down to the banks of the Ohio River. She clambered over a concrete barricade, cars rumbling overhead on the nearby bridge, until she stood on the rocks just at the edge of the water, the broad blue river stretched out in front of her. She glanced around nervously. There was no one around, save a few passing joggers who seemed oblivious to all else but the pounding of their legs and the music in their ears. She cleared her throat and called out in what she imagined to be a clarion tone.

"Salmon of Knowledge! Hello, Salmon of Knowledge! I need to talk to you!"

Nothing happened. She tried again.

"Salmon of Knowledge, I...I summon you! I summon thee, Salmon of Knowledge!"

Nothing happened. And although shouting at a river was embarrassing, it was not as embarrassing as the next thing she wanted to try. A thought had come to her, while she slept, that if calling didn't work, perhaps singing would. And so she sang, out over the water, her plaintive voice sailing across the river, carried out by the currents of the breeze, the only song about a fish she knew.

> *Oh help me, Jesus,*
> *Come through this storm,*
> *I had to lose her,*
> *To do her harm.*
>> *I heard her holler,*
>> *I heard her moan,*
>> *My lovely daughter,*
>> *I took her home.*
> *Little fish, big fish, swimming in the water,*
> *Come back here, man, gimme my daughter.*
> *Little fish, big fish, swimming in the water,*
> *Come back here, man, gimme my daughter.*

She waited. There was no reaction, except for a city worker, emptying a nearby garbage can, who was staring perplexedly at her as she sighed and clambered back up to the sidewalk above.

Chapter Twenty-Four

She found three different fish documentaries at the library and spent an entire evening watching them. This, Brynn realized as she closed her computer, was the most monumental waste of time so far. She couldn't believe she was spending all this time looking for a stupid magic fish.

Chapter Twenty-Five

Brynn dug out every bit of allowance money that was hidden in her sock drawer and took it all to the sushi restaurant. She ate until her money ran out. She kind of knew in advance that this one wouldn't work, but it was delicious, and she thought she deserved it.

Chapter Twenty-Six

Brynn raided the craft supplies in the closet, and with felt and glitter and glue, she made a beautiful, sleek, silvery fish, with scales and eyes and everything. She spent fifteen minutes trying to have a conversation with it before Conn walked in and started laughing. He didn't stop for three days.

Chapter Twenty-Seven

At the grocery store, using her newfound powers of invisibility, Brynn stole a box of organic salmon nuggets. She felt guilty about this, but she had used up all her money at the sushi restaurant. She took the box of nuggets home, cooked them up, and then dissected each of them carefully, looking for some kind of hidden message. There was none.

Chapter Twenty-Eight

At the seafood market, Brynn wandered around, examining the vast array of fish and other ocean creatures, recently dead or soon to be so, but they were all slimy and cold and none seemed remotely communicative. She found an isolated corner, where a whole haddock rested on ice, its bulging eyes staring at her. She looked it right in those bulging eyes and solemnly pleaded her case to it.

"Can you tell me how to find the Salmon of Knowledge?"

The haddock did not respond.

Chapter Twenty-Nine

Brynn slipped out of visibility, slipped onto the bus, slipped off again, and then slipped into the zoo, unseen by visitor and exhibit alike. Once again, she felt guilty, but she couldn't afford the entrance fee or the bus fare. She found the curiously-named Herpaquarium and padded as noiselessly as she could in front of the fish tanks, murmuring under her breath to the incarcerated denizens within, to the piranha and the alligators and the frogs.

"I'm looking for a salmon," she whispered. "I'm aware that none of you are salmon, but maybe one of you could point me in the right direction. I mean, honestly, weirder things have happened to me recently."

No one answered, not the piranha, nor the alligators, nor the frogs. She knelt down and pressed her cheek against the glass tank in front of her, startling a number of brightly-colored angelfish.

"Come on," she begged them, "just help me out. Just give me a sign."

Chapter Thirty

Still unseen, Brynn boarded the bus back toward Jeffersonville, back toward home, feeling thoroughly discouraged. She had only one clue that could possibly help her, and it made no sense at all. She slumped in her seat and listened to the vague whisperings of the sad, twangy music escaping from the headphones of the college student in front of her, snatches of lyrics of lost loves and lonesome nights and the moon over silent sidewalks.

When the bus pulled up to her stop, Brynn disembarked in a disagreeable stupor, barely able to lift her eyes from the ground. She allowed her body to coalesce into visibility (surprising some nearby pigeons, who squawked off in a huff) and leaned against the brick wall, unable to face the last few blocks that would take her home.

When she finally raised her eyes from the ground, she saw the sad man in the sad fish costume, and in her current mood, he seemed even sadder than usual, his grubby costume even grubbier, his dingy sign even dingier. She stared at him. She wondered who he was. She wondered what his life was like when he wasn't working here. She wondered if he struggled to get out of bed each morning, knowing he would have to stand in front of the same run-down restaurant all day long, knowing he would have to wave the same shabby sign on the same empty street, knowing he would have to put on the same battered costume he did every day, the same blue and silver foam rubber fish.

The anger and the realization hit her at the same time, both smacking her in the frontal lobe with the force of a thousand bees.

"You!" she shouted at him, marching over until she was just inches from the red felt tongue that drooped from the side of his foam rubber maw. "It's you, isn't it? It was you all along. You're the freaking Salmon of Knowledge!"

The man in the fish costume just shrugged, although Brynn thought he might have frozen in fear for the briefest of moments before he did so. She sensed apprehension in his bearing, even if she couldn't see any actual parts of his body. He turned away from her and returned to haphazardly waving his sign, although there was no one else on the street to see it.

"No," Brynn insisted, "no, no, no! If you are the Salmon of Knowledge, and I'm pretty sure you are now, I need your help. And I need it now. Please. My friend is in danger."

The man in the fish costume steadfastly ignored her.

"Okay, fine," she said, "be that way."

She reached in quickly, snatched the stained foam core sign from his hands, then retreated to a safe distance, dancing on the balls of her feet, holding the sign just out of his reach. He tried to grab it back from her, but as deeply ensconced as he was within layers of foam rubber, he had little mobility, and his arms flailed in muffled futility.

"How about this?" Brynn called to him, her cheeks

flushed. "I need answers. You need the sign. Honestly, I suspect the answers I need are significantly more valuable than this sign, so I understand my bargaining position isn't great, but let's start there."

She paused. The man in the fish costume did not respond. He made a quick grab for the sign, but she pulled it out of his reach once again.

"If you give me answers," she said slowly and sternly, "I will give you back your sign."

He stared at her. Or at least, Brynn thought he was staring at her. She wasn't exactly sure where his real eyes were, but the big, fake plastic eyes on the sides of his fish costume, those were definitely staring at her. He reached for the sign again, but when she held her ground, he crumpled slightly with an inaudible sigh. From within the recesses of his thick, foam rubber sleeves, the scales painted on them mostly worn away, he retrieved a small, yellowed pad of paper and a stub of a pencil. He scribbled hastily on the pad, then tore off the top piece and handed it to her. The note said:

Please give me back my sign.

"No," Brynn declined, shaking her head, "not until you help me."

He wrote again and handed her another sheet.

I don't know what you want from me.

I just work here.

Brynn looked at him scornfully from under her eyebrows.

"No," she repeated, "you are the freaking Salmon of Knowledge and I need your freaking help."

He made one final, halfhearted grab at the sign. When Brynn pulled it out of his reach yet again and held it behind her back, he gave a quick flail and stomp of frustration, and then a very audible sigh. His shoulders slumped. He took the pencil and wrote very slowly and deliberately on the pad, then passed over the note.

Fine. You may ask three questions,
and I will provide three true answers.

Brynn allowed herself a small, triumphant smile before she spoke.

"Are you the Salmon of Knowledge?"

He wrote quickly this time, practically flinging the paper at her.

Yes. Not a great choice for your first
question, though. Two more.

Brynn realized this was true. She'd now wasted a full third of the assistance she'd been searching for so desperately. For her next question, she spoke slowly and deliberately, thinking each word out in advance.

"My best friend. Makayla. She was taken away. Where is she?"

The man in the fish costume seemed to look deep into her eyes before turning back to his notepad. When he handed her the note this time, Brynn saw that, instead of the lazy scrawl he had used before, these words were in an ornate cursive hand, intricate and looped.

Your friend is held in the Unseemly Court,
in the Swallowed Hall, in the Land of Annwfyn.

"What does that mean?" Brynn stammered, staring at the strange words in front of her. "Those words don't make any sense. I need to find her. What do I do?"

The man in the foam rubber fish costume wrote again, deliberately and slowly. When he handed over the paper, the words were written in block capitals, forceful and tall.

You must find the Second Settler.

You must find the Mad Dog's Bone.

"Well, that's kind of cryptic," she said, cocking her head at him and pursing her lips.

He wrote quickly this time and flung the paper at her. This note had returned to the previous untidy scrawl.

Well, you were kind of a dick about my sign.

"Okay," she said, "I'm sorry. Just tell me…please…how do I get there? How do I find her?"

The man in the fish costume just shrugged again and held his hand out for the sign.

"Oh, right. You already answered three questions."

He nodded and thrust his hand forward.

"Any chance I could get a bonus round?"

He just shook his big fish head. Brynn put the sign back in his hand, and he returned to his slumped, sign-waving ways, an oracle no more, just a sad man in a sad suit, battered and dull. She gathered the notes he had given her and thrust them into her pocket.

Brynn McAwber had found the Salmon of Knowledge, but she wasn't any closer to her goal. She knew where Makayla was now, if a handful of cryptic gibberish could be called knowledge. She had received answers to all her questions, but questions were still all that remained.

Chapter Thirty-One

Brynn stopped by the library on her way home, a brief detour from her usual route. An older gentleman, clean-shaven, with silver hair and an argyle sweater vest, was at the reference desk.

"Can I help you?" he said.

"Yeah," she said, "I hope so. It's just a quick question. Can you tell me what this word means?"

She pulled out the papers that the man in the fish costume had given her, and showed the one on top to the librarian, pointing out the word 'Annwfyn.'

"I mean, is it even a word? I think it's missing some vowels or something."

"Hmm," he said. "One second."

He typed a few words into his computer, the glow of its archaic CRT screen reflected in his glasses. After a few seconds, he beckoned to Brynn, and she followed him down a narrow aisle, past several twists and turns, until they stood in a section of the stacks that were clearly rarely used, in front of shelves and shelves of books bound in dusty leather. He quickly found the volume he was looking for and set it on a nearby table. He flipped through the index and located the desired page.

"That is what I thought," the librarian said, "but I wanted to make sure. I would hate to give an incorrect answer. Those are rarely much help."

"So, what is it?" Brynn asked nervously.

"Well, that...that is a very old word. From a very old language. And yes, it is a real word. But one that derives from Welsh, which is why the construction may appear strange to your eyes. The 'w' here, as in most Welsh words, would take on an 'oo' sound, as in 'zoo,' almost as if it truly were a double 'u.' And the 'f' carries what would be a 'v' sound in English, so one would say something close to: a-NOO-veen."

"That's great. Absolutely great. Thank you. But what does it mean?"

"Ah. Yes. That would be the important bit here, wouldn't it? It means 'Otherworld.'"

Chapter Thirty-Two

That night, Brynn disappeared. She'd tossed and turned, unable to sleep, plagued by thoughts of every unanswered question. The world she currently resided in seemed to be almost more than she could handle lately. How was she supposed to find an entirely other world, let alone locate a single person within it? When she finally did fall asleep, she awoke hours later, her body invisible, standing face-to-face with the woman with the sword.

Brynn stared groggily at the figure in front of her as the world came back into focus, and wondered what the woman was doing there, on the still and silent street, on this night of all nights. The sword was sheathed on her back, as usual, and the rain (which Brynn only noticed at that moment) was beading on the woman's long braid as she stood poised and alert, her hands at the ready. Her eyes were bright and focused, but clearly oblivious to Brynn's presence.

The woman appeared young, although Brynn's parents had implied that she was perhaps hundreds of years old. Her hair was not as tidy as usual, golden wisps escaping from the thick braid all along its length. She bore a fresh cut along the back of one hand and another low on her neck. Perhaps she was hunting more than one goblin. Brynn wondered about the outcome of the scuffle that had caused the wounds. She wondered if the other goblin had escaped, or if it had fallen to the woman's wrath.

The scabbard strapped to the woman's back was of thick leather and embossed with strange writing. The dragon's head on the pommel was intricate and fierce, more lifelike than Brynn had imagined it could be, and the tiny jewels inset for eyes seemed almost to glow with a life of their own.

They stood there together in the rain, mere feet from each other, pursuer and prey, woman and child, hero and goblin. It was strange, now that Brynn knew. Now that she knew that this woman was the hero, and that she herself (from any reasonable point of view) would almost certainly be seen as the monster, the villain of this particular tale.

After all: never mind Brynn's true heritage, the countless families her ancestors had apparently ripped apart for century upon century. Never mind the wiry, green imp which lived inside her, enough to make a stranger scream if she changed shape and let it forth. Never mind the 'maleficence' (whatever that was) that supposedly resided deep within her being. Set all those things aside, and there was still the indisputable fact that a member of her family, her very own father, had stolen three children recently, which certainly painted her in a less than heroic light. And then there was also the theft of the fish nuggets, and the sneaking into the zoo without paying, and she still had some overdue library books and was clearly failing spectacularly at saving her best friend. Might as well stamp 'villain' across her forehead and be done with it.

And maybe that was the truth. Maybe she deserved to be

hunted. Maybe she deserved to be slain. Maybe she deserved to be swept aside, with all her fears and all her failings, her best intentions lost to the gnarled wickedness within her.

She looked up to the rain, held her hands to the sky, saw the moon shining through her fingers, felt the raindrops mingling with her tears once again, felt them dancing down her cheeks. She thought of her friend, stolen away to another world, with no one to save her but a frightened goblin, lost and alone. Was it possible, Brynn wondered. Was it even possible to change her own story? What if the blond-haired, sword-wielding battle-maiden stepped aside? What if the goblin—with all her flaws, with all her doubts—what if the goblin was the hero this time?

Anyone who took one look at this woman, though, Brynn knew, would see that this was fantastically implausible. She just oozed righteousness and morality and true-heartedness, and that was before you even took a closer look at the high cheekbones, the ice-blue eyes, the presumably magic sword, and the hair that somehow seemed to be perpetually wafting in the wind. If anyone was the hero here, it was clearly her.

Brynn gave a silent sigh and began the long, cold walk back to her house. It worried her that she had lost control of her abilities again. It was the first time she had disappeared in weeks. It was the first time she'd seen the woman with the sword in quite some time too. Neither boded well.

Chapter Thirty-Three

The appliance store had been closed up tight since Brynn first learned of the Salmon of Knowledge, but the next day, as she walked home from school, she saw that the lights were on, the 'OPEN' sign was turned outward, and the old woman was dusting the vintage stoves in the window. A scratchy recording of a blues singer trickled through the door, her voice mournful as she crooned the familiar words of an unfamiliar song.

The old woman checked her watch and gave a slight smile, retreating to the counter as Brynn entered, the unseen bells tinkling gaily above her as usual.

"You're open again," Brynn stated suspiciously.

"I am."

"I wasn't sure I was going to see you again, after...after last time."

"I told you, dear, this place is always open when it needs to be. Today, it needs to be."

Brynn nodded, sensing that this was the only explanation she was going to get, as unsatisfying as it was.

"Well, I found him," she said.

"Found who?"

"The Salmon of Knowledge."

"Good for you, dear," the woman said, sounding genuinely pleased.

"You know, he's not an actual salmon."

"I never said he was. How is he?"

"I don't know," Brynn shrugged. "He didn't say much."

"He never does. Did he give you the answers you were looking for?"

"Maybe. I don't know. He gave me some answers, but I'm not sure I get what any of them mean."

"Sometimes the difficulty is not in finding the answer," the old woman said, arching her eyebrows, "sometimes the difficulty is knowing just which question to ask."

"Yeah. I think I failed pretty hard on that score."

"What did he tell you?"

"Okay, so according to him, my friend is trapped in a place called the Unseemly Court, which is in something called the Swallowed Hall, which is somewhere called the Land of Annwfyn. Which doesn't have enough vowels."

The old woman nodded sagely.

"That sounds correct," she said.

"You knew that?" Brynn snapped in disbelief.

"I suspected it was likely."

"Then why didn't you just tell me?"

"I wasn't certain, and I would hate to give you incorrect information," the woman said. "Incorrect information is so rarely useful. But in any case, I couldn't have simply told you. There are rules, my dear, and rules must be followed, especially rules such as these."

"Well, whatever this Annwfyn place is, I need to figure out how to get there, so I can find my friend."

"You wish to travel to the Otherworld?" the woman said slowly, in a hushed tone.

"Yes. Of course I do." Brynn forced herself to speak calmly, even though her heart wanted nothing more than to scream in fury. "My best friend is there, and she might be in danger. I have to go."

"Well, visiting the Land of Annwfyn...I can't recommend that, dear."

"That doesn't matter," Brynn said stubbornly, "I'm going."

"Can I talk you out of it?"

"You can't."

"Well," the old woman said, giving a deep, melodramatic sigh, "if you're going to go, perhaps I have a few things that could help you out along your journey. And I should also probably state that I am not generally in the habit of offering assistance to goblins. I can't remember ever having done so, and my memory goes back much farther than you can probably imagine, dear. In fact, I feel fairly certain that one of my brethren may at some point have specifically forbidden me from offering aid or succor to any of the Tylwyth Teg." She leaned in close to Brynn and whispered conspiratorially. "But I've never been much of one for listening to what men tell me to do."

The old woman gave Brynn a wink and began rooting around in the drawers behind the counter.

"You know I'm a goblin?" Brynn asked in befuddlement.

"Well, yes, my dear. I mean, just look at you."

"But...but I thought I looked just like a girl."

"You do, of course, you're just lovely."

"Well then, how—"

"Trust me, my dear, to one who knows how to look, there's no hiding it."

Brynn just stared, flabbergasted, while the old woman continued to dig.

"So, let me see, what do I have here that might be of use?" she said under her breath. She wiggled her eyebrows as she seemed to find what she was looking for. "There we go. Are you ready?"

"I am. I guess."

"Very well." The old woman spoke dramatically, each syllable crisp and sharp. "I shall give you three objects to aid you on your quest. One contains within it the ability to unlock the mysteries of the Land of Annwfyn. One holds the power to guide your way should you manage to cross the threshold. And the last of the three may help you escape should your situation become dire."

She laid three objects on the counter. The first was an apple, shiny and candy-red. The second was a narrow metal tube with a button on the side. The third was an object Brynn had only seen in old movies and history books.

"There you are, dear. Use them wisely," the woman intoned, "use them well. May they aid you on your journey."

"Are you...are you serious?" Brynn asked slowly, her mind reeling. "An apple, a laser pointer, and a...I'm sorry, but is that a grenade?"

"Yes," the old woman nodded shrewdly, "yes, it is."

"Okay, I kind of feel like these are just some things you had lying around. And the fact that you had an actual grenade in the back of a drawer at your appliance store is kind of worrisome."

"The assistance you expect is not always the assistance you receive," the old woman declared sagaciously, pursing her lips.

"The amount of cryptic BS that has been spouted at me recently is astounding," Brynn responded.

"Language, dear."

"Yeah, I know." Brynn took a deep breath. "Okay," she said, "so these three things will help me...supposedly...do whatever I have to do...wherever it is I'm supposed to do it."

"They have that power within them. But only if you are clear of mind, brave of heart, and stout of will. For I did not say that they would help you, only that they could."

"Great. So, a magic apple, a mystical laser pointer, and an enchanted grenade?"

"You may call them what you will. To my mind, if there is any magic in this room, the only place it resides is here."

And with this, the old woman touched the girl's forehead with her index finger, very lightly, but Brynn felt a light tingle spread outward from the fingertip until it crept downward to her neck and arms, and made her squint and shudder.

"If you say so," Brynn said, disoriented and woozy. She leaned against the counter, waiting for the world to come back into focus.

"Here, let me help you," the woman said, retrieving a canvas shopping bag and laying the three objects neatly inside.

"Let me guess, a magic satchel?"

"No. Just a bag. Very useful for carrying things."

The woman held the bag out and Brynn took it, feeling more than a little uneasy in her heart and unsteady on her feet.

"So, now what?" she asked. "I know where I'm supposed to go. I have these...things you gave me. What do I do now? How do I get there? Where is the Land of Annwfyn?"

"I have offered you all the assistance I am able. The question you ask of me, I cannot answer. As I said, there are rules."

"You can be very frustrating, do you know that?"

"Indeed, my dear, I do."

The old woman took Brynn by the arm and ushered her briskly toward the door.

"Time to go now," she said officiously.

The old woman thrust Brynn through the doorway, out into the world, into the brisk air and the biting wind, Brynn attempting to interject all the while, but the woman paid no mind. Brynn stood there, pounding on the door and shouting, as the old woman pushed the doors closed, turned the locks and flipped the sign to 'CLOSED.'

"But where do I go?" Brynn yelled. "Where is it?"

Out of nowhere, a sneeze came upon her, and when she opened her eyes, the store was dark once more, and the old woman was gone.

Chapter Thirty-Four

Brynn was back in the stacks once more, in the oldest part of the library. She thought she remembered where to find the book the librarian had shown her, but it took almost half an hour among the crackling leather bindings to find it again. She lugged the heavy volume over to a nearby table, set it down gently, and then set her green canvas bag down even more gently, as it contained the (presumably) live grenade.

Besides the sack of junk the old woman had given her, all Brynn had were cryptic clues upon cryptic clues. No one she knew seemed to have the ability to simply tell her truth, to simply answer the questions she was asking. Books, though, she thought, books contained facts and figures and information. And this particular book, which sat right in front of her now, had provided her the sole, verifiable speck of knowledge she had gleaned so far. 'Annwfyn' meant 'Otherworld.' Perhaps more lay within.

She ran her fingers over the words 'The Myths and Traditions of the Celtic Peoples,' embossed in gold, as she opened the cover. She flipped through the rough-cut pages, examined the chapter headings, the diagrams, the illustrations, but nothing caught her eye. The Second Settler and the Mad Dog's Bone, she knew those words had to mean something. She flipped back to the index. She scanned through the long lists of words, but there was nothing about settlers, nothing about dogs, nothing about bones. Or rather, those words appeared numerous times in the index, but not in any way that would seem to relate remotely to her current predicament.

Her father had stolen her best friend, and now her best friend was lost and in danger in a different world. The mere thought of this would have seemed incomprehensibly absurd to her only a few weeks ago, but now all it led her to was anger and a despair that sought to take her breath. Brynn slammed the book shut in frustration.

"Can't find what you're looking for this time?" a voice said timidly.

She looked behind her and saw the bespectacled librarian, the one who had helped her before, shelving a tottering pile of slim volumes.

"No," Brynn admitted glumly. "Sorry about the noise."

"It's not a problem. Not really anyone else in here but us right now. If you tell me what you're looking for, I might be able to help." He adjusted his glasses on the bridge of his nose. "It's what they pay me for. I have a degree and everything."

A weary smile escaped from Brynn.

"Maybe you could," she said. "I don't know. It's so hard sometimes to know which question to ask."

"Very true," the librarian responded. "There is more information contained in this room than any of us could ever hope to learn in a lifetime. Unless you know what you're looking for, unless you know just which crumb of knowledge you need, this building is nothing more than a maze without a map. Lucky for you, however, this particular maze does have a map. All you have to do is ask, and assistance shall be provided. Which, as I think I mentioned, is my job."

"Are you good at your job?

"I am."

"That must be nice."

"It is," he answered with a twinkle in his eye, setting down his pile of books. "Why don't you tell me your problem, and I'll see if I can point you in the right direction."

Brynn paused, turning the questions over and over in her mind, trying to think of the best way to phrase what she needed, or even a small part of what she needed, that wouldn't make her sound completely insane. How could she tell the librarian what she was looking for without using the words 'goblin,' 'changeling,' or 'Salmon of Knowledge'? When she was finally ready, she spoke steadily and calmly.

"Who were the first settlers here?" she asked him. "Or, actually, I guess what I really want to know is...who were the second people to settle here?"

"Ah," the librarian answered with a genuine smile, "well, this part of the continent was first settled, of course, by the Mound Builders, six or seven thousand years ago. They and their descendants were here until the explorers and the European settlers arrived in the seventeenth century. The question I think you are asking, though, if I may try to rephrase it, is this: 'Were there any unexpected guests here between the arrival of the Native Americans and their subsequent conquest by the Europeans many thousands of years later?' Does that approximate what you're getting at?"

It wasn't at all, but Brynn agreed, wondering where this path would take them.

"If so, I think you may be looking in the wrong book. Come with me."

Brynn picked up her bag and followed him, as he led her to a shelf along the back wall of the building, full of atlases and guidebooks and bound bundles of gazettes and newsletters. He pulled a slim volume off the top shelf and set it on a nearby table. The cover read, 'An Early History of Indiana.' He flipped to the middle of the book and gestured to a nearby chair.

"Legend has it," he said as she took a seat, "that a man came here from across the sea, hundreds of years before the other European settlers, all the way back in the twelfth century. They say he came from Wales and was searching for Tír na nÓg, the Land of Youth, a mythical island rumored to be far to the west, across the water."

Brynn nodded, poring over the pages in front of her.

"When he landed on the North American coast, he saw that it wasn't what he was looking for, so he kept moving inland. This man took his small band of adventurers across this vast, unknown continent, where no Europeans had trod before. According to this legend, he never found Tír na nÓg, but he did find Indiana."

The librarian gave the smallest of smiles.

"They say his name was Madoc, sometimes given as Madog. And when he died, they buried him at a place called the Devil's Backbone."

He pointed out a hand-drawn map on the page.

"Do you think that's what you might be looking for? It's

only about ten miles from here, right on the banks of the Ohio River. Whether he's actually buried there or not is anyone's guess, but there have been several burial mounds found on top of the ridge."

"Burial mounds?"

"Mm-hmm. Says here that nine were found during the original excavations. No one goes up there much anymore, though. I guess the archaeologists found all they wanted to, and now that place is just home for cottonwoods and ghosts. Of course, this is all just myth and superstition, but it's a fascinating piece of local history, don't you think?"

"Yeah," Brynn said faintly, nearly stunned into silence. She'd just discovered that a man named Madog had been buried at a place called the Devil's Backbone, which was practically in her backyard. This had to be what the Salmon of Knowledge had meant, she thought, didn't it?

"What is this for," the librarian asked as she read the entire page again, and then a third time, "some kind of research paper? Some kind of school project?"

"Yeah," Brynn agreed hastily, "something like that."

"Well, good luck with it."

"Thank you," she said. "Really. You don't know how helpful you've been."

"My pleasure," he said. "Happy to be of service."

He began to leave.

"You know, his people...Madoc's people," the librarian said quietly, turning back to her but speaking almost to himself, "used to think that burial mounds were...well, that they could be used sometimes to enter fairy lands. That they were gates into other planes of existence, or into the realms of the gods, what have you."

"Really?"

"Mm-hmm. The oldest stories say that if you want to enter a fairy realm, a burial mound is one of the best ways to go about it. Circle the mound nine times, clockwise, of course, never in the other direction, and the door would be revealed. Of course, finding a door is not the same as opening a door, but the legends differ as to what needs to be done once you've found it. They all agree, though, that it's never easy. Only the quickest of wit and the purest of heart are able to enter the Land of Annwfyn."

Brynn stared at the page, her breath shaky, her pulse quickening.

"And, of course," the librarian said, "it would have to be during a full moon. Always a full moon."

"Huh," she said, "that's strange. It's a full moon tonight, isn't it?"

"No. Tomorrow."

Chapter Thirty-Five

"I'm scared," she said to the man in the fish costume.

Brynn hadn't told her family what she'd learned. After leaving the library, she'd returned home and had spent the evening barely talking, barely able to make eye contact, worried her parents would be able to see what she was planning written all over her face. She'd fretted herself to sleep, and once she did, she woke up, invisible and disoriented, three times: once in the hall, once at the front door, and the last time, climbing out the window. After that, she couldn't fall back asleep.

"I know where I'm supposed to go now. I figured it out. And I know when I'm supposed to go. It's tonight. Tonight is the full moon, and I'm going to the Devil's Backbone to try and find my friend."

She'd spent the day barely aware of everything around her. Finian and Makayla had teased her mercilessly in class, but she'd barely noticed. When she didn't respond, they'd returned to making out, as usual.

"I have no idea what I'm going to do when I get there. Try to open a door to the Land of Annwfyn, I suppose. And then walk through it. But I'm scared. I mean, I'm just...well, I was going to say I'm just a girl, but I guess that's not true, is it? I'm not a girl. I'm not a person. I'm a goblin and I'm not even supposed to be doing this kind of stuff. I'm not supposed to be the one rescuing kids. I'm supposed to be the one stealing them."

The bag from the old woman was hidden in her room. She'd laid out the clothes she supposed might be best suited for exploring whatever she might find on the other side of the door. It might be friendly. It might be hostile. It might be warm. It might be cold. There might be mountains. There might be dragons. There was no way to know. This, of course, she thought, meant that she should probably wear jeans and tennis shoes and a t-shirt, just like always.

"But I have to go. I do. I feel like this is all somehow my fault. Maybe if I hadn't been friends with Makayla, maybe she wouldn't have been stolen. Maybe I could have figured out a way to protect her, to tell the strange little man to stay away from her. Maybe if my parents had never had me, they never would have had to go back to stealing children."

She stifled a sob and wiped her nose with the back of her hand. The man in the fish costume hadn't responded this whole time. He still stood there, waving his sign as listlessly as he always did, the hard plastic eyes on the side of his big fish head as dull and lifeless as usual.

"I came to talk to you because I wanted you to know. I don't know who you really are, but I wanted you to know that I figured it out. I figured out where to go, and I figured out when to go, and I just needed to tell someone about it. And I thought you'd be the safest one to tell, I guess. You're the only one who's not going to try to talk me out of it. Because I have to go. My best friend needs me."

She wrapped her arms around herself, shivering in the brisk air.

"Thanks for listening. Thanks for answering my questions, even if I didn't understand the answers at first. Maybe...maybe if something goes wrong, you could tell my parents. I mean, you must know who they are, you're the Salmon of Knowledge, right?"

The man in the fish costume stood as silent as ever, barely moving now.

"Okay. I'm going to go. I've got to figure out how to get there and then I've got to figure out how to find the door. I mean, the Devil's Backbone isn't small. Or at least I don't think it is, from the maps I looked at. But the door is up there somewhere. It has to be."

She gave a thin smile.

"Maybe I should have saved one of my questions, huh?"

Brynn turned and walked away, and as she did, a stiff breeze came out of nowhere. It blew from behind her, causing her teeth to chatter and her skin to prickle. It picked up some of the trash on the street and whisked it around, tiny eddies of hamburger wrappers and discarded lottery tickets, swirling together and then falling silent once more.

A sheet of paper brushed against her leg, and then skittered ahead on the sidewalk before catching against a parking meter. It was small and yellowed with age. Curious, she bent down and picked it up. On the underside, there were four words, written in pencil, in a bold, cursive script.

It's the third one.

She turned back to the man in the fish costume, but he didn't seem to have moved. Another piece of paper brushed against her leg and stuck there. She picked it up and saw that this one was written in a familiar, untidy scrawl. It said:

Good luck.

Chapter Thirty-Six

Brynn ate dinner in silence, haunted by the thoughts of what she planned to do once the sun had set. She once again tried to avoid any eye contact with anyone else at the table, fearful they would see her pending disappearance writ large, fearful she would uncontrollably tell them, fearful she would simply burst into tears and not follow through.

When the time came for bed, she hugged her father fiercely.

"I love you, Papa," she whispered against his chest. "I'm still...I'm still upset about the things you've done. I'm still trying to figure out what it all means. But I love you."

"I love you too, sweetie," he said, holding her close. "I'm not proud of all the choices I've made. Maybe some of them weren't perfect. Or...well, I know they weren't perfect. Even if the reasons were good. Protecting you and your brother is always a good reason in my book. But that's in the past, and the most important thing now is that we stick together, right? That's what we do. We're a family. And we're goblins in a human's world. The only way for us to find our path in a world that doesn't really want us here is hand in hand and shoulder to shoulder. I know that, deep in my heart of hearts. This is our place, this is our home, and we'll find our way in it together."

Brynn nodded and wiped her eyes with the back of her hand.

"Is everything okay?" her father asked.

"It will be. I think it will be. I hope."

"I hope so, too. Good night."

"Good night, Papa."

She found Conn in the hall and hugged him goodnight, as fiercely as she had hugged her father. He only stared at her suspiciously and backed slowly into his room, peering out warily from behind the door until she felt obliged to retreat herself. She didn't expect anything different. But she still needed to let him know she loved him, any way she could.

She walked to her room, climbed into bed, and pulled the covers tight around her. When her mother came to tuck her in for the night, Brynn said, "Would you...could we do the rhyme tonight, Mama? Please?"

"You know we don't need to do that anymore, right?"

"I do, it's just..."

"We did it for so long."

"We did."

"It was part of this," her mother said, with a gentle hand on Brynn's cheek, "of going to sleep for you, for so long. Maybe it kept away the night, even a little bit." She paused and looked into Brynn's eyes. "Are you scared?"

"I am."

"Of course you are. A different world than you could have possibly expected opened up to you. There's nothing wrong with feeling scared. Whatever you feel is how you feel, and there's nothing you can do about that. The emotions you have are your own and every single one of them is part of you. It's what we do with those emotions that tells us who we are as people."

"Or goblins."

"Yes, my brave girl. Or goblins. Never be ashamed of your emotions. Let them inspire you. Turn them into bright fire and conquer the challenge in front of you. Release them into the air and let them heal you. Take them, hold them, and make something wonderful."

"Yes, Mama," Brynn said quietly, tears of unexpected joy in her eyes.

"Of course we can do the rhyme. Here." She put her hand on Brynn's heart and looked into her eyes. "Like this?"

"Yes, please."

"Say it with me?"

Brynn nodded, and they said the words together.

> *Egg and Iron encircle this heart,*
> *Fire and Clay crumble apart,*
> *We need no gold,*
> *We need no luck,*
> *There is no child here, nothing but dust.*

Brynn hoped very much that these wouldn't be the last words they ever said to each other.

Chapter Thirty-Seven

The sky was clear, the full moon brighter than she had ever seen, as Brynn slid her window open with transparent hands. She whispered a final 'good night' to her parents and brother, who she hoped were now soundly asleep, then climbed out and dropped to the ground below. Her unseen feet tapped along the wet grass as she crossed the lawn, found the sidewalk, and left her house, and her entire family, behind.

She looked down, double-checking that no part of her was visible, but she saw nothing but pavement and grass and the detritus that filled the border between them. She felt the secure bundle against her skin. Try as she might, she hadn't able to make the green canvas bag disappear, so it was tucked under her shirt, which seemed to do the trick.

She had only a vague plan as to how she was going to make her way to the Devil's Backbone. She would head toward the highway, find a bus or truck that seemed to be heading in the right direction, slip out of visibility, and hop aboard. Failing that, she might have to hitchhike, which she thought seemed like a terrible idea, but she had very few to begin with.

It only took her ten minutes to make it into town at an easy jog. And now that she was away from home, she dropped her concentration and let herself flicker back to visibility, pulling the bag out from under her shirt and slinging it over her shoulder. She took a deep breath and closed her eyes to gather her wits for the next portion of her journey. All of this would quickly turn out to be a horrible mistake.

"Coblyn! I do see thee," shouted a familiar voice, velvet wrapped in steel. "We meet again under the full moon. And this time I do promise to finish what was begun upon our last encounter!"

Brynn turned, searching, trying to find the source of the voice, when suddenly it was upon her. The woman leapt out of a nearby alley, her sword already drawn, her eyes bright with fury, her long braid aloft in the wind.

The sword swung with deadly force toward Brynn's neck. She screamed and something slipped deep within her. Her body twitched out of sync with itself, and then she was running. She felt suddenly powerful, as if she could run with the wind and just as far. She ran, as fast as she could, in any direction, toward any place that wasn't here, anywhere to escape the blond statue of towering virtue that pursued her.

Brynn glanced over her shoulder at the woman, close behind her, and when she did, she saw something she hadn't expected to see. She saw a tail, and it was only then that she realized what that curious feeling had been. She looked down, saw the green skin, saw the elongated fingers, and felt her senses expand. She was a goblin now, but this didn't seem to be a problem, as far as she could tell. It wasn't a problem at all. This body was clearly faster than the other, and she pulled away from the woman pursuing her. She also discovered that her night vision was vastly more keen, which guided her as she darted into a darkened alley, trying to lose the hunter beneath the yellow moon.

Brynn pressed herself against the wall, and focused on the hollowness deep within, and she disappeared once more. She held her breath. The woman with the sword skidded to a stop at the end of the alley, and cocked her head, looking curiously into the dark.

"You Tylwyth Teg have such an intolerable assortment of these damned tricks," the woman cried. Then she spat. She seemed to be fond of spitting. "I do see no coblyn here, but thy parcel, now floating unsupported in the air, betrays you. Thou shalt not escape. Have at thee!"

Brynn glanced down and saw that, yes, she had forgotten to tuck her bag away, and, yes, there it sat, hovering in midair. The discovery shocked her back to full visibility. The woman ran toward her, and Brynn ran as well, leaping across overturned garbage cans and piles of flattened cardboard boxes. She quickly discovered that this body could jump surprisingly high and surprisingly far (which felt surprisingly good as she bounded through the air) but she had little time to focus on her enjoyment as she attempted to escape the bundle of keening fury behind her.

As she ran, she tried to pull the bag off her arm, tried to tuck it somewhere under her clothes, anywhere at all, but it seemed to be tangled up somehow. She also tried to focus downward, back to the nothingness, back to the hollowness, but trying to run, disappear, and disentangle the bag, all at the same time, while in a state of blind panic, left her without concentration enough to do any of them particularly well. As she ran, her concentration faltering and coalescing and faltering again, she could feel her body flickering in and out of visibility like some sort of deranged fluorescent bulb.

She hurtled out of the alley and onto a street. Maybe, Brynn thought, maybe she was faster now. Maybe she could lose the woman simply by running faster. She poured on the speed and sprinted as fast as her sinuous goblin legs could carry her.

"Thy newfound coblyn form shall not avail thee!" the woman resounded effervescently, her voice as pure as ever, no sign that this pursuit was even winding her. "Nor shall thy disappearing tricks! Neither shall save thee from my righteous quest to rid the world of all thy kind. No more children shall be taken! Not while Gwenllian ferch Gruffydd has aught to say about it. Not while my mother's daughter draws enough breath in these her lungs to pursue thee wherever thou and thy wretched kin do seek to conceal thyselves!"

Brynn looked behind her. The woman had ungodly strength, each stride seeming to propel her faster and higher until she was practically airborne. Brynn was keeping her distance, but she wasn't gaining any ground. She knew she had to try something else.

She cast her thoughts back. What had her mother told her about the abilities of their people, about their aspects? There was something about a bird, wasn't there? She remembered. Her real name, not Brynn but Branwen, was an old name, and it meant 'white raven.' Her mother had told her that her name was there to protect her. If she could find it, the white raven was within her as well.

She felt down deep within herself. There was the

hollowness, the part that made her disappear. There was the ancient, gnarled burl of thorn, the part she barely had a grasp on, that she had found only a handful of times so far, the part within her that was the goblin. And there was the part she thought of as human, her fair folk essence, the part that she had known as herself for so long.

There was something else in there, though. She knew there was. There had to be. She had to keep searching. She found it difficult, though, with a hero in pursuit, righteous utterances flowing from her throat like knives slicing through silk.

"Thou canst not escape me, coblyn! I shall hound thee to the ragged scraps at the far edges of this world, and of all the worlds, if need be! Hast thou traveled there, fiend? To the far-flung dark places at the fringes of the worlds? For in sooth, I have. I have pursued thy kind there, and farther still. I have slain greater than thou, more powerful than thou, in far more dangerous dens than this, this borough of stench and nonsense that thou dost call Jeffersonville. I long to be rid of this hellish conurbation. But that I cannot do until thou breathest no more, until thy bones descend into the dust from whence they were most damnedly brought forth!"

Brynn could feel that this body was stronger, was faster, was keener than the other she had worn her whole life. But she also could tell that, no matter how far she ran, the woman pursuing her could run even farther. She kept searching, deep down inside, the slivers of herself that made up the whole. There was the gnarled piece, there was the hollow, and there was the fair. The goblin, the disappearance, herself. Skin of green, skin of glass, skin of white. And as she found each one, she felt her body transitioning between them as she ran, as she fled from the hero behind. Her body flickered in and out of forms, from human, to goblin, to nothing, and back again, as she tried to find the white raven within her.

She tried to think of a raven, she tried to think of white, she tried to think of wings, but all she felt was pounding pavement, and burning lungs, and the necessity of escape, and her body changing and changing and changing again, in vain pursuit of a transformation she didn't know how to access, and frankly didn't know if it even existed at all.

The changes were coming faster and faster as she tried to find something, anything within herself that would unlock the white raven inside. Skin of white, skin of green, and skin of glass cycled faster and faster. Pale then green then nothing, pale then green then nothing, pale then green then nothing, until she was practically a self-propelled strobe light hurtling through the dark.

It was so hard for Brynn to do any of this when all she felt within was fear, a fear that was growing, an all-consuming fear. Fear of the woman behind her, fear of the air burning her lungs, fear that her body would collapse before she could escape. Suddenly, she heard her mother's voice in her ear, a faint memory, an unbidden ghost.

"Never be ashamed of your emotions," the voice whispered. "Take them, hold them, and make something wonderful."

And then, instead of searching for a thing within herself, a thing she couldn't find, a thing that might not even be there at all, Brynn focused on the fear. She held it within her hands as she ran. She allowed it to be. She embraced it as part of herself. She took the fear, and she saw it, and she held it close. And then she turned it into bright fire and made something wonderful.

She felt that new something within herself, this new creation engulfing her and pouring forth, born from the fire, and born from the fear, and out of the cascading blur of changing hues and forms, another shape emerged, and this one was as white as the driven snow.

Brynn looked below her and saw the ground drop away. She looked beside her and saw strong, broad wings propelling her into the night sky. She looked beneath her and saw that, somehow, during the change, she had grasped the canvas bag with her feet, and her talons, as bone white as the rest of her now, clutched the handle and carried the bag upward with her.

She was flying. She was in the air. And the woman below was screaming in unbridled rage at the loss of her quarry.

Brynn was flying. She was floating on the wind. The air rushed past her, and her wings felt marvelous as they beat the air, and she could see so, so far, and she could hear so, so much, and the whole thing felt simply unbelievable.

She swooped and dove. She banked and twisted. Gravity had no hold on her. She was free, unfettered, aloft in the starless sky and there was profound freedom there, her snow-white feathers carrying her through the blackest night. She sang her joy to the full moon. And the full moon beamed her joy back at her.

This was much better than hitchhiking, she thought. So, so much better.

Chapter Thirty-Eight

It was 11 p.m. in Jeffersonville, Indiana, and Brynn McAwber was flying above the city on wings as white as bone. Her senses were keener than she would have thought possible. Her raven's eyes could spot an open window a mile away. She could hear even farther than that, or so she imagined. She flew above the city, clutching the bag below her, and knew she should find the river, because the river would lead her to the Devil's Backbone, and she needed to find her friend.

But her raven's heart told her otherwise. Her raven's heart told her to soar on the winds and let them carry her far, far away, far from the tribulations of her goblin family, far from the pursuing eyes and swords of vengeful heroes, far from the burdens of her teenage life. She could let the bag fall from her talons, the threadbare bag with the ridiculous artifacts the old woman had given her. She could let the bag fall to the earth below, and let that act free her from her former life. There might even be a nice explosion to watch from the air if the grenade happened to be real.

A chill prickled her feathers. No, she thought. She knew she couldn't, she knew it deep down inside. It was tempting to let the raven overcome her, but that would mean leaving her family behind, and leaving Makayla in danger. She had a task to do, and now she had wings to carry her on her way.

She trained her eyes on the water, banked sharply, and moments later, she was above the river. The current ran thick and dark below her, and Brynn followed the river upstream, away from the city, away from her family, away from all that she knew, toward the unknown, toward the Land of Annwfyn.

Her wings were powerful, and they carried her swiftly. The librarian had shown her the map of the river, of the ridge she sought, and only a dozen minutes after taking flight (or so she estimated, although she couldn't be sure how this raven body sensed the passage of time), she saw the fork in the river.

There, on the left, was the narrow channel diverging from the river. And there, between the creek and the river sat a tall, rocky ridge, covered in trees. Craggy and dark, the ridge looked as if it could indeed have been the spine of a devil, hunched in the deeps. Brynn was flying over it now. She was over the Devil's Backbone. She remembered the map in the library, the one that had shown the burial mounds on top of the ridge. And as she flew, she could see them now, could just make them out through the trees.

There were nine of them, and they stretched in a ragged line along the ridge, beginning where the creek met the river. And it was then that she understood the note from the Salmon of Knowledge, the one that had floated to her on the wind. From the end of the Devil's Backbone, she counted the mounds: one, two, and there was the third.

She slowed the beating of her wings, drew them in close,

and sailed downward through the trees. She fluttered her wings and bumped to a fairly graceful landing, thankful that her raven body seemed to know what to do. She focused down within herself, found the part of herself that she still thought of as a teenage girl, and drew it forth.

When her hands and feet and eyes and hair had returned to her, she was grateful to find that her clothes had returned as well. Setting out into the unknown without a stitch on her would have been a challenge she hadn't foreseen.

And then she stood there, bag in hand, a skinny girl on top of the Devil's Backbone, in front of what she hoped was a burial mound, in front of what she hoped was the correct burial mound that would take her, somehow, into another world.

She stared at the large mound in front of her. She stared at it for a long time.

"That," she said aloud to herself since there didn't seem to be anyone around to overhear, "that is just a big pile of rocks. What the hell am I supposed to do now?"

Chapter Thirty-Nine

It really did look like no more than a pile of earth and stone, grown over with moss and brush. Just a mound of dirt on a ridge in a river, that's almost certainly what it was, if Brynn's doubts were to be believed. It was time to find out if all the clues she'd amassed meant something, or if (perhaps and more likely) she was crazy. Because either this was a doorway to another world, or she was slowly losing her mind.

Nine times, the librarian had said, nine times around clockwise, never the other direction. She set her bag down on the brush to mark her place. Then she walked around the burial mound once, back to where she had started, back to the bag with the apple and the laser pointer and the grenade. There was no change to the mound in front of her. She walked around again and again, checking the sky, the dirt, the jumbled rocks, but there was no sound but the river, nothing to see but the moonlight filtering through the branches above.

Brynn kept walking, keeping tally each time she passed her bag of oddities: four, five, six, seven, eight, and she held her breath as she completed the ninth circle. Then she waited. There was the mound, just as it had been. There were the trees, there was the moon, there were the brush and moss covering the earth. Nothing had changed.

She bit her nails, counting the seconds, waiting to see if something would happen. But it didn't. The mound was just a mound. The trees were just trees. The dirt was just dirt.

She waited for several minutes, weariness and despair nearly overtaking her, before she heard it, far off in the distance: the cry of a hawk. It was answered promptly by another. Somewhere across the river, under the moon, they called to each other. The cries circled above her, but she could not see their source, could see nothing above her but the moon and the trees, and then she heard another sound, a softer sound, from somewhere behind her: a sibilance moving through the brush, along the ridge, coming from the river.

Her breath quickened, her pulse raced, and a scream caught in her throat as a serpent, glistening and bright, slithered toward her through the trees, so fast that it was nearly upon her before she could react. Its eyes were dusky jewels, and its scales were the color of autumn corn. It was longer than her arm, far longer, thicker as well, and it slid by her quickly, across the forest floor, toward the mound. A cool breeze brushed her cheek as it passed, chilling her to the bone.

Brynn shivered and clutched herself tightly as a second snake approached, and then a third. Each ignored her completely, moving directly to the burial mound on top of the ridge. With each snake that passed, the air grew colder and colder, and by the time the fourth snake went by, she could see her breath on the air.

The snakes were dancing on the mound now, all four of

them, intertwining with each other, circling, separating, and then meeting again. A fifth snake joined as Brynn backed away, her eyes wide, her breath coming in short gasps. They were talking to each other, she was sure of it, their hisses distinct and sharp as they slithered over the top of the mound. A sixth snake passed her, and then a seventh, and the limbs of the trees were covered in frost. An eighth snake went by and the ground crackled beneath her feet. A ninth snake joined and she could barely feel her toes.

The snakes paid her no mind as they palavered and pranced upon the mound. They came together, head to tail, to form a rippling ring which slowly began to spin, the overlapping snakes sliding across the frosty earth beneath. The circle of serpents moved faster and faster, the air now so cold that Brynn was shuddering uncontrollably. Needles of pain pricked her with every breath as she drew the frozen air into her lungs. Her back was against a tree, a dozen feet from the mound, and its frigid bark pressed into her as the snakes moved faster, nine segments of an undulating wheel, fire moving over ice, their sharp hiss discordant over the running water far below.

Faster and faster they went, nothing but a blur now, a slithering circle of glistening striations, when suddenly there was a blinding flash of light and a peal of thunder, and when the stars had cleared from Brynn's eyes, all was still, and all was silent. A sheet of ice lay across the burial mound. It was roughly circular and bore the imprints of the snakes which had flowed across the earth, but of the serpents themselves, there was no sign. Brynn could feel the air warming, and as she approached the mound, the frost was already leaving the trees which ringed the clearing around it.

The sheet of ice was thick, perhaps three inches through, and cloudy enough that she could no longer see what lay beneath it. She poked at the ice nervously with her finger, but it did not move. It did not appear to contain any snakes within it. It was simply a sheet of ice where there had not been one mere seconds before. It was nothing but cold and solid and inscrutable. She ran her hand across it, and her hand came away wet. The air was warming quickly, much more quickly than she would have thought possible, and the ice was already melting.

There was a slight crack, the sound of a frozen pond on the first day of spring, and the sheet of ice shifted slightly, a fraction of an inch. Brynn caught a glimpse of something underneath it, something bright and smooth. She clambered up the side of the mound, sat down above the sheet of ice, and pushed at it with her feet. She pushed and kicked and kicked again until finally there was movement. The sheet slid down the face of the mound, crashed to the forest floor below, and splintered into a thousand pieces, which rapidly began to melt, until scant seconds later, there was no sign left of the ice, or the snakes, or the freezing air which had haunted the ridge only moments before.

There was, however, a door. She had circled the mound nine times, and a door had appeared. Okay, she thought, achievement unlocked: not crazy.

The door was circular, set directly into the sloping surface of the mound, with a distinct line running from top to bottom, which (she presumed) would allow it to open. It was ringed with heavy, square flagstones, ancient and pitted, but the door itself was smooth and clean. An unbroken string of indecipherable writing ran all along the outer edge, but try as she might, not a single character could be understood to her eyes. A beam of moonlight had broken through the trees, ephemera floating in the glow, and the beam landed squarely on the center of the door, where a metal disc lay, about the size of her hand. At the center of the disc was a hole, about the size of her finger. There was nothing else. No instructions, no handle, and above all, no key.

Brynn had thought, perhaps, that once she found the entrance, she could simply walk into the Land of Annwfyn, and there would be Makayla waiting for her, waiting to be rescued. Apparently, it was not going to be that simple. She'd found a door, as she had hoped. But the door she'd found was large and heavy and very, very solid and very, very closed.

She pounded on the door as hard as she could, but there was no response. She tried to read the writing which curved along the edge, but she could find no meaning. She tried to dig around the edge of the door, but the underbrush grew thick and heavy right up to the flagstones, and she succeeded in doing nothing but scraping her knuckles on brambles and thorns. She pulled at the seam that ran down the middle of the door but could gain no purchase, although she did manage to break a fingernail.

She slid her hand over the door. It felt cold and smooth and unyielding. This didn't seem remotely fair. She'd come so far, she'd deciphered all the clues, and now there was nothing but this frustratingly inaccessible stone circle. She stared at the door again for several minutes, lost in confusion. So far, the teenage girl atop the Devil's Backbone had found no luck with this door. Maybe, Brynn thought, maybe a goblin could do better.

She found the ancient core, down within herself, and brought it forth. She stood there, in her green skin and barbed tail and pointy ears. She could sense so much more than she had moments before, but the door looked just the same. She prodded at it with her goblin fingers, but there was still no result.

She found the hollowness within her, and flickered out of visibility, and slid her disappeared hand across the surface of the door, but it remained impenetrable and obscure. The white raven had no better luck, as she pecked at the stone with her porcelain beak.

Brynn shifted herself back to normal, now thoroughly flummoxed. She picked up the bag which sat at her feet. The old woman said that one of the objects within could help her enter the Land of Annwfyn. She pulled the grenade out and held it in her hand. She supposed she could try to blow the door open with it, but this seemed unreasonably dangerous. She decided that she would try this only as a last resort. She pulled out the laser pointer and pressed the button. A bright red dot appeared on the stone door, but nothing else happened. She waved the dot over the surface of the stone, but it was just a red dot dancing in the dark, through the thick beam of moonlight, across the cold stone below.

She pulled out the apple and looked at it. It looked red and juicy and delicious. She couldn't think of any way an apple could help her to open a door. But the longer she looked at the apple, the more she wondered about it. Weren't there magic apples, she thought, in some of the old fairy tales? Or was she thinking of the poisoned apple from Snow White? Maybe, if she ate it, this apple could give her the mystical power to open the door. Or perhaps it would grant her supernatural senses that would reveal a handle, or a key, unseen to her now. Or maybe the apple granted massive strength, enough to pry open an immovable door. Or, of course, perhaps it would kill her.

The old woman told her that one object could help her enter, one could guide her within, and one could help her escape. Maybe she was supposed to use the apple to escape, or to find her way, not to open a door. Why, she thought, why did all these people have to be so cryptic with their advice?

Brynn looked at the apple again and shined it against her shirt. It was a beautiful apple, she had to give the old woman that. With no better ideas offering themselves to her, she took a bite. She chewed, tasted, and swallowed. It was just as she had suspected. It was delicious. She examined her fingers, felt along her abdomen. She sensed nothing inside her that would seem to presage untimely death. So, she thought, perhaps not poison then. She gazed at the stone door. She saw nothing she hadn't seen as a girl, as a goblin, or as a raven.

She took another bite. It was still delicious. She examined her body again. She continued to not be dead, but her senses had not expanded to supernatural proportions either. The third bite yielded more of the same. The apple was clearly a bust. The only thing she learned was that fleeing from a vengeful hero and then flying ten miles up a river had left her ravenous. She finished the apple, eating it down to the core, while she stared at the door, her brow knotted in concentration.

She wondered if her quest would end before it had really begun. Perhaps she would just have to slink back to town and, in all likelihood, be slain by the hero who had been watching her for months. That's what goblins were supposed to do, weren't they, she thought, be slain by heroes?

Brynn took one last bite, frustration and discouragement all that remained in her heart, and was pulled from her gloom only when she noticed how unusually solid the core of the apple felt in her hand. This seemed strange to her, considering how tender and sweet the flesh had been. She held the core aloft, and the singular beam of moonlight shone along its surface. Angular grooves seemed to trace themselves up and down its length. The marks left by her teeth protruded sharply, and the seeds lined up in a neat row. The core was substantial and intricate, unlike any apple she'd seen before.

Only one small chunk of the apple's remains seemed to stand apart from the complexity, from the solidity of the rest. The upper tip of the core still held the stem and a few pulpy bits of flesh, and it hung by a few tendrils to the rigid base of the center. Curious, she pulled at the stem, and the pulpy tip came cleanly away, leaving a dull, triangular point on the far end, and an intricate, notched cylinder behind, just about the width of her finger.

"It can't be that simple, can it?" she said to herself, as she placed the point of the apple core against the hole in the middle of the door and gently pushed. It slid in noiselessly, and she heard a faint click as the base of the core settled into place.

Brynn set her fingers against the remains of the candy-red apple and turned it clockwise. Instantly, she heard a dull rumbling, and the seam of the door rose outward on hidden hinges, revealing a long, stone corridor beyond.

Chapter Forty

She stood there, on the threshold of another world, and there was nothing to do but take one step and then another. There were torches, she saw, actual torches, lining the walls of the passageway, darkening the walls behind them with soot and smoke. They sputtered periodically but never faltered. Brynn wondered how long they had been burning, or if they had been lit just for her.

The walls curved over her head as the path led her downward, underground, farther into the burial mound, farther from the only world she knew. The vaulted passage continued onward and onward, and her feet trudged dutifully along, the multitudes of torches causing a multitude of shadows, which danced along the walls and the floor in front of her as she walked.

After ten minutes of walking, when she thought that she must be far underground, or perhaps even underneath the river (although the walls and floors were perfectly dry), the passageway suddenly opened onto a grand, domed chamber. The room was round and vast. The ceiling, far above, was painted to resemble a sunlit garden, although the colors were faded with age. The floor was tiled in thick, blue flagstones which ran from wall to wall, their complex pattern unbroken except at the very center of the room, which was occupied only by a ragged circle of earth. In the center of the earth was a thick, metal pole. And atop the pole was a head, the base of the neck neatly severed. The head looked human, and looked as if it had recently been attached to a body, although where one would have expected to see blood or viscera dripping from a newly decapitated head, the wound was dry and clean.

On the far wall stood three immense doors, tall and narrow, gilded with bright metal and inset with jewels. The ubiquitous torches were here as well, and their light reflected from the gleaming doors and shimmered across the room. Brynn stepped carefully into the chamber, and her footfalls echoed through the still air.

She examined the earthen circle as she approached the center of the room. The impaled head within was not unpleasant to look at, and Brynn suspected that the decapitated man would have been considered handsome while he lived. The skin was fair, and the hair was long and dark. Several heavy gold rings dangled from each ear, and a pointed beard hung from the chin.

As her foot stepped onto the final flagstone at the edge of the circle of earth, the eyes of the head snapped open, causing her to start in surprise. Its jaw moved tentatively, as if it had not moved in some time, which Brynn hoped was the case, and was in great wonderment as to why it was moving now. Somehow, she was not surprised when the severed head spoke to her, in a voice both raspy and sonorous.

"Halt, traveler!" the head intoned, fixing its eyes upon her. "Do you seek to enter the Land of Annwfyn?"

"Umm, yeah," Brynn said, unsure how to address a head absent a body, her previous life having left her unprepared for such a development, "I do."

"Then I have grave news to impart, for I am here to deny your passage! Your path led you here, here to the Devil's Backbone, to the final resting place of Madoc ab Owain Gwynedd. You have revealed the door upon the burial mound. You unlocked the door and found your way to the very threshold of Annwfyn. Few of your kind have made it even this far, a mere spider's breath from the realm of the fair folk themselves. But here, mortal, here your journey must end! Whatever you sought within the Otherworld must be forever lost to you. For only those of the Tylwyth Teg may enter this land. It is for them, and them only. Those such as you have no place here!"

The eyes of the severed head snapped shut, its mouth closed, and it moved no more. Brynn couldn't tell whether whatever presence was within it had departed, or if it was merely playing possum. She stepped onto the dark, loamy earth beneath the head, and gently poked at the pole with her finger.

"Excuse me," she said politely, "I'm sorry to disturb you, Mr. Severed Head, but I really need to find out how to get into Annwfyn. My friend is in there, and I need to find her. She might be in danger. You could tell me which door to use, or I guess I could just go try them, but I thought maybe you could help me. If you wanted."

The severed head made no response to any of her entreaties.

"I just...I really have to go in."

She waited again, but sensing that no further answers were forthcoming, she left the head behind and walked toward the doors at the far side of the room.

"Mortal!"

Brynn shrieked and jumped in alarm as she heard the cry from behind her. She turned and saw the severed head rotating slowly to face her, using its neck muscles to slowly jostle itself around the pole. She waited patiently, as each twitch only moved the head a fraction of an inch. When the severed head had finished its tortuous circumnavigation, it spoke again.

"Mortal," it repeated, "do you insist on following this path? Even if it should mean your certain doom?"

"I...I have to go in," Brynn said. "I don't think I really have a choice."

"Very well then!" the head bellowed, as a hollow echo resounded through the chamber. "If you will not desist (a decision which is certain to lead to your gruesome and untimely demise), it is my obligation to inform you that any mortal who wishes to enter the home of the Tylwyth Teg must face one of three challenges. Behind each of these doors lies an impossible task, and only by completing one of these may you pass out of the burial mound and into the Land of Annwfyn!"

The severed head paused, arching its eyebrows skyward, as if to give Brynn a chance to respond. When she did not, it looked slightly discomfited but continued onward with its soliloquy.

"Behind the first door lies a fearsome beast which has never fallen in combat, which has never been outwitted. Its rage never abates, its strength never flags, and its hunger is never sated. To pass through, you must defeat this foul creature, vanquish it mercilessly, or it shall devour you! Every mortal who has chosen this door has been consumed, has been swallowed whole, even before a sword could be raised to challenge the foe within!"

At the far end of the chamber, the first door opened slowly of its own accord, and through the tall aperture, Brynn saw only brief flashes of the beast that paced and howled beyond: massive, hooved feet; a thick tail, spiked and covered in scales; claws longer than her arm and thinner than paper. There were flames, and there was horror. The beast bellowed, and the rage in its voice shook the entire chamber. Brynn could smell blood and the pent-up stench of eternal fury.

The severed head paused again, a satisfied smile upon its lips. It raised its eyebrows once, for dramatic effect, before continuing on.

"Behind the center door lies a riddle, written on parchment. To pass through, all you must do is answer the riddle. Simple enough? Perhaps! But this riddle is still being written, and the scribe within has been composing it for a thousand years! He writes faster than the wind, the thoughts flowing from his quill like water from a fall, and with every line he writes, the riddle grows more inscrutable, its answer more unattainable to any but the infinite minds of the wisest of the gods. Every being who has ever attempted to answer this riddle has been driven mad before their eyes finished the first sentence. The question is more than a mortal mind could ever hope to comprehend, and the answer is as unknowable as the universe itself!"

The second door opened slowly, and within, Brynn saw a massive wooden table, on top of which lay a long sheet of parchment, anchored down by a series of what appeared to be skulls, some human and some otherwise. The end of the parchment trailed off the end of the table, and continued onward, lying in limp rolls all across the floor. The rolls were stacked up along the walls and hung from chandeliers. They were wound about chairs and layered haphazardly upon the bookcases that filled the walls of the enormous room, from floor to ceiling.

A spindly, wizened little man sat high in an alcove, his fingers and clothes so ink-stained as to be nearly unrecognizable. He wore a pot of ink strapped to his back, which must have held several gallons at least, and he continually reached his quill behind him, over his shoulder, as he wrote lines and lines of text on the seemingly never-ending roll of parchment, throwing off more and more curls of script to dry in the wind. When the door opened, the slight current in the air brought Brynn a faint whiff of ozone as she stared at the madness within.

The severed head paused once again and pursed its lips, eyes rolling feverishly in its head, as it chortled at Brynn's reaction. Its voice dropped into an awestruck whisper as it continued its speech.

"And through the third and final door lies a table set for a King. Any food you could possibly desire is there, and every food as well. Upon these platters are delicacies from far-off lands, delicacies from countries that no longer exist, delicacies from worlds that have been wiped from the catalogue of existence, except for their place at this table. You shall see sweets from the farthest reaches of the universe, viands from the depths of the earth, a goblet filled with the essence of the wind. To pass through, you must sit at this table, a table set for the gods themselves, and finish the meal upon it. You must eat every morsel, from one end to the other, before you may leave. But this table has no end, for it was set for those whose appetite is as boundless as time! You may sit at this table, and you may eat, and every bite you take shall bring you pleasure heretofore unknown to any of your kind. But beware, for every bite you take shall only serve to increase your desire for the next, and within mere moments, you shall devour yourself into oblivion! No mortal has lasted more than nine and a half minutes at the heavenly table you see before you!"

The third door opened, and the odors that poured forth were indeed so tempting that Brynn could think of nothing else but rushing through to the table beyond, and gorging herself on every dish that lay upon it. The sole chair in the room was tall and magnificent and resplendent in white, and the table it sat before was loaded with foods that she was afterwards unable even to describe, other than knowing that she desperately wanted nothing more than a single taste of each.

Brynn stared at the three open doors, feeling utterly and hopelessly vanquished already, before she'd even made the choice of which challenge to face.

"So, what say you, Mortal," and here the head slathered the word 'mortal' with a condescension so thick that Brynn felt waves of it pressing into her skin, "do you still say that you wish to enter the Land of Annwfyn?"

"I...I do," Brynn said, her voice barely a whisper.

"Then which do you choose?" the head intoned. "The Unvanquished Beast? The Eternal Riddle? Or the Neverending Feast? For as I have told you, only those of the Tylwyth Teg may enter the Land of Annwfyn! You may choose one of these three challenges if you wish, but for such as you, each is certain to mean your doom!"

Brynn cocked her head at him.

"Wait a second," she said.

"Yes?" the head glowered, its eyes fiery, a menacing scowl plastered upon its visage.

"You keep saying that mortals are forbidden from entering."

"That is correct!" the head bellowed. "Any mortal who attempts to pass through these doors will meet a certain and most unpleasant doom!"

"Yep. You've said essentially that same thing a bunch of times. But what about...I don't know, what about non-mortals? Can they enter?"

"Of course!" the head intoned, its voice echoing throughout the vast chamber. "The Land of Annwfyn is for the Tylwyth Teg, and for them alone! The boundaries of the country of the fair folk may not be crossed by any others, unless they should face the challenges I have set before you! Now, mortal, the time has come! Choose! And choose wisely! For else, you are sure to meet your doom!"

"Oh, well, you see," Brynn said with a shrug, "you see, here's the thing. I'm not actually a human. I'm a goblin."

She felt down within herself, found the ancient, gnarled

feeling within, and brought it forth. Her human form flickered away, and now she stood there changed, green skin and sinuous tail and pointed ears and all.

"Oh," said the severed head, "you are?"

"I am."

"Oh," the severed head said again, clearly deflated. "Well, you could have just said so. You can use the service entrance."

The three massive doors closed slowly, the terrors and beauties within faded from sight, and Brynn could no longer smell the horror and madness and exquisite deliciousness that lay beyond. Once they were firmly shut, a small plain door, previously unseen, creaked open, and it was to this entrance that Brynn ran, as fast as her feet would carry her.

Chapter Forty-One

This hall was much narrower than the one Brynn had followed to the chamber with the severed head, and the torches were smaller and less frequent. She moved from illumination to illumination, but spent much of the long walk along this corridor in darkness, seeking out each burning torch to guide her way to the next.

After ten minutes or twenty or a hundred (she feared she was losing track of time as she traversed the tunnel), she came to the last visible torch. She stumbled past it, feeling along the wall with one hand, while the other clasped her bag tightly against her. Her hand traced the edge of the rough stone until she found herself obstructed by a solid mass in front of her. Whatever it was, her hands told her that it felt like wood. She gave a tentative push and was surprised when the surface moved on silent hinges, a door springing open into a brightly-lit expanse beyond, the sudden illumination nearly blinding her.

The room in front of her was huge, and loud, and full of movement and smells and creatures she knew she couldn't even hope to recognize. There were long tables and tall rows of shelves and wide iron sinks and barrels taller than she was, and far in the back, she could see enormous earthen structures filled with flame. It was then that Brynn realized she had stumbled into a kitchen, but one unlike any she'd ever seen before.

The ceiling was so high that birds were nesting in the rafters overhead. The winged creatures, sharp of eye and beak and wing, far darker and far faster than any she'd ever seen back home, would swoop down to claim any unguarded scraps and then retreat to their airy perches above.

There were dozens and dozens, perhaps hundreds, of beings at work, chopping and baking and cooking and sautéing and cleaning and sweeping. And she was fairly sure that 'beings' was the proper word here, because, of the vast multitude she saw, she didn't think a single one was human.

There was a regiment of creatures with green skin and tails, who she thought must be goblins (or coblyns, as her father preferred) like her. At a long trestle table, assembling what seemed to be crusts for the largest pies she could imagine, were a dozen or so creatures of intensely black hue, with bright, phosphorescent hair, and the constellations within their skin swirled ever so slowly, and Brynn realized that these must be the xana, like her mother. At the back of the room, clustered around the tall earthen ovens, were huge bunches of knotted muscle, as tall as trees, with faces like carbuncles and eyes like coal, who manned the bellows which kept the massive ovens aflame.

A coterie of tall, spindly beings, with pointy ears and grey skin and uncommonly pointed shoes and saucer-shaped eyes of icy blue or icy yellow, moved carefully through the chaos, wearing crisp, white aprons. Their features were delicate, and their clothing and hair were fancifully appointed and impeccably maintained. As each pan was brought from the ovens, the spindly creatures would arrange the components of the dishes on plates and in tureens and on platters and then whisk the completed meals out of the room, off to destinations unknown.

Along the wall stood a bank of sinks and tubs, steam and profanities billowing forth. Scrubbing the pots and earthenware within were a group of creatures whose skin seemed as translucent as the water itself, so much so that it was difficult for Brynn to tell just where the beings left off and the water began. They sang as they worked, and although she did not understand the words, the song left her head light and her throat parched for drink.

Her gawping was interrupted by a tall man, more familiar in appearance than any other she'd seen in this immense room. His face was craggy, his eyes were golden, and his dark hair was long, trailing in a thick mane down his back. She would have thought him human but for the long, horse-like ears that jutted from the sides of his head, and the long tail of wiry hair which twitched impatiently behind him.

"You!" he shouted, striding toward her between tables piled high with mountains of vegetables being diced at inhuman speeds by a company of goblins. A thick sheaf of parchment, soiled by vinegar and dusted in flour, was clutched in his hands. He flipped through the lists and charts and recipes until he finally found the page he sought.

"What are you doing?" he bellowed at Brynn, finally making eye contact and drawing himself up to his full height, his tail swishing menacingly.

"Umm...nothing," she hesitated, her eyes sliding

surreptitiously around the edges of the room, seeking any options for escape.

"Are you supposed to be here?"

She shrugged uncertainly. He squinted suspiciously at her.

"You appear to be idle. Is that correct?"

She gulped and then nodded.

"I guess so?" she said.

"Excellent!" he cried victoriously. "Then I have a task for you, one of utmost urgency! Take...hmm...this one with you." He reached out his hand, without looking, and grasped a nearby goblin by the collar, whom he then pushed against Brynn. The hunched goblin stumbled and mumbled an apology, his eyes never leaving the floor.

"The wind giants in Tir fo Thuinn are demanding their Millennium Soufflé, several decades before its appointed time," the horse-eared man announced ominously. "We have shown them a variety of calendars, lunar and solar, mystical and mundane, to highlight their error, but they will not be appeased. Their most recent howls of complaint emptied a small sea and diverted the migration patterns of several subspecies of the Intrepid Spiderhawk. It has been decided, by those who decide such things, that it will be best to simply allow them their unscheduled indulgence."

The tall man nodded knowingly, as if Brynn should be able to understand the serious ramifications of this statement, but she could only stare in slack-jawed confusion.

"A delicate dish such as this," the man continued stridently, "typically requires a year and a day of preparation, whereas we shall be creating this confection in mere hours!"

"But what—," Brynn started to say, but the man took no pause for her inquiry.

"It will take at least two of you. Procure other assistance if you should find it necessary. Now," he said, handing Brynn a rusty tin bucket and a tuning fork as big as her head, "go shear the Zephyr! Go!"

"What?" was all Brynn managed to utter.

"The Zephyr! It needs to be sheared and I need one full bucket of zephyric leavings nearly before yesterday, but I am straight out of time-traveling sous chefs, so you two will have to do!"

"But—"

"No more delays! To the Tower of Intolerable Ascension! You will need to take the Serpentine Corridor, and then the Staircase of Woeful Appetite to the tower's entrance. Ask the Wardens of the Seventeenth Gate there, and they will direct you to the Chamber of Shrieking Winds, in which the Zephyr usually resides. When you have completed the shearing, return here to me!"

He turned away, his nose buried once again in the shambolic pile of stained parchment, but then turned back, uttering one final pronouncement.

"Should your essences become transmuted, we shall send a party after you in one week. Now go!"

And then he disappeared into the mass of culinary activity that swirled throughout the room.

Brynn stared after him in wild-eyed horror, before her eyes fell to the bucket and tuning fork which now rested in her hands. She was relieved to have escaped discovery, but alarmed to have been tasked with what was apparently an extremely dangerous duty, and was now unsure how best to proceed. She stood there, lost in her quandary until the goblin at her side cleared his throat nervously.

"Well," he mumbled, "we should, umm, probably get to it. I guess."

"Yeah. Yeah, I guess we should," she said, and followed him as he led her between tables and around massive bins of unidentifiable vegetables to a broad corridor which led away from the kitchen.

"I'm Chwilen," he offered after they had been walking for some time.

"I'm...Branwen," Brynn responded, struggling to remember precisely how her mother had pronounced the name.

"Great," he sighed. "You been working here long?"

Brynn shrugged.

"It's not so bad," he continued. "The Head Pwca, he's not so bad once you get used to him."

"That guy back there, the one with the...horse ears...he's in charge? And he's a...he's a what?"

"A Pwca. Don't say the word 'horse' to him, though. He'd flay you with his teeth."

Brynn shuddered, and followed the other goblin as he led them onward. She re-adjusted the bag on her shoulder and the bucket in her hands. Her guide kept a brisk pace, and she struggled to match it as they veered through corridor after corridor. She tried to remember each twist and turn, in case she needed to find her way back, but within moments, she was utterly lost and at the mercy of her companion for any navigation.

"Hey," she called out, as she quickened her pace to match his, "have you ever heard of a place called the Swallowed Hall?"

"Yeah, I think so," he shrugged. "It's out beyond the plains, even past the Dunes, isn't it?"

"I don't know," she hedged. "Someone told me I need to go there."

He looked sidelong at her, his eyebrows raised apprehensively.

"We...we need to get to the Tower," he said suspiciously. "Didn't you hear the Pwca?"

They continued on for some time before Brynn found a moment to bring the subject up again. They were ascending a steep incline in the vacant corridor, and the goblin in front of her had slowed his pace somewhat.

"Can I tell you a secret?" she whispered to him, struggling to match his strides.

"I guess," he mumbled, his eyes on the irregular stones that tiled the floor of the passageway.

"I'm not supposed to be here. I really...I really need to get out of here, but I'm not sure how."

He gave a quick glance over at her.

"What do you mean, you're not supposed to be here?"

"I'm not...I'm not really working in the kitchens. I just accidentally ended up in there because I'm looking for someone. I'm looking for my friend. She's lost, and I think she might be in danger."

"Really?"

"Yeah. I'm worried about her. I'm really scared something bad is going to happen to her."

He nodded as they continued their walk.

"I think I can relate," he said. "My best friend, his name is Mwydyn, he's always getting into scrapes. He always wants to go places that little goblins like us shouldn't go, you know? Always wants to see the top of the tower, always wants to find the deepest dungeon. He got trapped down in the mud at the Ineffable Channel once, it took me a week to find him." He gave a sad nod of his head, the tips of his ears waggling with emotion. "I know what it's like to worry about a friend."

"So, do you think you could help me out?" she asked him quietly.

He gave a shy smile.

"Yeah, I guess so."

"Really? Oh, that's amazing. I just need to find my way out of here, out to the...the plains, I guess, and then see if I can track down the Swallowed Hall."

He glanced around and then wiggled his eyebrows mischievously.

"Wait a second," he said. "I have an idea."

The corridor was widening, and ahead, she could see a large, ominous staircase, but her companion grabbed her by the elbow and led her down a small tunnel which branched off from the main passageway. The ceiling was low here, low enough that she had to duck her head in several places. He led them past several more twists and turns before they arrived at a small, stone chamber with a pointed roof, and three wooden doors on the far wall.

"I thought we were pretty close," he said to her, then gave a quick gesture with his head toward the third door. "That door will take you out of here. Straight through there, down a couple ladders, and it'll drop you right onto the foothills. I'll head back to the Staircase and see if I can handle that Zephyr myself."

Brynn handed him the bucket and the tuning fork.

"I'm sure you'll do great," she said. "Go back and ask the Pwca for help if you need it, okay? No sense getting your...essence...transmuted or whatever it was he said."

"Yeah," he said, his eyes still glued to the ground, "that would suck."

"Thank you," she said to the goblin. "I mean it. Thank you. You really saved me here."

"It's no problem," he said, a nervous smile playing on his lips.

"Good luck with the Zephyr."

"Good luck finding your friend."

He stared shyly at the floor, as he had for almost the entire, brief time she'd known him.

"Thanks," she said, "I should go." She opened the door. "See you around, Chwilen."

Brynn stepped across the threshold as the other goblin raised his eyes to hers to say goodbye.

"No, not that door!" he shouted, but she was already falling.

Chapter Forty-Two

Brynn found her raven's wings in midair and struggled to keep herself aloft, but there was little room to maneuver in the narrow shaft. She attempted to find her way back up, back to the door she had fallen through, but all was dark above her, and she made no progress. Eventually, she allowed herself to drift downward, and soon her talons found soft ground below her. She brought her wings in close and shifted herself back to the form she was used to, the one with the copper hair and the pale skin. She reclaimed her bag from where it had fallen to the ground and fitted the handles back onto their now-accustomed place on her shoulder.

All around stood tall pillars of white, in two long lines, which moved away from her in gentle curves. They towered over her, their tops clouded by the darkness above. Everything she could see was lit in a cool, blue glow, the color of the moon on a clear winter night. The light seemed to be coming from all around her, but as she looked closer, she found the source of the illumination: a smattering of round, flower-like formations scattered along the white pillars. The flowers were as big as her torso, with innumerable tiny petals on each, cascading outward from the center. Each pillar held several, with no seeming pattern to their distribution or arrangement.

Brynn walked to the nearest pillar and gently touched one of the flowers, whereupon it promptly exploded in a flurry of iridescent wings. She looked to the glowing cloud which now floated about her head and saw that the flowers were composed of droves of resting moths. Their wings were the color of mother of pearl, and they glowed with a pale light. Each moth emitted only a pinprick of light, but the host which now swarmed around her emitted enough to bathe the entire area in their glow.

She felt the surface of the pillar which had been exposed by the departing moths. It was stark white, very hard, and the surface bore faint pits and cracks. She ran her hand along the curving surface and thought that it appeared like nothing so much as a massive column of bone, and as soon as she'd had this thought, she immediately wished she hadn't.

"This doesn't bode well," she said softly to herself.

She walked between the bone-white monoliths, suddenly feeling as if she was traversing the ribcage of some otherworldly behemoth, and her head and her heart feared for what might come next. The two rows of pillars gradually curved toward each other as she walked, until they formed a narrow path, the columns running in parallel lines beside her, the gaps between them decreasing as she proceeded. The pillars were six feet apart, then three, then a few inches, and suddenly she was walking down a hallway, between massive plates of bone which soared above her into the darkness and the unknown.

The cloud of moths continued to follow her, and she saw more resting in their curious flower formations, bathing the corridor in their sterile blue glimmering. Ahead of her, the darkness began to subside, and soon she discovered why. Another towering plate of bone rose from the earth, reaching for the darkness above. She stood in front of it and saw that she had arrived at a junction, the path continuing to either side, to the left or to the right.

She stared for several minutes in either direction, but with nothing to guide her other than the cloud of iridescent moths, who did not seem willing or able to assist her, there did not seem to be anything to do but make a blind guess. She chose the right-hand passage, which she followed for only a few minutes before it branched again. She continued on in this way through several more intersections, each time trying to remember which way she had turned, hoping to move in the same direction as the original passage she had followed, but she soon had to admit that she was hopelessly lost.

"Lost in a maze of bones in another world, and nothing to show for my trouble but aching feet and a bag full of junk," she said aloud, and the words echoed back to her, ever so faintly.

She sat on the ground, her back against one of the plates of bone, and tried to quell the panic that was beginning to bloom in her breast. She looked into the bag that was slung over her shoulder, significantly more scuffed and grimy than it had been when she received it.

Once again, the grenade offered itself, but she really didn't want to try to explode her way out of here, and besides, even if she could blast a hole in one of the plates, she'd probably just find another portion of the maze beyond. She'd still be lost and she'd be down one grenade.

She pulled out the laser pointer and pressed the button. A bright, red dot appeared on the opposite wall of the passage. She traced the point over a nearby formation of Bone Moths (as she was now thinking of them) and they fled from its pinpoint precision. She swooped the point through the cloud that formed in the air, and found she could drive them this way and that, upward or downward, by simply alarming them with this mundane import of the technology of another world.

Brynn realized she was simply distracting herself, though, from the task at hand, and her current state of utterly failing at it. She sighed and aimed the laser pointer at the bone plate directly across from her. She stared at the bright, red dot, but nothing else happened. She moved the point down a few feet, and there was still more nothing. She moved it down to the next junction, about thirty feet along from her current position, and it remained the same as ever, bright and red and lasery.

Or had it?

She pointed it again at the bone plate at the end of the passage, and stared, curious. She picked herself up and walked to where the passage branched again to the left and right, holding the pointer out in front of her. As she approached, she saw that, indeed, the dot of light had changed slightly. It was no longer just a simple point of light, no longer a bright, red dot, but had transformed instead into a bright, red arrow, one which pointed distinctly to the left.

She shook her head and blinked hard, unsure if what she was seeing was real, sure her eyes must be playing tricks on her, but the arrow remained, shaking now as her hand trembled slightly. She followed the arrow's suggestion and took the left-hand turning, continuing on between the towering planks of bone. She aimed the dot at the wall next to her, and it resumed its dot-like ways. But at the next intersection, she shone it at the wall in front of her, and another arrow appeared, this time pointing to the right.

She followed the red arrow again and again, her breath quickening, wondering if she might escape the maze after all, might make it to Makayla before it was too late. Her pace increased, the red arrow switched back and forth, she made turn after turn, left and right and right and left, when suddenly the red beam she held in front of her flickered and went dark.

Brynn stood at the end of a passageway, the pitted bone plate looming before her, but there were no exits to either side. The geometric arrangements of bone moths were arrayed around her, and another cloud of them swirled above her, as they had her whole journey through the alabaster maze, but there was nowhere to go. The arrows had led her to a dead end and then they had disappeared. She tapped the laser pointer, shook it, but nothing happened.

She stood, unsure what to do next, lost in the silence, when she suddenly heard a noise behind her: a scritching in the soil and a metallic grinding. The moths swirling about her fled to the nearest wall, assembling yet another glowing flower, and then lay still.

The sound was growing nearer. With no relevant options leaping to the fore, no apparent means of escape, she decided to try the pointer one last time. She slowly pressed the button, and the red beam sprang back to life. She pointed it at the wall in front of her, but no arrow appeared. The beam of light now formed letters upon the wall, and the letters spelled out, 'DANGER.'

Chapter Forty-Three

Brynn pounded on the walls of bone, but it was clear that the only way out was the way she had entered. She considered using the grenade again, but was still fearful that she stood more chance of damaging herself than finding any means of egress. Far down at the end of the corridor, she could hear the sounds growing louder, and then she saw a faint shadow, thrown by the light of the wings of the moths that lay still and silent upon the pitted walls.

The shadow grew larger, dancing upon the whiteness of the walls, taller and taller, an ominous harbinger, she was sure, of what was to come. And then she saw the source of the sounds as it waddled around the corner into view. It was about three feet tall, made of burnished silver plates, and resembled nothing so much as a giant chicken. The sounds she'd heard were the scritching of its metallic claws on the dirt beneath it, and the clanking of machinery (gears and pulleys and levers, she surmised) that lay within it. Periodically, it let off a puff of steam through a vent on the back of its neck.

As it drew closer, Brynn saw that fine, silver plates were fitted neatly together over its body, and the comb on top of its head was formed of intricately engraved tines. The feathers on its wings were convex circles the size of her finger, and its eyes were made of thick glass, banded in steel. The legs moved stiffly, rising in succession, clanking upward, and then driving the claws firmly down into the earth. Its head jerked from side to side as it moved, as if it was searching for unknown sustenance.

The lenses of its eyes were emitting steady beams of bright, white light, which scanned fitfully across the walls as its head shifted unsteadily back and forth: forward, then to the left, then forward, then to the right, and back again. Its beak was thick, and sharp blades were bolted to the edges of it. On its back, she saw a large, iron key, with two looped handles, which rotated slowly as the chicken moved, as if the curious creature had been wound up, and the spring was slowly winding down as it continued its patrol.

The metallic chicken clanked and scritched down the hall. Brynn retreated until her back was against the wall of bone, and then could do nothing but wait. When the automatous fowl was no more than ten feet from her, it stopped. Its head rattled jerkily to the front until the white beams of its eyes landed upon her face. She heard several loud clanks from somewhere deep within the interior of the peculiar contraption, and the vent on the back of its neck emitted a large blast of steam. The chicken then settled downward, its head dropped solidly onto the neck, and its knees bent, with a grinding rasp, to accommodate the now-motionless weight. The noises within ceased, and it was still, other than the bright beams which continued to shine from the glass eyes.

Brynn stared at the silent machine, unsure what her next

course of action should be. The machine was immobile, other than the slow ticking of the key upon its back. She wondered if she could simply walk around it, or if she might be able to establish communication with it, if communication was even possible with such a device. She gave a tentative wave to the shiny fowl to test the waters, and this provoked an immediate reaction.

The chicken cocked its head to the right with a querulous clank, and the beams of light from its eyes grew in intensity. The beak clacked open and, from some source deep within, a siren issued forth, the claxon echoing off the walls.

The moment after the alarm sounded, two things happened: Brynn screamed, and the chicken attacked. The metallic fowl dropped its head downward, thrust its neck forward, lowered its brow, and began a quick march directly at the teenage girl. With its head now lowered, Brynn saw that both the comb and the beak were bright and sharp and honed to fine edges, and both were moving steadily closer.

In a panic, Brynn took the bag on her shoulder, the only object she had at hand, and dropped the handles into her hand. She swung the bag with all her might at the advancing contraption, striking it square in the side of its head, interrupting its forward momentum and twisting its trajectory, its clanking feet now marching it toward one of the bone walls which flanked the corridor.

She suddenly remembered what the bag still carried, and gave silent thanks that she hadn't blown herself to kingdom come. However, the blow had diverted the chicken enough that she was able to scamper around the side of it and make a beeline for the far end of the corridor.

Recalling the power she had felt in her goblin form, she quickly switched, pouring on her newfound speed as soon as she felt her tail appear behind her. However, looking back over her shoulder, she saw that the chicken had increased its speed as well. The eyebeams were now the color of flames, as if some fire had been lit within it, and its metallic chicken legs were no longer scritching and clanging, but were now a blur of motion as the chicken sprinted in pursuit.

Brynn felt something cold and sharp wrapping around her ankle, and she fell to the ground as it pulled her legs from beneath her. The chicken had cast forth a long, slender, barbed tongue, which had shot across the dozen or so yards between them and was now cutting painfully into her skin. Before she could even catch her breath after her fall, the tongue retracted with astonishing force, throwing her into the air, over the chicken, back toward the dead end she had only recently escaped from. As soon as she was airborne, the chicken released the tongue, and Brynn was on a collision course with the towering bone plate.

She heard an unfamiliar scream and realized it was her own, her goblin's throat screaming in a voice that she both recognized and did not. Her vision was still blurry and her stomach roiled from the assault, but she managed to find the raven within herself, quickly enough to avoid a presumably fatal impact with the maze of bone.

As the white raven, she pounded her wings in midair, but before she could even find her bearings, the chicken had shot its barbed tongue toward her again. She barely escaped a coil attempting to loop itself around her throat, and dove downward. She had no faith in her ability to maneuver quickly enough in the air to avoid the lash and thought she would have better luck in one of her humanoid forms.

She came in for a rough landing on the earthen floor, promptly switched back to her goblin form, and then, thinking quickly, found the hollowness within, and her body disappeared from view. She'd hoped this might dissuade the beast, but she had no such luck. Whatever senses the mechanical fowl possessed, her invisibility clearly had no effect on it. The tongue lashed forward again, and she leapt aside, rolling across the ground to avoid it.

Brynn scrambled back to her feet, but the chicken's tongue was already in motion again. It shot forward, lashing her once more around the ankle. Another sharp retraction and she was thrown to the ground as she was pulled inexorably toward the chicken's sharp beak. She wondered if she would survive even a single bite. The barbs bit into her ankle and the rough dirt floor bit into her skin as she was dragged across it. There were only a few yards left between her and the beast.

Casting about her with her arms, clawing at the dirt, trying to slow the pull of the tongue, she spotted the bag and the laser pointer which she had thrown aside when she attempted to escape on her raven's wings. She dug her fingers into the earth and managed to stall her momentum. The pull of the tongue increased, the barbs slicing into the skin of her leg, and she felt the blood begin to flow. She held on with one hand and stretched the fingers of the other as far as they would stretch. She landed a single finger on the laser pointer, and then another, and then it was in her hand.

She pressed the button on the side and shone the bright,

red dot into the glass eyes emitting their fiery beams, hoping to disrupt the beast, blind it, confuse it, anything. Surprisingly, her last-ditch effort had an immediate effect.

The chicken stumbled and the tongue slackened. Brynn regained her footing, and finding a strength within herself she had no idea even existed, she ran directly at the deadly chicken and swung her leg. Her foot connected with the side of the chicken's head, throwing it even farther off-balance. The tongue was still bound to her ankle, however, and seeing as flight was not an option, she leapt at the beast, landing on its side, clutching the metallic feathers as firmly as she could. All the weaponry of the beast seemed to be attached to its head, she realized. If she could avoid the head, she might have a chance at survival, however slight.

The chicken bucked and thrashed, attempting to dislodge her. The tongue began retracting again, pulling her ankle directly into the beast's maw. Steam was billowing forth from the vent on the back of its neck continuously now, and the key on its back spun faster, as the beast increased the intensity of its attacks.

Brynn was losing her grip, and once she did, there would be nothing between her and a beakful of doom. She tried to clamber higher and was able to slip her fingers around the looped handles of the key on the chicken's back. Finding a more secure purchase here, she pulled herself away from the mouth, but the tongue drew her back. Brynn felt a sharp tug on her ankle as the chicken attempted to dislodge her once more. The chicken gave another yank, even stronger this time, and one of her hands lost its grip.

The beast gave another jerk, the strongest yet, pulling

her off the chicken's flank and toward the mouth. She had not, however, loosened her grip with the one hand that still clutched the looped handle of the key, and as she was tugged through the air, the key came with her, pulling forth with a raspy hiss from the aperture on the beast's back. As Brynn collapsed to the ground, the chicken ground suddenly to a halt. The beams from its eyes went dark, the fire within them instantly extinguished, and the vent let forth one final, perfunctory cough of steam before the chicken toppled sideways, landing with a hollow thud on the ground beneath.

Brynn stumbled to her feet, scrambling to disentangle herself from the barbed tongue, but it unlatched easily now that the beast had lost whatever mechanical life had animated it. Blood was flowing freely from her ankle, and she clutched at it as she stumbled backward. She collapsed to the ground and stared at the deadly metal automaton that she had seemingly and inadvertently defeated.

Sensing no further movement, she hobbled forward. She prodded the chicken with a hesitant toe, but the creature was clearly no longer animate. She stood there over its body, her blood seeping into the ground as she wondered what on earth she should possibly do next. Probably tend to her wound, she supposed.

She retrieved the bag, the canvas bag the old woman had given her, from where it had fallen. She pulled the grenade out, still amazed that it had survived intact through all that had happened, and that it had yet to destroy her (or anything else for that matter), and slipped it into her back pocket, followed by the laser pointer.

Using the sharp tines of the chicken's comb, she sliced

the fabric of the bag into long, wide strips which she used to bandage her ankle as best she could. It still hurt, and she couldn't move as fast as she had, but she was no longer losing blood (or not as much, anyway).

She hobbled around the body of the chicken, her leg already starting to feel marginally better. Perhaps her goblin body healed faster as well, she thought. She stared at the apparatus in front of her, and she wondered what purpose it served, wandering about a maze of bone, attacking whatever it saw. It seemed strange that someone would go to all the trouble of constructing something this complex, solely on the offhand chance that someone like her would fall through a doorway and into the maze.

As she stared at the contraption, she noticed another aperture in the chicken's head, similar in size and shape to the one she had pulled the winding key from. Curious, she retrieved the key from where it had fallen, and fitted it into the hole on the chicken's head and gave a tentative turn. She encountered resistance and tried again, but it still did not move. She applied both hands to the key and leaned the full weight of her body into the attempt.

Metal ground against metal, but the key turned, and with an echoing sproing, the top of the chicken's head released and opened, revealing the mechanisms within. Countless, intricate gears and notched cylinders lay inside, along with tiny levers and minuscule springs. The lamps which presumably powered the eye beams took up the rest of the space, and when Brynn touched a small lever on the back of their casing, they sprang to life once more, throwing their bright beam on the dead-end wall.

At the center of it all lay a smoky jewel with innumerable facets, held in place by delicate wires and a golden frame. She touched it delicately with one finger, and an unmistakable bristle of electricity buzzed beneath it.

She clasped her fingers around the jewel and twisted firmly. The gem released with a barely audible crackle and hiss, and she held it between her fingertips, staring at the luminous fog which seemed to swirl within it. The beams from the beast's eyes still shone, and she walked to the wall to hold the jewel in the light, to examine it more closely.

As she did so, however, she noticed that one of the lights fell upon a shallow hollow in the wall that she had not noticed before, covered in powdery sediment. She gave a hesitant blow, coughing at the layer of dust that flew away, and a tarnished golden framework was revealed beneath.

Hesitantly, she took the jewel in her hand and fitted it against the opening in the wall of bone, and to her amazement, it fit precisely, as if it had been designed for nothing else. As the golden framework accepted the jewel, the electricity beneath her fingers buzzed once again. She heard a crack, and then a slender line appeared in the wall where none had been before. The line grew to a fissure, and the fissure grew to a gap, and then she heard the unmistakable rasping of hinges long unused. Two panels within the wall were swinging outward, and suddenly she was blinded by the light of day as a doorway appeared, a doorway that appeared to lead out of the maze, away from danger, and out into a wooded glen in the Land of Annwfyn.

The hidden brain of the clockwork chicken had freed her, and she stepped through the revealed doorway, and onto the surface of a different world.

Chapter Forty-Four

It was much brighter here than it had been in the maze of bone, where the only illumination came from the geometric constellations of moths. And although the blue sky above her was clear, Brynn could see no sun, could find no source for the crisp light that bathed the land around her.

She stood on the lightly wooded foothills of a mountain range, which thrust into the air like jagged, snow-covered teeth behind her. Squat, broad trees littered the ground, and the brush that grew below them was wiry and gnarled. A narrow, dusty path in front of her, that looked as if it had not been walked in many months, led away from the door in the mountain and wound downward through the rolling hills.

Below her, she could see a large plain spreading across the land, and in the distance, on the horizon, she saw mounds of sand, impossibly high. Those must be the dunes that Chwilen had told her of. And if they were, the Swallowed Hall lay beyond them.

In the midst of the plains, not too far from where the hills ended, she saw a road, which appeared to run from the mountains she had come through and out toward the dunes. She gathered her wits about her, tested her ankle, which seemed to be feeling better by the minute, and set her goblin feet to treading the thin footpath before her.

As she approached the edge of the plains, she saw that they were covered, for the most part, by a tall grass, which grew higher than her head, with serpentine creeks and rocky hillocks interspersed throughout. She stepped into the field of spiky, brown grass and pushed her way through until, only minutes later, she arrived at the road she had spied from above.

It was empty and paved with flagstones of dusky black, so tightly fitted that nothing grew between them. She checked her only possessions, the grenade and the laser pointer, still safely ensconced in her back pocket, and began her trek down the road. Nothing seemed to change as she walked. The stiff grass stood over her on either side, and little could be seen through it, save the occasional muddy creek or rocky mound. No birds flew overhead. No crickets sang in the field. There was nothing but the sunless sky and the towering grass and the ebony road.

Her feet carried her on and on, her goblin feet, trudging through a world they seemed to know, and she was beginning to wonder just how long this road actually was when a faint sound broke the stillness. Something was clacking along the road, far behind her, a rumbling clatter accompanied by a low-pitched squeak. She feared the return of the clockwork chicken and thought to hide in the grass, but before she could locate a promising spot, the source of the sound appeared around a bend in the road she had passed not ten minutes before.

It was a wooden cart with four tall, wooden wheels. The sideboards of the wagon were long planks of bright yellow timber, which rose several feet above the bed, and held within a tottering heap of something lumpy and brown. The man (or man-shaped creature) driving the wagon sat on a bench perched over the front, and he seemed to be nothing but hair. Bright eyes peered from underneath shaggy brows, and the long, mottled hair which covered his face and head was pulled back into innumerable ponytails, tied in thick blue ribbons. Some sprang from the side of his face, some from his neck, some from the top and sides and back of his head, and the ponytails themselves were gathered back into a knot on the top of his head, which then flowed behind him like a firework or a mane or both. His body was covered in a set of thick leather coveralls, from which erupted his alarmingly hairy hands and feet, which were also, it appeared, festooned with blue-ribboned ponytails.

At the front of the cart, and Brynn was surprised she hadn't noticed this first, was yoked a massive black beetle, the size of...well, Brynn realized it was probably the size of a Volkswagen Beetle. Its six legs clacked along the road as it pulled the wagon, and its antennae danced merrily in the wind. Brynn wasn't certain, but she thought she heard it humming, and despite the size of the load it pulled, it seemed to move effortlessly with the burden behind it.

Above all, though, she noticed the odor, which was putrescent and from the moment she saw the wagon, it was difficult to think of anything else.

She squinted against the horrific smell wafting to her on the wind and waited for the wagon to pass. It was moving so fast there was little time to do anything else, and seconds later, it was upon her. The hairy man at the front of the wagon pulled the reins short, and the gigantic insect skidded to a halt, its antennae wiggling in such a manner that it appeared they were waving at her. She shuddered and turned her attention to the driver.

"Ho there, little lass!" he called to her. "What do ye be doing here upon the Ebony Road? Have ye happened to find yourself a teensy trace of troubling tribulation?"

The voice that emanated from the mass of hair was deep and raspy, but not unkind.

"No," she said, "no trouble. I guess. I'm just...I need to get out to the dunes."

The enormously bushy eyebrows of the man, which extended a full foot outward from his head, raised and lowered precipitously.

"To the Dunes, do ye say?" he glowered ominously. "I do not ken if the Abattoir Dunes be a fortuitous place to set your compass to, especially for such a wee bit of a coblyn as stands before me."

"The...the Abattoir Dunes?" Brynn gulped.

"Aye, lass!"

Brynn shivered, the tide of panic that had threatened to engulf her since she first set foot inside the burial mound rising once again.

"Well, yeah," she nodded weakly, "yeah, that's where I need to go. I have to. It's important."

"If ye do say so!" the hairy man obliged. "Well, if ye are insistent, perhaps I can offer a slight spot of succor. As it does so happen, my path will be taking me to the very base of the Dunes. 'Tis not the most glamorously appointed vehicle I do employ, but would ye perchance care to allow us to dispatch you to your destination?"

"That would be wonderful," she said with some relief, "thank you."

"'Tis my pleasure, lass. Climb aboard!"

As she climbed up on the bench beside the hairy man, Brynn was slightly alarmed and more than slightly nauseated when she discerned that what the cart was hauling was a mountain of dung. She was even more alarmed when she noticed that the huge mound of dung seemed to be moving. The layers of putrescent gunk wriggled and throbbed as she watched, and she turned around quickly, not wanting to give even a second's thought as to what might be causing them to do so.

The man turned to her, extending his bushy hand.

"I be known as Gwallt. And who do ye be?"

"I...my name is Branwen," she said, shaking his hand, noting that even his palm was coated with a fine layer of brisk fuzz.

The hairy man turned back to his reins, and the wagon was soon careening down the road of dusky stone once more. Brynn realized that, after all her efforts to avoid it back in Jeffersonville, back in what seemed like a different life, she ended up hitchhiking after all.

"So, what is...what do you do with this wagon?" she asked, trying to engage the man in some kind of conversation that wouldn't lead to her discovery as an unwanted interloper.

"Oh, miss," he said with a languorous sigh, "it can be a hard grind, and the odor, I'm sure ye have kenned, can be none too pleasant. But the dung must be hauled out and yon to the Olfactory Factory if they are to continue on with their most important labors. The drudgeries of an abbey lubber do know no end."

He sighed again and Brynn nodded, unsure how to respond to this.

"Can I inquire of you, lassie," the man continued, "why your peregrinations do carry you to so ominous a place as the Dunes?"

"I'm, uh, I'm looking for someone."

"Oh, girl," he said with sadness and alarm, "if ye be seeking any living creature within the Dunes, it is fair unlikely that ye shall be finding their blood still quick and their heart still beating. Ye do understand that, lass?"

Brynn nodded, tears springing unbidden to her eyes. She had come so far, but she knew that, even if she found Makayla, it might be too late. It might have been too late long before she even began.

"I do. I know."

The man nodded.

"Well then, I shall convey you there, as promised, and I hope ye do find what ye seek. But for the nonce, we must needs take a momentary hiatus on our journey."

He pulled the reins up short, and the beetle again skidded to a halt. The hairy man looped the reins over the bench and leaned in to Brynn.

"If ye will pardon me, I must excuse myself for a twinkling. I find it is time to drain the snake," he said with a knowing waggle of his eyebrows.

Brynn looked at him distastefully, and then watched as he jumped to the ground and thrust his arms up to the shoulders into the putrid muck which lay in the bed of the cart. He looked to the sky as he waved his arms within the dung, clearly searching for something, and then finally gave a smile of victory as he found that which he sought.

"Got you," he said, as he gave a grunt and pulled out an emerald serpent a dozen feet long and as thick as Brynn's waist. She looked at him even more distastefully.

"I shall return," Gwallt said, and moments later, he and the snake had disappeared into the lofty grass.

Chapter Forty-Five

"Psst. Hey, Branwen," said the beetle. The hairy man had only been out of sight for a fraction of a second when the gigantic bug twisted its eyes around to look at her, as much as its squat body would allow.

"Hello," Brynn said hesitantly, unsure how one was supposed to respond to a giant insect.

"It's me," the bug chirped, "Chwilen. We met in the mountain."

"What?" Brynn stammered.

"I'm sorry I couldn't say 'hi' before, but I have to be a beetle right now, and I'm not supposed to talk, 'cause I'm being punished. I'm really glad you're okay, though. I'm sorry you fell through that door. I hope the chicken didn't find you."

"It was...I'm fine. You're being punished?"

"Yeah. The Head Pwca gave me a month on dung duty for helping you."

"Oh, Chwilen, I'm so sorry."

"Ah, it's no big deal," the bug demurred. "I actually like being a beetle. I'm way bigger like this, and it means I don't have to talk to anyone that much." The bug paused. "I'm kind of shy."

"I noticed."

"Yeah. Plus, I can sing while I work, and no one really cares."

"I heard you when I saw the wagon coming."

"You did?" the bug said nervously.

"Yeah, it was nice."

Brynn couldn't be sure, but she thought the beetle might have blushed.

"I wanted to tell you—," the bug began, but then broke off and snapped its head sharply to the side, its antennae quivering. "He's coming back! I only have a second. He'll drop you off at the base of the Dunes. Don't go into the Dunes if you can help it. What else can you change into? Has your invisibility developed yet?"

"Yeah," Brynn stammered, "it has, I can disappear. And I...I can change into a raven. A white raven."

"Great!" the bug chirped. "Then fly. Fly over the Dunes and don't land. Fly straight over them, the same way the road is heading right now. When you get past them, you'll see a forest. Keep to the right, following the tree line, and eventually, you'll find a crater. That's what you're looking for. I'll try to come back for you if I can." The bug's antennae flailed in panic. "Oh no! He's here!"

The giant beetle fell silent, but for a gentle, chittering melody which floated from its mandibles. At the same instant, the hairy man appeared, pushing the grass aside, carrying a snake which was just as long, but now no wider than a garden hose.

"Snake drained!" he assured Brynn as he clambered back up onto the bench beside her, thrusting his deflated burden back into the mountain of dung. "Are ye ready to proceed?"

"Yeah," she said hesitantly, "I am."

"Then let's be off!" he shouted, with a snap of the reins.

The giant bug, who was also apparently a goblin, took off again at a frenetic pace, and they were soon bouncing down the road of black stone. Gwallt spoke little as they drove, his eye on the road, which curved sharply through the field of tall grass, bending around tall, rocky hillocks, murky ponds, and the deep crevasses which now began to dot the landscape.

Half an hour later, Brynn at last saw the dunes over the top of the looming grass, and such was the speed of the bug-drawn carriage that, once the dunes were visible, they arrived at their base only minutes later. The road here curved off to the left, toward a rocky ravine that dipped sharply downward. The hairy man pulled the wagon up short.

"Well, here ye be, as promised," he said kindly, "the very outskirts of the Abattoir Dunes. I cannot imagine why ye would wish to set your feet anywhere near them, and to speak sooth, I would much rather if ye would stay aboard my carriage, and continue on with us to a destination of less unpleasantness."

"I can't," Brynn said, "I'm sorry. This is where I need to be."

"I can understand full well the weight of an obligation." Gwallt reached under his leather coveralls and pulled out a dull, jagged rock, the size of his fist, which hung from his neck on a thick, black chain. "I do have an obligation meself, and 'twill be many a year afore it is fulfilled. So, I will not try to dissuade you from yours. I would only plead with you to be careful, and offer up that, if ye do hear the howl of the beasties that do dwell within these dunes, a howl which keens as if 'twill siphon the water from your eyes and turn your brain to jelly, 'twould almost certainly be a fair-minded choice to step quickly in the opposite direction."

"If I hear such a thing," Brynn said, "I will certainly do my best to avoid it."

"That be all I can ask, then. Good luck be upon you, lass, and may ye find what ye seek."

"Thank you, Gwallt," she said with a smile. "Look after that beetle, huh? Seems like he does a good job."

"That he does. 'Tis his first day upon the road with me, but so far, I must say I approve. Take care, Miss Branwen! May fortune smile upon you!"

Gwallt flashed a smile, which was incongruously white amidst the dark sworls of hair covering his face, then he flicked the reins, and the beetle took off at its usual alarming pace. And as the wagon drove away, the only sound Brynn heard floating back to her was the chittering melody of a song she'd never heard, but which she somehow knew told of a raven of the purest white.

Chapter Forty-Six

The Abattoir Dunes were full of bones. That was the first thing Brynn noticed about them. The steep mounds of sand towered far above her head and extended onward as far as she could see, but all of them were full of bones. The coarse, white sand was littered with the remnants of creatures of all shapes and sizes.

A skull near her feet could have been human, but for the single, arching horn which sprang from its forehead. The curved bone several yards away could have been a kneecap, but one so huge she might have curled up within it to take a nap, if she so chose. (She did not.) Farther away, she saw an impossibly large skull, big enough to contain her house, with massive, curving tusks. Beside it lay a leg bone as long as a city bus, and just as wide.

When she scooped up a handful of sand, Brynn saw that it wasn't actually sand at all, but countless tiny bones. There were skulls no larger than a pinhead and arm bones no thicker than an eyelash, which must have come from a creature so small she could have held it on the tip of her finger. And the smallest grains were either bones that had been ground to dust, or bones so small that her eyesight was not fine enough to make them out.

Brynn let the tiny bones slip between her fingers, and watched as they cascaded to the ground at her feet. She agreed with Chwilen. This was no place she wanted to walk, not if she could help it. It was time to take to the air. She closed her eyes, slowed her breathing, and concentrated. Soon, she felt the powerful wings within her, yearning to be free. She let them forth, and seconds later was high above the dunes, floating on wings of white.

As Chwilen had instructed her, she flew on in the same direction the road had brought her. The dunes seemed endless. She saw no movement within them, nothing but the bleached white bones, mammoth remnants of the creatures of this world, half buried in the dust of their fallen companions.

Brynn was surprised, once again, at how powerful the wings felt, how they never seemed to tire. She felt as if she could fly forever, and was tempted to, as she had been before. The raven she was wanted nothing more than to ascend to the heavens, to soar with the clouds and never return. But she knew that she couldn't. As Gwallt had said, her obligation weighed upon her. She pounded her wings in the still air, carrying her forward, onward to whatever was to come.

Half an hour later, she at last spied the end of the dunes. And again, Chwilen had spoken true: there was a forest in front of her. Minutes later, she was over the tree line. She banked sharply to the right and followed the edge of the dunes until she saw the crater she had been told of. It was immense, possibly a mile across, she thought, and the cliffs which ringed the edge dropped off precipitously. At the bottom of the jagged, vertical cliffs, she saw a lake of the deepest blue, ringed by a beach of rippling grey.

Brynn flew over the edge and found that the face of the cliff was broken and pitted, as if the ground had been ripped from within by unthinkable force. She glided downward, far downward, hundreds of feet, and then buffeted her wings, alighting for a landing on the beach. As she returned to her human form, she felt a curious sensation beneath her.

Looking down, she saw that the beach she stood upon was composed of nothing but pearls, covering every dry bit of land below the cliffs. She picked one up between her fingers, and it emitted a faint whisper, a lingering remembrance of a chateau in France and an overheard revelation at a dinner party. Another spoke of countless nights wasted at a backwoods bar, waiting for a rendezvous that was never to occur again. Yet another told her of a door that should never have been opened, of a sight that should never have been seen by a child too young to understand.

Scanning the area around her, she found a signpost a few dozen yards down the beach. When she approached it, she saw that the letters on the ragged wood spelled out:

The Beach Of Unwanted Memories

Walking closer, Brynn noticed how unusual the letters appeared, how irregularly they were shaped, how oddly formed. As she reached out a tentative finger to trace the letter 'B,' the letters began to move, and she saw that each was formed by a coalition of white and green inchworms.

The letters wriggled about, disrupting the meaning, crawling over and under one another until they reassembled themselves into formation once again. This time, the form they had chosen read:

Hello, Branwen.

"Um, hi," she replied.

She stared at the sign, but no further movement seemed to be forthcoming. She was just about to turn away when the inchworms began to squirm again. When they had reconvened, the letters said:

You should not tarry.

The Swallowed Hall awaits.

"I know," Brynn said, "I just don't know what to do. This world is so confusing."

The worms did not reply, but crept down to the ground and, as a unit, uprooted the sign from the beach and carried it away. Moments later, the worms and the sign disappeared into a small hole in the face of the cliff.

Having nothing whatsoever to guide her now, Brynn walked to the edge of the water. As it had appeared from the air, it was nothing but the deepest blue, and to her eyes, it seemed incredibly broad and incredibly deep. She was sure this must be her destination, but she had no idea what to do next. She'd come so far. This was the place. She knew it was. This was where the Swallowed Hall was supposed to be, but there was nothing here but an enormous lake full of water and a bunch of rocks full of other people's memories.

"I need to find the Swallowed Hall," she whispered, fighting back tears. "What do I do next? Why won't someone tell me what to do next?"

There was no response. There was the soft sound of the water lapping at the pebbled shore, and there was a gentle whistle as the winds swirled around the edge of the cliff, far above her, but that was all.

She felt one tear roll down her cheek, and then another, and as Brynn reached up to wipe them away with the back of her hand, she heard another sound, a different sound. Something was moving in the water. And nearly as soon as she heard it, she saw it as well. A wide, flat-bottomed boat was approaching, from far across the lake. It was empty, as far as she could tell, and there was no apparent means of locomotion. The wooden boat had no sail, no oars, no motor, but it moved quickly toward her until its hull scraped against the pearls at her feet.

"Hello," she called softly, but there was no response.

There appeared to be only one choice in front of her, and so she took it. Brynn stepped into the boat, sat down, and the boat began to move across the surface of the water.

Chapter Forty-Seven

The flat-bottomed boat sailed swiftly across the lake of deepest blue, at the bottom of the towering cliffs, in the middle of a forest in the Land of Annwfyn. And Brynn could do nothing but wait and find out what would happen next.

And she soon found out that what would happen next was not very much at all. The boat sped toward the center of the lake, and once it reached the center, it stopped.

"Hello," she called out again, a note of anxiety creeping into her voice, but there was still no answer. Whatever was propelling this boat, it did not appear to be willing or able to communicate.

Brynn crept to the edge of the boat and peered over the side. She was glad to learn that the vessel was surprisingly stable in the water, and it barely moved at all as she shifted her weight and leaned out. Below her, she could see the water, as blue as ever, as deep as ever, but the longer she looked, she thought she could make out a shape beneath it, a long shape, blocky and dark.

The boat had brought her to the right place, she realized. The Swallowed Hall was here, directly beneath her, beneath the surface of the water. If only the old woman had given her scuba equipment, she thought, instead of the stupid grenade. But she hadn't, and all Brynn had in her pockets were the grenade and the laser pointer and a couple dollars in change, and none of those had the slightest chance of helping her as she stared at the blurry outlines of her destination, rippling with the waves, far underneath the surface of the lake.

As at the shore of the lake, there appeared to be only one choice in front of her. She did not know where this one would lead, but that had been the case at every step along the way, since she'd first decided to find Makayla, since she'd first learned of the Salmon of Knowledge, since she'd first set her foot on the path that would lead her to this other world.

She stood up, walked to the low beam at the stern of the boat, put one foot hesitantly on it, and then the other. She steeled herself, looked up to the sunless sky, took a deep breath, then stepped off the back of the boat and plunged into the deep blue lake.

Chapter Forty-Eight

She sank quickly, feet first, eyes wide, into the depths of the lake. After a few seconds, as her body began to attempt to float upward, once the force of her plunge had abated, Brynn turned herself downward and tried to put the swimming lessons her parents had insisted on to good use.

The building below came into view quickly, and she saw that it wasn't as far under the waves as she had originally thought. The hall was long and gothic, with a peaked roof and walls of dark stone slabs. Directly below her, at one end of the submarine hall, she thought she spied a door, and it was to this that she directed her efforts.

She kicked and stroked, her strength beginning to flag as her lungs began to burn, but she soon grasped the handles of the carved, wooden doors that stood at the front of the hall. She was nearly out of breath as she put her feet to one of the doors and her hands on the handle of the other, and kicked inwards with what strength remained to her. To her surprise, the door opened easily. Brynn was not sure what she had expected, exactly, but no air poured out of the Hall, and no water poured in. She released her grip on the handle and gave one strong stroke with her arms, which jetted her across the threshold of the Hall, and as soon as it had, gravity took hold of her and threw her to the shockingly dry floor.

Brynn clambered to her feet, gasping for the air which she realized was all around her now, and as she struggled to fill her lungs, she stared back at the entranceway she had just passed through. A wall of water stood in the tall, arched doorway. She stepped toward it, and saw the clear demarcation, just at the edge of the doorframe. On her side there was air, and on the other side there was water, and nothing seemed to be preventing the water from entering, but there it sat, a wall of blue, streaked with the dregs of sunlight that penetrated from above. As she watched, a fish swam by, a golden fish with ghostly fins a yard long, but it didn't seem to notice her.

She reached her hand out. Her hand slid easily into the water and came back wet, but the water remained in place. She realized that whatever was happening here was likely far beyond her comprehension, so she eased the door closed over the water without and turned to face the Swallowed Hall within.

The floor was laid with tiles, an intricate pattern of white and bronze, thousands of them, and not a single one appeared to be anything other than spotless. Arches lined the walls, and in the recesses, Brynn saw urns flowering with exotic plants, chests filled with glittering treasure, and tapestries of untold beauty. The ceiling was high and vaulted, and on it was painted a vivid and complex mural, running from one end to the other, of monsters and gods engaged in holy combat.

There were no signs of life. Nothing moved within the hall, and no sounds were to be heard. At the far end of the chamber was another set of doors. These ones were smooth and bright and looked as if they were made of liquid gold. It was toward these that she set her feet.

The soles of her tennis shoes padded softly on the tiles as she walked down the lofty hall, and Brynn suddenly realized that they were dry, and the rest of her was as well. Her footsteps echoed in the immensity of the room, and her heart was pounding so loudly she thought it would echo as well, and then the doors were in front of her. She checked her ankle, which seemed to be completely healed, or nearly so. The grenade and laser pointer were still lodged firmly in her pocket. She had nothing else, nothing but determination and obligation and maybe a less-developed sense of self-preservation than she should.

She took a deep breath. Either her friend was behind these doors, or she had come all this way for nothing and perhaps was about to die. She really hoped it was the former, but the pit of her stomach told her otherwise.

She swung open the golden doors. A jeweled court was revealed beyond, a world of brocade and luxury. Two golden thrones sat at the far end, on a high dais, all gilded finery and overstuffed luxuriousness. White marble pillars ringed the circular room, and on the ceiling was a chandelier of diamonds and gold. Between the pillars lounged a coterie of alarmingly attractive courtiers, men and women of such gorgeousness that Brynn could only assume she'd arrived in a land of immortal divinity. They were sipping drinks from jeweled goblets, and nibbling on delicacies from ivory platters, and everything smelled so delicious that she was nearly intoxicated by the fragrance alone.

Every head turned her way as Brynn opened the doors, and the room fell silent. In front of the dais, she now saw, were three low pedestals, each bathed in a warm pool of light. The first pedestal held a baby, motionless, suspended a few inches in the air, that couldn't have been more than a year old. The second pedestal held a boy of no more than five. And on the third pedestal was Makayla. Her friend's eyes were closed, and she looked peaceful, but Brynn couldn't tell from here if she was alive or dead.

In front of the pedestals knelt a woman in tattered clothing, with a long, golden braid and a scabbard strapped to her back. Brynn couldn't see the woman's face, but she knew immediately that it was the hero who had pursued her, back in Jeffersonville, back in another world. Bands of light tethered the woman's wrists and ankles and bound her to the floor.

Brynn had somehow found her way here, to a glittering court full of lords and ladies and luxury and thrones and prisoners and magic, and in the middle of it all, and somehow she wasn't surprised, was Finian.

Chapter Forty-Nine

Finian grinned as if he had never been so pleased with himself, as if he thought that no one else could ever be as pleased with themselves as he was with himself at that very moment.

"Welcome, my good lady," he crowed in a voice thick with self-congratulation, "welcome to the Unseemly Court!"

Brynn just stared at him.

"What are you doing here, Finian?"

"This is my Court! And I...I have brought you here to join me in my revels!"

"I don't know what's going on. I don't know who you really are, but I came to get Makayla." She looked at her friend, immobilized in the shimmering glow. "Why is she here? What did you do to her, Finian?"

"We can dispense with that name," he said grandly, with an insouciant wave of his hand, "now that you and I are here, here in my Kingdom beneath the waters of Annwfyn. Finian was but a name I did put on in order to beguile you and your fellow schoolmates. But in truth, my eyes saw none but you. You were the jewel I sought amongst so much sand. See me now for my true self, fully revealed to you only here, here in my Unseemly Court. For the one you knew as 'Finian' is in truth Efnysien fab Euroswydd, the King of the Swallowed Hall!"

Finian raised both hands high in the air with this proclamation, and the assembled courtiers all burst into raucous applause. Brynn waited, and waited, and slowly the applause died away into silence. Finian held his position, waiting for Brynn to respond, but she did not. There was a long moment of nothing. One of the ladies coughed.

"I don't care what you're calling yourself now," Brynn finally offered into the stillness. "You are still clearly a massive jerk."

"You should not speak to me in this manner, my sweetness," Finian said, a knife's edge behind the syrupy sugar of his words. "Look where you are. See all that is around you. The grandeur. The magnificence. The untold opulence of my court. The unrivaled beauty of my courtiers. This could all be yours if you would but lend an ear. I worked so hard to bring you here. Spun so many webs. Plucked so many heartstrings. Slew so many underlings who disappointed me with their efforts to achieve this end."

"I don't care about any of that, Finian," said Brynn. "I just want my friend back."

"I told you. My name is not Finian!" He stamped his foot as his voice rose sharply in volume, and Brynn saw a brief shower of sparks erupt from his eyes and drift slowly to the gilt tiles beneath his feet. "Listen now, most delicate flower." He spoke crisply now, and the fire remained in his eyes. "I gave you this choice once before, the choice of me, and you foolishly denied it. I shall now offer you another choice, and this time, I know you will choose wisely."

The coiffed courtiers around the room had given nothing but rapt attention as Finian spoke, but now they tittered in a chorus of anticipation.

"That is correct, my flock," he cooed to them, "I spoke to you of this one, of this Branwen. I told you she would be coming here to our palace. I shall now offer her...the choice."

The assemblage fell again to silence. Makayla and the two other children remained in their suspended glow, completely immobile, but Brynn noticed that the woman bound to the floor was struggling against her bonds, her long, blond braid quivering with the effort. Finian returned his attention to the teenage girl in front of him, gesturing dramatically as he spoke.

"I met you as Brynn, but from the first, I knew you to be a coblyn named Branwen. I lured you here, to the Swallowed Hall, and you performed admirably on the journey. You deciphered the secret locks of the burial mound. You faced the trials of the Severed Head of Madoc ab Owain Gwynedd. You survived the Labyrinth of the Clockwork Chicken. You ventured along the Ebony Road and flew across the Abattoir Dunes. So now, at the end of it all, it comes down to a simple choice."

From the dais, he retrieved and held aloft a slender, jeweled goblet. He stood between the bound woman and the pedestal that held Brynn's best friend in thrall, and delicately dipped his fingers into the effervescent glow that surrounded Makayla's immobilized form.

"I offer you a choice among three," he said in a dramatic whisper. "You may choose only one, and that choice shall determine your fate. You may choose the woman, you may choose the children, or you may choose...this chalice." His voice rose in volume as he relished this clearly rehearsed moment. "Choose the woman, and I shall spare her life. She shall be freed, and you may do with her as you wish, but the children will remain here as my ornaments forever. Choose the children, and they are free to go. My hold over them shall be broken, and you may take them home. Or," and here Finian lowered his voice and walked steadily toward her, the goblet outstretched in front of him, "drink from this chalice and you shall be my Queen, the Goblin Queen of the Unseemly Court, the Lady of the Swallowed Hall in the Land of Annwfyn. You will rule at my side until the stars fall from the sky, here at the center of everything. One sip, and you shall have knowledge and power unimagined by any goblin since the dawn of time!"

He smiled at Brynn lasciviously, and traced a witheringly hot finger along the line of her jaw, causing her to shudder in revulsion.

"Once you are my Queen, all within our domain shall be as you desire. This woman, who pursued you, who sought to slay you, her life would be held within your hand. You could crush the life from her eyes with but a thought."

The woman bound on the floor struggled still against the mystical bonds, and as she pushed against them, she twisted her body until, for the first time since she had arrived in this room, Brynn saw Gwenllian's face. She saw no fear in the woman's icy blue eyes, only hot, righteous anger.

"This woman, this so-called hero," and here Finian (for Brynn refused, even in her mind, to call him anything else) spat in Gwenllian's face, "has slain countless of your kin.

Should she leave this Hall, she will undoubtedly slay many more. She will certainly seek your family: your father, your mother, your brother, and a baby on the way, yes?"

Brynn shuddered, her breath shaky. This wasn't at all what she had expected to find. She knew she would be putting her own life at risk by coming here. It hadn't occurred to her that she might be putting her family at risk as well. That shouldn't be possible, she thought, it wasn't fair.

"Don't talk about my family."

"But they are part of you, my pet," Finian countered silkily, "and it is you that I want. Become my Queen and they shall be safe. No being from Annwfyn shall ever have cause to cross their shadows again. The Queen of the Swallowed Hall may do as she wishes, may do anything that she wishes. You could even free this woman, if your heart somehow finds within itself the gift of mercy. And all three children, if you so choose, you could send them skipping back to their sickly human families, to live their stunted, sickly little lives. Every living thing in the Land of Annwfyn shall be yours to command. All shall be just as you desire."

"I have a feeling there's a catch," Brynn said, in as steady a voice as she could find within herself.

"But a small one. Should you drink from this chalice, you may never again leave this land," Finian replied with a sickly-sweet smile. "You shall be the all-powerful Goblin Queen, but you may never leave the Land of Annwfyn. A Queen may not leave her Kingdom."

"My family?"

"Lost to you forever."

Brynn stood in silence, the knot in her stomach growing

every second that Finian spoke. Every option that Finian had offered seemed utterly terrible. The four lives in front of her had just been put into her hands, and there didn't seem to be any way to save everyone. The children didn't deserve this fate, she thought. Makayla certainly didn't. Even Gwenllian didn't deserve this. To be sure, the woman had tried to kill her, but she was obviously a good person, and Brynn didn't think she could leave her at the hands of someone who was clearly revealing himself to be a monster.

If she chose to free the children, she could take them home, but the woman would almost certainly suffer, or be tortured, or killed, or worse. If she chose to accept Finian's offer and remain here, Makayla would be saved, but she would never see her again, and she would never see her family again, which was a thought too monstrous to consider. If she simply turned on her heel and walked out of here, no one would be saved at all. She could return to her family, but the four people before her would remain under Finian's control.

Finian stared at her silently, a wry smile playing on his lips, clearly enjoying her internal torment. Brynn stared at the goblet in his hand. She had to admit, there was a part of her that was being pulled by this choice, that wanted to march up, drain the goblet, throw it to the ground, and become the Goblin Queen. That is what the goblin within her wanted, the maleficence that existed in her core. The ancient, gnarled evil locked inside her, the natural state of the goblins for millennia, the part her father had warned her about, desperately yearned for one sip of the draught that Finian held in his hand. But she couldn't do that, she knew, she couldn't leave her family forever.

"What if I just turned around and left?" Brynn asked. Her thoughts were a blur, and her words came out tinged with the panic and anger that threatened to swallow her until she was lost beneath them. "What if I walked up and punched you in the nose? What if I took that drink and threw it in your face?"

"Listen to me!" Finian shouted, and sparks once again flew from his eyes. "I am offering you the chance of a lifetime, the chance of a thousand lifetimes! You are a bloody goblin. The lowest of the low. The very bottom rung of the Tylwyth Teg. Your people carry the dung and steal the babies and empty the chamber pots and mend the shoes and everything else that none of the rest of us wants to do! The most you could ever possibly aspire to is passing as human for another year or two, until some hero finds you and obliterates you and your family into absolute nothingness! Okay? Do you understand? You are nothing, and I am offering you something. More than something. I am offering you me. I am offering you the chance to be a Queen. My Queen! I am Efnysien fab Euroswydd, the King of the Swallowed Hall, and I get that you don't know what that means, since for some reason your parents kept you utterly ignorant of the world you come from, but I am just going to need you to trust me when I tell you that I am a big...damn...deal! I'll get you a book later and prove it to you, okay, but it is time to make your choice. Be my Queen. Take the chalice, have a drink, and feel power and knowledge beyond comprehension descend upon you. Become the Queen that I know your soul wants you to be." His voice again descended to a haughty whisper as he sought to bring himself back under control. "This is literally the best offer you will ever receive in your life. You said 'no' to me once. I would think long and hard before you say 'no' to me again."

He held forth the goblet once more, his arm quivering with rage, the sparks now venting from his eyes relentlessly, showering the air with golden electricity. Brynn looked at the woman on the floor, at her tattered clothing, at the welts on her back, at the fire in her eyes. Brynn looked at the three children frozen on the pedestals: the baby, the child, and the young woman, her friend, her best friend, Makayla, the reason she'd set her foot to this path in the first place. And she looked at the young man she'd known as Finian, but who, she now realized, wasn't named Finian, probably wasn't young, and almost certainly wasn't a man. She struggled to form the chaos of her mind into the words she knew she needed to say.

"So, you're the one who decided that Makayla would be stolen?" she asked, simply and directly.

"Indeed," Finian responded with a smug smile and a wiggle of his nose. "It was clear that she was the best pawn to use to bring you to this place."

"The strange little man, the good neighbor, did he have anything to do with this?"

"Very little. He knew naught of my involvement. But another pawn for my arsenal. He thought he was working for the usual directorate, when in fact it was I who pulled the strings."

"Were you the one who threatened my father?" Brynn asked, still trying to keep her voice under control. "Made him think he had to steal children again to protect his family?"

"I did no threatening," Finian scoffed, and then gave a petulant shrug, "not directly, anyway. I uttered a few whispers, impersonated one or two minor deities. Nothing that could be traced back to me. But it had to be that way. It seemed too perfect to have your own father be the catspaw that brought you here to me, my jewel of impish perfection."

Brynn felt the anger and the panic rise within her again, and other emotions too, almost too many to count or comprehend: fear and revulsion, love for her friend, concern for the children, mercy for the woman. She found them all within herself, and she held them tight. She knew what she was going to do with them. She was going to follow her mother's advice, the advice of the wisest person she knew. She was going to take her emotions and turn them into bright fire. She was going to take them, hold them, and make something wonderful.

"Then I've made my choice," she said to Finian.

"Very well," he said. "It is time, my glorious courtiers! It is time for our Queen-to-be to announce her choice. Attend, and marvel at what is to come."

The ears and eyes of every luxuriously-appointed being in the room turned to focus on Brynn and Brynn alone. Finian smiled an unctuous smile and held the goblet out to her. Brynn walked over slowly, on unsteady legs, her nerves keening with anxiety at what she was about to say. She plucked the chalice from Finian's fingers and held it in her own, looking deep into the fiery liquid that swirled within the golden cup.

"You have chosen, Branwen the Coblyn?" Finian intoned, his eyes afire, his breath husky with anticipation, his lips quivering with delight.

"Yeah," Brynn said, "I have chosen. I thought about it. I thought about what you did to these kids here. I thought about what you did to my best friend. I thought about what you did to this woman here, and what else you're obviously going to do to her soon. And I thought about what you made my father do, and about how you nearly broke him. So, yeah, I made my choice."

She looked up from the golden chalice and straight into Finian's eyes.

"I choose the woman."

As soon as Brynn spoke the words, the glowing bands that held the woman captive dissipated into the air and she leapt to her feet, her eyes full of fury, her hands full of vengeance. Finian staggered backward.

"Wait," he said. "What? Why?"

"Because," Brynn said, "I think she's even more pissed at you than I am."

Chapter Fifty

Gwenllian punched Finian across the jaw and his world crumbled. The marble of the pillars sloughed away, and all that remained were rotten, blackened posts, infested with maggots. The golden chandelier decayed into a cluster of bones, each with a thick candle on its end, stinking of tallow. The dais was a tumbled pile of lumber and stone, and the gilded thrones were overturned washtubs. The only remnants of the previous finery were the three pedestals, which glistened still, and the glowing columns of light which continued to hold their prisoners immobile and pristine.

Brynn looked into the goblet that she had taken from Finian, and saw that it was now nothing but a cracked wooden cup, filled with dust. She cast it away from her, and it clattered across the rotting planks of the floor.

"What happened?" she cried to Gwenllian, who stood panting nearby, her eyes locked on the cowering Finian.

"The Court of the Trickster King is nothing but lies," the woman responded icily. "Much like he himself. There was naught here but illusion and trickery."

Finian spat out a gob of blood, rubbing his jaw where the fist had landed.

"Your cowardly blow will not stop me, hero," he hissed at

Gwenllian. "The incandescent souls that make up my court will provide the death I promised you, and the other punishments I spoke of as well."

Brynn wondered if the exquisite courtiers had simply disappeared, but then she saw what they had become. Rotting, shambling mounds of flesh slumped against the walls, gnawed on the timbers, and pawed absently at the empty eye sockets and gangrenous limbs of their companions.

"It's time, my pretties," Finian called to them, "time to turn every living being in this room to mincemeat!"

He turned his attention back to Brynn.

"You should have chosen better," he sneered. "You could have had everything. You could have been a Queen! Now all you shall be is a bitter feast for my minions, who will strip the flesh from your frame and suck the marrow from your bones."

The desiccated heaps were shaped like humans or goblins or something in between, with eyes of black and nails of red. They hissed and howled and began a slouching march toward the center of the room, their arms thrashing in anger and hunger.

"I'd love to stay and chat, but I'd hate to interrupt my lovelies' meal," Finian jeered with a mirthless giggle. "Mother always told me it was rude."

He scurried away amongst the hissing horde and disappeared through a door that had lain hidden in the shadows of the thrones that were no more. The fiends that remained howled louder and quickened their pace. Gwenllian leapt into their midst, bashing one on the side of its head with her forearm as she dashed to the mound of rubble that had once been a grand dais. There, laying on one of the washtubs, was the dragon-pommeled sword. It had disappeared amongst the glittering glory of the thrones, but now, in the scabrous world that remained, it shone like the sun.

She lunged for the sword, and the instant her fingers touched it, she was already whirling around, the blade neatly lopping off the head of the nearest ghoul, which promptly collapsed to the ground in a pool of putrescent muck.

The rotting heaps of flesh were closing in on both of them now, half moving toward Gwenllian and half moving toward Brynn. The teenage girl attempted to land a kick on the flank of the nearest assailant, but the ghoul did not so much as flinch. Sensing further efforts would yield similar results, Brynn chose the better part of valor, and discreted herself between the flailing limbs of her attackers, until she found what she thought would be a safer position: near the badass woman with the magic sword.

Gwenllian swung again, slicing off another head, and with the return stroke, she sunk the blade deep into the festering chest cavity of another.

"What art thou doing here?" she asked Brynn between gritted teeth, as she continued to fend off the wall of foes before them.

"What are *you* doing here?" Brynn retorted, as the horde of ghouls pushed them back toward the mound of rubble.

"Forsooth, I did come here to rescue these purloined children."

"That's what *I'm* doing here."

Brynn kicked at a pair of outstretched, grasping arms rising from a recently bisected ghoul.

"I did surmise it wast thou who hadst stolen them," replied the golden-haired woman, casting a suspicious sidelong glance.

"No." Brynn shook her head. "My father did. It wasn't his fault, I promise. He was forced to. They threatened him. Threatened his family, us. I'm trying to make things right. That one there," she said, pointing to Makayla, "that's my best friend. I'm here to save her. If I can."

"Why didst thou free me then, coblyn? Thou couldst have taken the choice the Trickster King offered, saved thy friend and walked away from this Court unhurt and unbound. Down!"

"What?" Brynn cried, but did as she was told, diving to the ground.

Gwenllian's sword sliced a ghoul asunder, from neck to hip, and then circled around, beheading another that had lurked directly behind Brynn.

"Thou dost owe me no loyalty," the woman continued. "Thou dost surely realize that I have pledged to kill thee and all thy kith and kin."

"I couldn't leave you here with him," Brynn said, clambering back to her feet. "Even if you did try to kill me, he's clearly a monster. I saw in his eyes what he was going to do to you, and I wouldn't subject anyone to that. Besides, all those things he said about leaving me and my family alone...I don't think he would have. I didn't believe him."

"Then thou didst show fine judgment. Nothing that falls from the lips of Efnysien is the truth. He would not, I trow, have raised thee to be his Queen. He would have lowered thee to be his very slave."

The conversation was cut short as a trio of ghouls rushed Gwenllian at once, engulfing her with their thrashing limbs. Brynn screamed as the woman, who seemed to be her only hope of leaving here alive, disappeared from view. The rest of the rotting heaps followed their three companions, moving as a mass toward the fallen hero. Brynn was backing away, her eyes locked on the ball of writhing flesh, when she felt hands around her throat.

She spun around, as best she could with the knotted fingers of a ghoul forcing the air from her body. The fiend in front of her was tall, with stringy, grey hair and hollow eyes. The hands around her neck insisted upon her death, and the long nails that grew from them requested her blood, and Brynn feared that both would be granted shortly.

She saw stars in her eyes, and her lungs screamed for air. She felt fissures open in her neck as the nails tore at her, and hot blood began to seep into her shirt. The ghoul slammed her body against a rotting post. Her head snapped back against the wood, her vision went blurry, and she felt maggots streaming into her hair.

She tried to scream, but no sound would come. There was nothing else, nothing but the cold breath of the ghoul in front of her, and the hollow eyes, and the preternaturally strong hands crushing her life away. She only had seconds left, she was sure of it, but nothing she had and nothing she was would be able to break the ghoul's grasp, and she was sure of that as well. She offered up a silent apology to everyone she'd failed, to the children, to her parents, to

Makayla, even though she'd been almost certain from the start that failure was likely the end result of this journey.

She stared into the hollow eyes in front of her and saw the hunger and the hatred that resided there when suddenly there was something else in those hollow eyes, and that something was a shining silver sword. It came from behind, stabbing upward through the ghoul's head, and as it erupted from the fiend's eyes, the hands around her throat released, and Brynn fell to the floor, gasping and retching.

When she finally regained enough breath to raise her head, and when the stars in her vision had finally subsided, she looked up, and saw Gwenllian, panting and covered in viscous filth, but there was nothing else. Somehow, while Brynn was failing to fend off even one of the creatures, the golden-haired hero had slain the rest.

"You...you killed all of them?" Brynn panted.

"'Twas but a minor nuisance," Gwenllian said as she wiped the muck from her sword with her sleeve. "They were but wretched inklings of Efnysien's depraved imagination, with naught but hunger and obeisance inside their breasts, and nary a single thought inside their heads."

"You could have just let me die, you know," Brynn said hollowly, her stomach seizing and her body shaking. "Might have saved you some trouble in the long run. I mean, you've been putting a fair amount of effort into trying to kill me for a while now."

"That was not a fate that thou deservedst. Besides, I must needs pursue Efnysien. He shall not be allowed to escape unpunished for all that he hath wrought here. But I cannot now fulfill the rest of my obligation without aid. It shall be left to thee to rescue these children and return them to their rightful homes."

Brynn looked to the three suspended souls, aloft in their pillars of light.

"Okay," she nodded. "Well, thank you. You saved my life. I guess...I guess I owe you...or something."

"Perhaps thou dost, little coblyn," Gwellian acknowledged with a grim smile. "But at present, the debt of thy life is not the matter that driveth my hand. Naught is of import now but that these three children be freed, and that the Trickster King doth meet his justly deserved fate."

"Okay," Brynn sighed weakly, coming to the realization that she might survive after all, "yeah. Okay. So, what do I do?"

"All thou must needs do is lift each child from yon pillars of light. Once outside, the spell shall be dissolved, and they shall return to sentience and to motion. But heed this now and heed it well: once a child is freed from this spell, the child must be taken from Annwfyn and returned home by sunrise. The child must cross the threshold of their own abode before the break of day. If they do not, forsooth, all will be lost. The child shall be returned to the Land of Annwfyn, and to Efnysien's power, and shall be trapped here forever." Gwenllian looked deep into Brynn's eyes and spoke in a steady voice, her jaws clenched. "Canst thou do this?"

"I don't know," Brynn admitted, shaking her head, "I mean, before sunrise? I came down here in the middle of the night, and I've already been down here for a few hours at least. I'm not sure exactly how long. It's been hard to keep track. A lot has happened."

"Canst thou do this?" the woman repeated.

Brynn took a deep breath and looked at Makayla frozen in the pillar of light.

"Yeah. I mean, I've come this far, right? Yeah, I'll get them home."

"Very well. Thou shalt save the children," the woman said, an improbable breeze once again arising and wafting her braid gently in its wake, "and I shall handle Efnysien."

Brynn nodded.

"Dost thou have any weapons?" the woman asked.

Brynn reached into her back pocket and pulled out the grenade that somehow still resided there.

"Just this."

The woman looked at it curiously and held out her hand.

"May I?"

Brynn handed her the grenade, and Gwenllian peered closely at it.

"Dost thou know what this is?"

"A grenade, I guess," Brynn shrugged. "I've never seen a real one before, just pictures in books."

"This...this is no grenade. Where didst thou find this?"

"I met this old woman who gave it to me. She said it could help me. I've been too scared to use it."

"Ah, yes," the woman breathed with a wry chuckle. "Methinks the Cailleach Bheurach hath been meddling again." Gwenllian rolled her eyes, a surprisingly human gesture. "Such is her way. Thou shalt need to activate this before thou dost depart."

"What do I do?"

"All thou needst do is grasp this pin here," Gwenllian

said, indicating the metal ring at one end of the grenade, "and pull, and set it upon the ground. Then thou must needs run."

"What will happen?" Brynn asked as her brows furrowed.

"Things will explode," Gwenllian said, as serious as ever. "Many things."

"So, it's a grenade."

"Call it what thou wilt. Place it in this room, in the very center of Efnysien's Unseemly Court, before thy flight. His Kingdom shall not be left standing."

"Here?" Brynn asked, confused. "But where will you be?"

"Not here," the woman said, fierce determination written upon her face. "My path shall follow that of the Trickster King."

"But...if this thing will destroy the Hall, won't you be destroyed too?"

"Believe you me, little coblyn," Gwenllian said, with a genuine smile, "I have survived worse. But the time has come for the end of idle chatter." The woman twirled her dragon-pommeled sword in her hand and strode on nimble feet to the door that Finian had escaped through. "Remember: thou must return the children before break of day or all will be lost. Now go!"

And the woman was gone, leaving Brynn alone with the oozing husks of the slain ghouls, and the stolen children, frozen in their pools of light.

Chapter Fifty-One

Brynn stood in front of the pedestal, reached out, took her friend's hands, and pulled. Makayla's body toppled forward, as stiff as stone, but then crumpled into mobility as it fell across the edge of the glimmering pillar of light.

Makayla tried briefly to stand, but then shuddered and collapsed to the ground. She shook her head and tried to look around, but her brain didn't seem to be able to process the sights it was taking in. Then her eyes found Brynn's and seemed to focus on the one familiar thing in this grossly unfamiliar place.

"Brynn?" she croaked out, her voice barely a whisper.

"Yeah," Brynn said, "I'm here. I came for you."

Brynn helped her friend to her feet and then clasped her in her arms, pressing her cheek against Makayla's shoulder.

"I came for you. It's going to be okay. I'm going to get you out of here."

"I was having this nightmare," Makayla said, her thoughts and body slowly coming back to life. "I dreamed I got stolen from my house and trapped in some other world and there were some really strange people around and nothing made any sense and—"

Makayla stopped mid-sentence and peered into the dank

and water-logged room.

"What the hell is this?" she said. "No, seriously, Brynn. What...the hell...is this?" She squinted her eyes in disbelief. "I wasn't having a dream, was I?"

Brynn shook her head.

"Where am I?" Makayla demanded. "What are you doing here?"

"Where we are is kind of hard to explain," Brynn said gently, holding her friend out at arm's length now, and looking into her eyes, trying to project as much confidence as possible. "But yeah, you kind of got stolen. And I'm here to rescue you."

"What do you mean 'rescue me'? What is this place? Why are there gross corpses everywhere? What is going on?"

"That is a really big question," Brynn said, releasing Makayla's hands and returning to the task at hand. "I can tell you all about it once we're out of here, but we're on a pretty strict timeline, so we need to go."

Brynn moved to the base of the next pedestal, to rescue the child within, but Makayla's voice snapped behind her.

"Brynn! What...is...going...on?"

The face of the newly rescued girl was ashen, her breath was coming in sputtering gasps, and she was trembling.

"I'm sorry, Makayla," Brynn said, "I know. You just woke up in a supremely strange place. It's...it's probably a lot to take in, huh?"

Makayla gave an insistent and forceful nod, her lips pursed, her eyes wide.

"Okay," Brynn sighed, trying to give a reassuring smile, "here's the quick version. I'm a goblin. I kind of have superpowers. You were kidnapped. It was Finian's fault. You were replaced by a fake version of you who was terrible. We're in a building at the bottom of a lake on another world. I'll explain the rest later. Right now, we have to save the others, blow this place up, and escape."

"Others?" Makayla stammered, still unable to make sense of it all.

She looked over, saw the other two children floating in the pillars of light, and staggered back.

"Holy crap! Who are they? Did they get...stolen...too?"

"Yeah," Brynn nodded, "they're the...remember when you told me about the kid who stole the beer truck, and then there was that baby who pulled a knife on her mother the year before? This is them. Only these are the real ones. The kids who went nuts were...well, they weren't really kids. They weren't even people."

"This is really messing with my sense of reality, B." Makayla stared at the frozen children, trying to take deep breaths but not succeeding greatly, then snapped her head around. "Wait! Go back. You just said you're a goblin. What does that even mean? Like, pointy-eared Halloween dudes?"

"I don't even know how to explain that, and we really have to go," Brynn said, at a loss, but then had an idea. "Wait a second. Maybe this will answer a bunch of your questions at once."

Brynn slowed her breath, closed her eyes, found the gnarled ancientness within and pulled it forth. She felt her body change, felt the tail, the ears, the heightened senses. She opened her eyes and saw Makayla staring at her with dropped jaw. Brynn gave a gentle wave, then pulled within herself and transformed back.

"Ta da," Brynn said softly, shaking her hands with fingers spread wide.

"Okay," Makayla said in a resigned tone, "so...so, yeah. Reality is really not what I thought it was, huh?"

Brynn shook her head.

"I think I might freak out, B."

Makayla was close to tears, Brynn knew, although her friend rarely liked to show emotion. She was holding herself tightly, her lips quivered, and tears welled up in her eyes.

"I really think I might need to freak out now," Makayla reiterated.

Brynn went to her, stood in front of her and took her hands.

"I know you're scared," she said to Makayla. "I know you don't understand any of this. I don't really, either. But here's the important thing: I have to get you and these kids back home. And we have to do it right now. Any of you who aren't back home by sunrise will get sent back here, and it'll be for forever, and I know this all sounds crazy, but I came a long way to find you...a really...long...way, and I've been trying to hold it together, but...I had to do it all by myself, and it's been really hard." Brynn shook her head, her eyes skyward. "I need help. I need help from *you*. So I know it's asking a lot, but I really need you to hold it together right now so we can save these kids, and so I can save you. You can freak out later. We can freak out later together. Like, for a whole weekend maybe. 'Cause I've seen some crazy-ass stuff the last couple of weeks, and I could really use someone to talk about it with. But my best friend's been missing. And I've been alone."

Brynn wiped Makayla's tears with her thumb, trying to muster up as much of a smile as she could, and Makayla hugged her then, as fiercely as she'd ever been hugged.

"I'm back," Makayla said. "You found me. You did. And you're right. You're absolutely right. I don't know what's going on, but you obviously do. So I'm with you. I'll freak out later. Let's do this. Call the shot."

Brynn smiled again, a real one this time.

"I missed you, Makayla."

"Well, I was apparently being kept in some mystically-induced nightmare dream state or something, so I didn't really know what the hell was going on. But yeah, I missed you too, B."

Somehow, in the middle of this festering court full of corpses, there was still a laugh or two within Brynn, and she let one forth, still in disbelief that she'd found her friend in spite of everything.

"Come on," Makayla said, "you said we were in a hurry! Call the shot. We should go, right? Save these kids?"

"Yeah. Let's save the kids."

Brynn walked to the second pedestal, reached into the glimmering pool, grabbed the sandy-haired five-year-old around the waist and lifted him out. As soon as his body crossed the edge of the light, he looked around for only a second before he started screaming. He thrashed his body and squirmed out of Brynn's arms, and sat splay-legged on the floor in his rocket ship pajamas, hollering at anything and everything around him.

"Hi," Brynn said in a gentle voice, giving a gentle wave. "Hi."

The boy quieted down, looked at her suspiciously for a full three seconds, and then started screaming again.

"Hey," she said over the surprisingly piercing din that his five-year-old lungs produced, "this is not what you expected to see when you woke up, huh?"

He shook his head emphatically, but the screams did not subside.

"How about this?" she said to him, forcing a cheerful smile onto her face. "What's your name?"

The scream wavered.

"There you go. What's your name?"

"M...M...Max," he stammered, allowing the scream to dissipate, at least for the moment.

"Hi, Max, I'm Brynn. I know this is a scary place, and you don't know what's going on. But we're going to get you out of here, okay? We're going to take you home. I just need you...I just need you to take some deep breaths and try to keep calm if you can. Okay? Can you do that?"

The boy nodded and struggled to draw deep breaths into his lungs.

"Great. We'll get you home as soon as we can. But you're going to see some weird stuff on the way."

His hand reached up and tugged on her pant leg.

"Am I...am I in a video game?" he asked in a tone that Brynn decided to interpret as hopeful.

She nodded at him with wide eyes, trying to come up with an appropriate response.

"Yep," she said after a long pause, the best solution that presented itself to her befuddled brain, and this seemed to send him into a state of curious contemplation.

"Really?" Makayla hissed to her, as Brynn moved to the third pillar.

"If it'll keep him calm while we get him out of here, I'll say whatever he needs to hear."

Brynn reached into the glimmering light and pulled forth the infant, in her diaper and her butterfly t-shirt. The baby began moving, as the boy had, as soon as she crossed the edge of the light. Brynn was just beginning to admire the cute little barrettes in her hair and was just beginning to comment on how calm the child was when she threw up all over Brynn's shirt and then began bawling at an even higher volume than the boy had.

Brynn tried to console the baby, and to wipe the spit-up off herself, and to figure out what to do next, but couldn't seem to do any of them. She adjusted her hold on the baby, but nothing she did seemed to help at all. The baby just felt like a kicking, screaming, lumpy octopus.

"Give her here," Makayla finally said. "Haven't you ever held a baby before? You look like you're holding a dinner tray."

Makayla took the baby, laid the infant facedown over her forearm, and then held her to her chest. Within moments, the child had calmed, and the piercing cries had been replaced by curious coos.

"Wow," Brynn said, "how did you do that?"

"I've had lots of practice. Three younger brothers, remember?" Makayla took a peek underneath the diaper. "She's clean, anyway. Let's try to get her home before that changes."

"Agreed."

"Time to go?" Makayla asked.

"Time to go."

Brynn turned to the boy who still sat cross-legged on the floor, watching everything with alternating suspicion and curiosity.

"Hey, Max, we've got to go. Can I pick you up?"

He nodded, so Brynn picked the boy up around the waist, his head and arms flopping over her shoulder, and the four of them left the Unseemly Court behind, throwing open the ramshackle wooden doors and running into the Swallowed Hall.

The last time Brynn had seen the Hall, she had been amazed by its elegance and radiant enormity. But now that the illusion was torn away, it was just a vast, water-logged warehouse, full of moldering crates and grimy heaps of scrap.

She led them to the tall set of doors she had entered through and set Max down in front of them.

"There's one thing I have to do before we can go," she said to Makayla.

"What's that?"

Brynn pulled the grenade from her pocket.

"This."

Makayla gave her a baffled look.

"Why do you have a grenade?" she asked suspiciously.

"It's part of that long story I'm going to tell you another time. And apparently, it's not a grenade."

She ran back down the Hall, pulled the pin from the grenade, and threw it into the shattered Court. It clattered against the floor and lay still. Brynn heard no ticking. It emitted no glow. There was nothing to indicate it was working at all, but she didn't want to take any chances. She sprinted back to the entranceway and threw open the thick, wooden doors.

The wall of water sat in front of them, as if they sat behind glass, an aquarium attraction for the denizens of this strange world.

"What's that?" Makayla asked her.

"Water," Brynn answered.

"Why isn't it coming in here?"

"Honestly, I have no idea."

"Okay," Makayla nodded, her knuckles white as she held the baby firmly against her, "chalk it up to just another thing I have no damn chance of understanding."

"Makayla!" Brynn scolded.

"What?"

"Language," she hissed, pointing surreptitiously at Max.

"Oh, right." Makayla shrugged. This was clearly not high on her list of concerns at present. "So, where do we go from here?"

"Well, we're in another world, under a lake, stuck in a rotting hall that I think is going to explode at any moment. There's nowhere to go but up."

Chapter Fifty-Two

"Up?" Makayla asked.

"Yep," Brynn answered.

"Up through that water there?" Makayla asked, hopeful that she had misheard.

"Yep," Brynn reiterated. "We're actually not that far underwater, but we're going to have to swim." She turned to the young boy, who was staring goggle-eyed at the illogical wall of water before them. "Can you hold your breath, Max?"

"Yeah," he said in breathless wonder, "one time, I held my breath for a whole hour."

"He probably means a whole minute," Makayla whispered to Brynn.

"That should be enough. What about the baby?"

"I saw my mom take my brother to swim lessons when he was tiny," Makayla said. "They dunked those babies underwater. Scared the bejeezus out of them, but they were fine. I'll hold her close, keep her mouth against my shirt, try to see she doesn't gulp in a big mouthful."

"You sure you can keep her safe?"

"Pretty sure," Makayla answered with a shrug and a squint.

"I guess that'll have to do. Okay, Max, I'm going to hold

you, and we're going to swim up to the top of this lake, okay?"

"Okay," the boy agreed obligingly.

"What happens when we get to the top?" Makayla asked.

"I don't know," Brynn answered hesitantly. "There was a boat that brought me here, but it might be gone. We might have to just swim to shore with the kids."

"What do we do after we get to the shore?"

"I don't know. We'll be at the bottom of a pit."

"A pit?"

"Yeah. Big, round crater. Huge, jagged cliffs all around."

"Can we climb out?"

"Doubt it."

"This is not inspiring a lot of confidence," Makayla said, pursing her lips and holding the baby close.

"I'm giving you all I got," Brynn responded. "One step at a time."

"Let's do it, then."

Brynn picked the boy up and held him against her shoulder again.

"Ready, Max?"

He nodded.

"Okay, big, deep breath in one...two...three!"

She took a lungful of air, and when she saw that he had too, she jumped across the threshold, into the lake. As soon as she did, she felt her body start to rise, buoyed by the air within her. She kicked her legs to help it along and held tight to the boy. Only seconds later, she felt her head break through the surface of the water, and she took a deep, gasping breath. She nudged Max, whose eyes were still squinted shut, and then he did as well, grinning with pride at his successful accomplishment.

She treaded water, as best she could while holding the boy, looked around, and was surprised to see the flat-bottomed boat, only feet away. She flipped onto her back, holding Max on her chest, and kicked to the wooden craft, which held its position steadily, despite the waves in the water caused by their arrival.

"Grab the edge!" she sputtered to Max.

He did, and Brynn did as well, just as Makayla appeared from below. She lifted the baby above the water, and it immediately began to squawl, even louder than before.

"Guess she's okay," Brynn gasped, still out of breath. "Good job."

Makayla did not respond, but with a few kicks and strokes, she had joined Brynn and Max at the boat.

"Yeah, this one's a trooper, I think," Makayla panted.

The baby continued to wail. Brynn didn't know what else to do for her, though, except to keep moving.

"Hold on," she said to Max and Makayla, and then attempted to pull herself up over the low rail at the rear of the boat.

Brynn was worried she would flip the boat over, but it barely budged as she hauled herself onto the deck. She reached down and pulled Max in, then lifted the baby out of Makayla's arms, who pulled herself in as soon as the rest were clear. They lay there, all four of them, dripping and gasping, in the middle of the lake, under the sunless sky. Makayla pulled the baby back against her, and the anguished cries soon subsided.

"So there's a boat," Makayla said between gasps.

"Yeah, it's the same one that brought me here. I don't know where it came from." Brynn gave a deep sigh, relieved that she'd managed to lead them out of the Hall, out from under the lake, and that, so far, they were all still alive and relatively uninjured. "We should keep moving." She looked toward the prow of the boat. "I need to get back to shore," she called out vaguely, unsure if anything would happen.

But, as before, the boat began to move smoothly and swiftly through the water, toward the beach.

"So there's a magic boat," Makayla said.

Brynn just shrugged. At that moment, an enormous plume of water erupted behind them, accompanied by a massive crack, as if of thunder. The water from the explosion rained down upon them, soaking them once again.

"What the hell was that?" Makayla shouted. "Was that from that grenade you had?"

"I don't know!" Brynn answered. "Maybe."

She looked behind them. Where the plume had arisen, a swirling eddy had formed, which swelled as she watched. Within moments, a churning whirlpool was sucking the surrounding water down into it, growing larger by the second.

"We need this boat to go faster, B," Makayla called. "We need it to go faster now!"

"Yeah," Brynn agreed, "yeah, we do. Boat? If you can hear me, please go faster!"

Thankfully, the boat obliged. The phantom craft sped through the waves, just outrunning the outer edges of the maelstrom, which continued to devour the water behind. Brynn watched in horror as the swirling chasm grew monstrously large, seeking to overtake them, but the boat kept them barely out of its reach. Each second was an agony of panic, but bare moments after the explosion, the whirlpool had somehow devoured every drop of water in the lake and then swirled away to nothingness. Their boat settled down onto the lakebed, now nothing more than a massive plain of murky pearls.

"Where'd the lake go?" Makayla asked her, but Brynn could only shake her head in confusion. "For that matter, where'd that huge building go? Shouldn't that still be down there? Or, I don't know, at least the remains of it or something?"

Brynn looked and saw that her friend was correct. There was nothing in the center of the lake, no rubble, no timbers, nothing that would indicate the Swallowed Hall had ever stood there at all.

"I don't know," Brynn said. "Yet another of the millions of things I apparently don't know about this place."

Brynn climbed out of the boat, since it was obvious the beached craft would carry them no further, and pulled Max out as well, who promptly collapsed against her shoulder again. Makayla clambered out with the baby, and all four of them stood there, staring at the remains of the lake that was no more.

"I hope she got out," Brynn said, although it was mostly to herself.

"Who?" Makayla asked.

"Someone who helped me. The woman who helped me save you." She saw that Makayla was squinting at her in confusion. "It doesn't matter. I just hope she got out."

Makayla nodded.

"What now?" she said.

"We should keep moving."

Brynn and Makayla, carrying the other two with them, trudged across the pebbled lakebed, back toward the cliffs that ringed the deep pit. As they drew closer to the beach, Brynn saw a greenish figure standing there, and as they drew closer still, she realized that she recognized the figure. He gave a tentative wave and began running toward them, and they met in the middle of the beach of cloudy pearls.

"Chwilen!" Brynn said, surprised to see him. "What are you doing here? I thought you were being punished."

"I was," he said, slouching with gaze downward, as usual. "I got away. Gwallt had to make a stop, and the snake got away from him. So I escaped."

"Won't you be punished even more?"

"Probably," he grunted. "But I thought you'd need help if you made it back out of there. I'm...I'm glad you did."

"You're right," Brynn said, agog at the arrival of this unexpected assistance, "we do need help. We need to get out of here. I can fly myself out of here—"

"You can fly?" Makayla nearly screamed.

"Later," Brynn assured her before turning back to the other goblin, "but I can't take the other three with me. And we need to get out of here pronto."

"Out of the pit," Chwilen asked, "or out of Annwfyn?"

"All of it."

"Oh."

"Yeah. We need to get home, and we need to get there soon."

"I think I can help," Chwilen said with a mischievous smile, flicking his eyes upward to meet hers for the briefest of moments.

He took a deep breath and squinted his eyes shut. His body shimmered in the breeze, and where the slender goblin had stood, there now sat an immense, shiny, black beetle.

"Are you serious?" Makayla asked. "What is going on with this place?"

But before Brynn could answer, Max shouted, "I love bugs!"

Makayla and Brynn both looked at him.

"I do!" he shouted. "Especially giant ones!"

There didn't seem to be any way to respond to this, so they turned their attention back to the massive insect, which lifted the covering plates off its back, revealing wide, iridescent wings beneath. The wings extended and fluttered noisily.

"Hop on!" the beetle cried. "Let's get you all out of here!"

"We get to ride a bug?" Max whispered reverentially. "This is the best video game ever."

Brynn sat Max on the bug's neck and climbed on behind him. Makayla straddled the neck behind her, and then the insect set its wings into ferocious, buzzing motion, and rose into the air.

Brynn looked down, saw the dry lakebed where the children had so recently been imprisoned, and then she and her friends left what remained of the Swallowed Hall behind, and flew away into the Land of Annwfyn, riding on the back of a giant beetle.

Chapter Fifty-Three

"Where are we going?" Brynn shouted to Chwilen, struggling to be heard over the sound of his wings.

"You said you need to get out," he said. "I'm going to get you out."

"But how?" she asked. "Are we going back to the mountain? Back through the kitchen? To the maze?"

"Nope. You said you need to get home, and you need to get there fast. I know what we need to do, trust me. We're going to the Pipeline."

Brynn didn't know what this meant, but Chwilen seemed confident, and it was difficult to talk over the noise of his wings and the rushing of the air, so she settled back and enjoyed the ride. Max was rapt with wonderment as they flew, and Makayla's comforting arms and the white noise of the beetle's wings somehow lulled the baby to sleep.

They flew deeper into the forest, over magnificent spires of trees with deeply grooved bark and crisp, green leaves tinged with blue. They flew for miles and miles, the panorama of trees broken occasionally by a river or a rocky clearing, but still the forest continued on.

Brynn had never seen so many trees in her life, and was just beginning to wonder if there was any end to the forest when, ahead of them, a swarm of birds broke through the treetops to swirl and cavort in the warm air above. As they drew closer, Brynn saw that they weren't birds at all, but instead were tiny figures, as big as her hand, human in appearance, with olive skin and dark hair. Shimmering, translucent, golden wings grew from their backs, and the tiny beings darted about through the air, chirping and hooting and hollering at each other in a language that Brynn did not know.

The flock of tiny creatures laughed and waved as the beetle flew on. Max waved back, but Brynn only stared in curious fascination as they passed, and wondered what else lay hidden beneath the canopy of leaves.

Soon thereafter, Chwilen's pace began to slow, and he began to circle, drifting slowly downward. Below them was a clearing, the largest they'd seen so far. The ground here was little but crumbling dirt, broken through by some hearty scrub, but nothing larger. As they approached the center of the circle, the land grew darker and darker, until Brynn saw that all under them now was scorched earth, charred and desolate, as if some massive explosion had cauterized the land here, ages ago. At the center of the clearing, the scorched earth gave way to nothingness, a jagged hole ripped from the ground, and the giant beetle carried them directly toward this fissure.

They saw no other signs of life as they descended into the deep shaft. They traveled past layers of loam, and sediment, and dark, broken stone, until they came to the bottom of the well, passing into a massive cavern below the surface of the forest.

The chamber was vast, hundreds of yards wide, and just as deep, and just as tall. Glittering stalactites and stalagmites littered the ceiling and floor, and veins of gleaming ore could be seen streaking the cavern's walls.

In the very center was a gigantic metal sphere, the surface a patchwork of metal plates, none of the same size, of a wide variety of hues. Protruding from the sphere were innumerable metal pipes, of all shapes and sizes, affixed to the exterior of the globe with thick, dark rivets. The pipes jutted out in every direction, but all of them extended from the sphere to the walls and floor and ceiling of the cavern, disappearing into the rock. Some traveled a straight path. Some took twists and turns along the way. Some intersected with other pipes, joining together to form larger conduits. Some split from one into many, branching and branching again on their circuitous journey to the outer walls.

"Hey, Brynn?" Makayla shouted over the buzz of the wings, now carrying them slowly through the vasty air of the cavern.

"Yeah?"

"Remember when we took that field trip to the aquarium last year?"

"Yeah?"

"Does that thing kind of look like a big old sea urchin to you?"

"Yeah. It kind of does. What is that?" she asked Chwilen.

"That's the Pipeline," he responded cheerily.

"What does it do?"

"It takes you home."

As they drew nearer to the sphere, they saw spidery

ladders, far below, climbing from the jagged floor of the cavern, teetering upward until they connected with dark doorways on the surface of the metallic globe. Tiny figures were ascending and descending along them, making their way into the huge globe, or finding their way back out again, but whether they were actually tiny figures, as she had seen in the forest, or simply seemed tiny due to their distance, Brynn couldn't be entirely sure. Her sense of perspective seemed to be slipping away the longer she remained in this land.

Near the top of the globe, a few round openings now were visible in the otherwise unbroken surface. Chwilen flew slowly around, peering briefly into each, until he seemed to find the one he was looking for. He drew his wings in closer and took them through the hole, which was barely large enough for his beetle's body and wings to pass through. Inside, they found a dim room of metal, with curved walls and a burnished floor. The giant beetle lit down, fluttered his wings closed, and the passengers clambered off, whereupon Chwilen immediately resumed his goblin form.

He held a finger to his lips and then tiptoed over to the single door on the wall. He opened it, peered quickly outside, then closed and locked it.

"Okay. We're safe for the moment," Chwilen said quietly.

"Man, I really don't think I'm ever going to get used to that changing shape thing," Makayla muttered.

"What do we do now?" Brynn asked the goblin.

"We'll have to sneak into one of the Egress Chambers. There's no one in the hall right now, which is lucky, so if we go invisible and move as quietly as we can, we should be able to find an empty one without anyone figuring out we're here."

"Invisible?" Makayla squawked loudly.

"Shh!" Brynn and Chwilen hissed in unison.

"We got to ride a bug, and now we get to be invisible?" Max asked in an awestruck whisper, his five-year-old brain barely able to contain his delight. "This is seriously the best game I've ever seen."

"Okay," Chwilen said to Brynn, "you said your invisibility had developed, right?"

"Well, yeah."

"Great. How many others do you think you can take with you?"

"With me?"

"Yeah, how many besides yourself can you make invisible?"

"Um, just me, I think."

"Oh," Chwilen frowned with furrowed brow. "You can't do that yet?"

Brynn shook her head.

"Don't worry, I'm sure you'll figure it out," Chwilen said hesitantly, trying to give a comforting smile. "So, I guess I'll get everyone else then, and you'll just handle yourself?"

"I can do that."

"Great. We should go. No telling when someone else could fly in here."

Chwilen held out his hands. Max took one, and Makayla, still holding the sleeping baby, took the other. The goblin squinted his eyes shut, and Brynn saw everyone else in the room flicker out of visibility. She found the hollowness within herself, and then she was gone as well. Although she couldn't see him, Chwilen made a distinct 'shh' noise, then flipped the lock and pulled the door open.

Brynn followed the sound of softly padding feet down the hall, around a corner, and past several closed doors. The hall was metal, like everything else here, all patchwork plates and dull rivets and scuffed sheen. At the end of the hall, a door stood open, and Brynn followed the sound of the feet inside. The door eased shut, the lock slid closed, and then Chwilen and the others flickered back to visibility, followed quickly by Brynn.

"That was quicker than I expected," Chwilen muttered. "The Pipeline seems pretty empty today. Wonder what's going on."

Brynn looked around the room they had found their way into. Near them stood a thick, wooden table, with a massive leather-bound book atop it, next to a long counter covered by rows of metal levers with leather handles. The rest of the room was filled, floor to ceiling, with doors and ladders. The doors were on the walls and on the floor. Some were free-standing in the middle of the room. Some of the ladders led up, ascending into the ceiling, and some led down, descending into the floor. A few leaned against the wall, leading apparently nowhere.

"Where...where do all of these go to?" Brynn asked in wonderment.

"Everywhere," Chwilen answered absently, as he heaved open the cover of the leather-bound volume on the table.

The book was as tall as she was, Brynn suspected, and it was several feet thick. Chwilen lifted a hefty chunk of pages, as thick as his waist, and with a grunt, pushed them over onto the cover. He began scanning the interior of the book, which was packed, margin to margin, with writing so tiny that Brynn could barely make it out.

"Where do you need to go?" Chwilen asked.

"Jeffersonville, Indiana," Brynn answered.

Chwilen flipped through a few pages.

"United States?" he asked.

"Yes," she answered.

He flipped through a few more pages.

"Earth?" he asked.

"Yes," she answered.

Makayla gave a nervous chuckle. Max gave a sigh of delight.

"Okay." Chwilen sang softly to himself as he flipped through page after page, almost faster than Brynn could see. "J...J...J...J...here we go. Jeffersonville. Indiana, you said?"

"Yeah," Brynn agreed.

"Okay."

He checked a minute line of text in the book, no bigger than his thumbnail, then moved to the long array of levers which lined the counter next to it. He adjusted the position of a few dozen of them, checking the book between each. After several minutes, he seemed to feel he had finished his task, and after double-checking his work once more, he nodded approvingly.

"There. That should be it." He turned to the rest of the group. "Ready to go home?"

"Yeah," Brynn said, "I am. We are."

Chwilen smiled.

"This way, then. It looks like we'll be using Ladder G-14."

He led them across the room, around doors that led nowhere, and holes in the ground, and ladders that must have been built for giants, and trapdoors that could only have been used by mice. Near the far side of the room stood a simple, wooden ladder, leading up to the ceiling and beyond. Bolted to the floor in front of it was a scuffed metal plate, which read, 'G-14'.

"Here you are," he said to them. "Right up there. You'll be home in no time."

"Really?" Brynn asked. "That's it?"

"That's it," he said.

"It was a lot harder to get in," Brynn said, mostly to herself, staring up the ladder into the darkness beyond.

"That's often the way with Annwfyn," Chwilen answered softly. Now that he'd delivered them to their exit, his task completed, he'd resumed his pensive ways, and was staring at the floor, unable to meet her gaze.

"We should go," Makayla said.

"Yeah," Brynn agreed, "we should. You go first with the baby. Max, you follow Makayla, and I'll bring up the rear."

"Sounds good," Makayla said. She gave Chwilen a punch on the arm, which made him smile. "Thanks...I'm sorry, but I'm not even going to try to say your name."

"It's okay," he said.

She held the baby against her and began to climb, moving slowly but careful with her one available arm. Max followed right behind her.

"Thanks for all your help, Mister Giant Flying Bug!" he cried, as he began to climb. "You're the most amazing thing

I've ever seen! I'm going to draw so many pictures of you when I get home!"

"I'm sure his parents will love that," Makayla's voice came floating back down from above, as the three of them disappeared into the darkness.

"You made quite an impression on him," Brynn said to Chwilen, but he only shrugged. "I should go."

He only nodded.

"Thank you, Chwilen. You really...you really saved us. I don't know how I could ever thank you enough. You didn't have to help me get away from the kitchen. You didn't have to help me out with Gwallt. You didn't have to come back for me. You didn't have to do any of that, but you did."

He stared at the ground.

"Aw, shucks," he said, "it was nothing."

"It wasn't and you know it."

In an impetuous rush of gratitude, she leaned over and kissed him on the cheek. His eyes went wide, he turned completely red, and with a barely audible 'pop,' he promptly disappeared. Brynn smiled.

"See you around, Chwilen," she said as she set her feet to the ladder.

"See you around, Branwen," his voice replied.

She climbed then, foot over foot, hand over hand, upward into the darkness, and out of the Land of Annwfyn.

Chapter Fifty-Four

The light had disappeared long ago, but the rungs of the ladder continued. Brynn's muscles were complaining, and she was wondering if they needed to stop and rest when she heard Makayla's voice.

"I think I'm at the top."

"Yeah?"

"Yeah. I can see light, but there's...something's in the way. I can't move it."

Brynn furrowed her brow in the darkness.

"Let me see if I can come up," she called into the gloom.

She climbed up the ladder, which luckily was wide enough to accommodate her as she passed the others, until she found her way to the top. A few holes of dim, blue light did indeed pierce the darkness here, but Makayla was right. If it was a door, it wasn't one she could open.

Brynn felt around the barrier, trying to locate a handle or a hinge or a lock, but she found nothing. She pushed against it, as hard as she could, but it did not move.

"Anything?" Makayla asked.

"Nope," Brynn answered. She thought for a moment. "Let me try something."

She closed her eyes, and concentrated, and sank down

within herself to find the goblin within her. She let it forth and opened her eyes, felt the heightened senses and the heightened strength that the change brought. She looked at the faint traces of light, and felt all around the barrier once more, but discovered nothing new. She braced herself with her legs against the ladder and pressed both hands against the unmoving obstacle. She pushed with all her newfound goblin might. The barrier moved, ever so slightly, with a faint scraping sound.

"It moved," she gasped.

"Really?" Makayla asked from the darkness.

"Yeah," she said. "Let me try again."

She took a deep breath, steeled herself, then pushed again as hard as she could, letting forth a wheezing grunt. The barrier moved upward an inch, another inch, and more, and then Brynn slid what she now realized was a manhole cover aside, onto the street above. She climbed up onto the asphalt and stood blinking and panting in the sterile glow of the streetlights.

Seconds later, she saw Makayla's head bob up, and held her hands out, offering to take the baby, but Makayla shook her head.

"I'll hold on to her. She's still asleep, and you're...you're kind of creepy looking right now."

Brynn looked down and saw the tail between her legs. She grimaced.

"Sorry," she said, before shifting herself back to her human form.

"No worries," Makayla said, "it's not like it's the weirdest thing I've seen in the last couple hours."

Makayla climbed nimbly out, followed quickly by Max, and then the four of them stood on the streets of Jeffersonville, in front of the appliance store, back in the real world, the Land of Annwfyn already feeling as if it had been a distant dream. The city was cold and dark around them, and there was no sign of the sun in the sky, only the full moon casting its icy glow on the empty street.

"We're back," Makayla said.

"Yeah," Brynn answered.

"Right in front of the weird, empty appliance store."

"It's actually not as empty as we thought."

"Yeah?"

"Yeah. I'll tell you about it later. Does your phone still work?"

With her free hand, Makayla pulled her phone from her pocket, pressed the button on the side, and the screen sprang to life.

"Yeah. It's been to another dimension and inside an exploding lake, but I guess it's still working."

"What time is it?"

"Almost six."

"We've got about an hour before the sun's up, right?"

Makayla moved her thumb quickly over the screen on her phone.

"Looks like sunrise is...7:09 a.m. today."

"An hour. To get all three of you back home."

"We better hurry."

Brynn hunkered down to look at the boy who now stood yawning in the quiet night.

"Hey, Max," she asked, "do you know where you live?"

"Yeah," he answered, "Hayworth Street. Right by the park."

"We're going to take you home now, okay?"

"Yeah," he said, "that sounds good. I'm sleepy."

Brynn smiled, and the four of them walked through the night. The streets were familiar, after all the hours she'd just spent in the unknown, although her feet were tired and her spirit was weary. They walked silently, each of them thinking of what they had seen and done since they'd left the Swallowed Hall.

Fifteen minutes later, they were walking across the park, next to the exceptionally mundane swings and slides, and then they stood on the sidewalk on Hayworth Street.

"Which one's your house, Max?"

"That one, right there," he said, pointing to a tall, brown house with a peaked roof and a swing on the porch.

"Great. Let's get you home."

Brynn started to lead him to the house, but Makayla grabbed her elbow.

"Wait a second," she whispered, "what are you going to do? Walk up and say 'here's your son'? They'll think we abducted him. We'd be in jail for the rest of our lives."

Brynn frowned.

"That's probably true. So, what do we do?"

"He's supposed to be missing, right? Ran off into the woods after stealing the truck?"

"Yeah."

"I think he just rings the bell," Makayla said.

Brynn nodded. They walked together to the tall hedge that surrounded the house's lawn, and then she let go of his hand.

"Time for you to go home now, Max, okay?"

"Okay," he said gamely.

"Your parents are really worried about you. They think you've been gone for a long time."

"It doesn't feel like I've been gone for a long time."

"I know," she nodded. "It's...it's hard to explain. But they are going to be so happy to see you. You might...you might not want to say too much to them about what you've seen for the last couple of hours. I'm not sure they'd understand."

"Okay. See you later!" he said to Brynn.

"Bye, Max," she replied, and he walked up to the door and rang the bell.

A haggard-looking couple in bathrobes opened the door a few seconds later, and stood there in stunned silence before they scooped the boy up in their arms, tears already streaming down their faces.

"Oh my god," the mother choked out, "is it you? Is it really you?"

The father said nothing, but only clutched his wife and son to him, unable to speak.

"Mom, Dad, I was in a video game!" Max shouted, unable to contain his glee. "I rode on a giant bug, and I turned invisible, and this lake totally exploded! It was awesome!"

Brynn and Makayla turned away, not wanting to intrude on this private scene between Max and his parents, and as they departed, they nearly tripped over Max, hiding in the bushes. Or, Brynn realized, not Max, but his duplicate, supposedly missing for weeks now.

"What are you doing?" he squeaked.

"We just sent the real Max back to his parents," she said, cocking her head at the impostor, "back where he belongs."

"What?" he squealed furiously. "You've ruined everything! I was just about to murder his parents! It was going to be so, so, so funny!"

"No murdering," Brynn insisted calmly.

"Oh, come on!" he pouted.

"No murdering!" she repeated.

"How did you get him back?"

"We saved him. That's all that matters. The question is: what do we do with you?"

"Well, what about—," he began slowly, his eyes shifting nervously, before attempting to dart away from them. Brynn was able to grab him around the waist before he'd gone two steps, however, and she clutched the fetch against her as he struggled and squirmed.

"We can't let him get away," she grunted. "There's no telling what he'd do. He's evil."

"No, I'm not!" the fake Max howled.

"Yes, you are," Brynn reprimanded him. "You're an evil stick. I know you think you're not, but you are."

The fetch did not respond, just kicked and thrashed against her, and it was all Brynn could do to hold on to him. She cast her eyes around, looking for anything that could help her, anything at all, and saw some landscaping materials in the next yard over. There were rakes, and bags of mulch, and rolls of sod, and there to the side was a pile of empty burlap bags.

She lurched over to the pile, the fetch arching and pushing against her the whole way, and somehow was able to retrieve a bag and stuff him inside. Once it was done, she held the top of the bag firmly closed, and the thing inside settled down somewhat, although she could still hear it muttering profanities to itself, in English and otherwise. Makayla had been staring wide-eyed through this whole ordeal, the baby still asleep in her arms.

"Brynn," she said finally, "you can't just stuff a kid into a sack."

"It's not really a kid," Brynn assured her. "It's just a fetch."

"A what?"

"A fetch. A stick of wood. Not real."

"It looks real," Makayla said nervously. "It sounds real. *He* sounds real."

"I know. It's not a he, though. It's an it. I promise. You're just going to have to trust me on this one."

Brynn tied the top of the bag closed with a length of rope she found in the dirt and threw the mumbling sack onto her shoulder.

"We're running out of time," she said determinedly. "Let's get that baby back where she belongs."

"Okay," Makayla agreed hesitantly, a concerned look plastered to her face, "I looked up the address on my phone from the old news reports. It's not too far from here."

"Then let's go."

The information was correct, and it took them only a few minutes to reach the house. They decided it would be best if Makayla took the real baby to the front door while Brynn retrieved the fake baby. She dumped the mumbling sack in the corner of the lawn and hoped no one would notice it.

The world was starting to wake up now. A few cars were driving by. Lights were flickering on in nearby houses. A paperboy rode by on his bicycle. Brynn gave Makayla a nod and allowed herself to flicker out of visibility. She quickly located the baby's room, which was on the ground floor, fortunately, and as soon as she heard Makayla ring the doorbell, she eased the window open and climbed inside.

"Hi, ma'am, I'm sorry to bother you," she heard Makayla say faintly, from the other side of the house, "but is this your baby? She was outside on the lawn."

Brynn tiptoed over to the crib where she expected to find a sleeping baby, but instead found a glaring, squinty-eyed bundle of fury. The fetch was standing up inside the crib, peering around, fists raised in a defensive position as it occasionally threw a ferocious jab at the empty air.

"I know you're there!" the baby hissed. "I can smell you! Coward! Skulking in the shadows! Show yourself and challenge me!"

"No chance," Brynn whispered as she scooped the fetch up under her arm, where it thrashed even harder than the other had. She held tight as she climbed back out the window, and added the fake baby to the sack with the fake Max. She tied the top up again with the rope, and the two fetches began loudly complaining and attempting to one-up each other with violent vulgarities.

"What do we do with them now?" Makayla asked, once she'd rejoined Brynn on the sidewalk outside the house.

"They come with us," Brynn said, hoisting the sack back up onto her shoulder.

Makayla nodded, clearly still uneasy about the whole

situation.

"So far, so good, I guess, huh?" she asked.

"I suppose so," Brynn shrugged. "It's just you now. What time is it?"

"Six thirty."

"How far is your house from here?"

"A couple miles."

"Then we'd better run."

Chapter Fifty-Five

They took turns carrying the sack full of squirming, fake children as they ran. It slowed them down significantly, but even so, fifteen minutes later, they were approaching the dusty red ranch house that Makayla lived in with her parents and three brothers. They tiptoed up to the wooden fence that surrounded the property. Nothing seemed unusual. The house was quiet. No lights were on, and they could see no movement within.

"Will there be anyone home?" Brynn asked.

"There shouldn't be. My parents take the kids to school, and they're usually gone by now. The only one home at this time of the morning would be...well, me."

"So...fake Makayla may be inside."

"Only one way to find out."

"I guess so," Brynn agreed. "Do you want me to check?"

"No. If there's something in there that took over my life, I want to look it in the eye."

"Yeah. I think that's what I'd want too."

Brynn dumped the bag of fetches over the fence while her best friend walked to the porch. Two things happened then: Makayla knocked on the door, and Makayla answered it. The eyes of the fake Makayla went wide, and it tried to run back inside the house, but the real Makayla was too quick.

"Oh no, you don't!" she insisted, grabbing the fetch by the shirt. "You're coming with me."

The fetch twisted and struggled, tried to scratch, tried to kick, but Makayla, her anger at the impostor giving her all the strength she needed, had no problem hauling the fetch out the door, off the porch, and into the backyard. Brynn followed, dragging the burlap sack behind her, howled profanities leaking from it all the while.

There was a shed in the backyard, with clouded glass and peeling paint, and it was to this that Makayla hauled the fetch. She pulled open the door and threw her doppelganger inside.

"What are you doing here?" the fetch hissed, as it licked the blood from a scrape on its hand.

"I'm here to take my life back," Makayla declared coldly.

"I'm not sure I want to let you do that."

"I don't really care what you want."

"Oh, come now," the fetch pouted, "I'm having ever so much fun being you. Such a nice little life. Such a quaint little city to outrage. Finian and I are finding so many extraordinarily scandalous things to do. We have an explosion planned for next week, you know."

"Finian's dead," Brynn interjected.

"I sincerely doubt that," the fetch scoffed.

"I would never be with someone like that," Makayla scowled, shaking her head. "I would never give someone like that the time of day."

"Oh, honey," the fetch said with an acrid smile, "someday you really must let yourself live a little. Boys are ever so much fun if you only let them be."

"No," Makayla responded, her lips trembling, "you don't get to decide that for me. My life. Not yours."

"Guess what, sweet meat?" the fetch purred, sensing a weakness. "Even if you do get rid of me, even if you do reclaim your life, it will never be the same. Everyone at school will only know you as Finian's lapdog, now and forever. I mean, if you're there, and Finian's not, what do you think the teachers will do to you? After all the fire alarms that were pulled, after all the classrooms that were trashed, after all the crap they had to endure? You think they're just going to let you waltz back into class, and sit down, and get on with your oh-so-predictable A-minus ways? I don't think so. Someone will have to take the fall for everything that happened, and when the superintendent comes sniffing around, tallying up the damage estimates, filing all the incident reports, those teachers are going to have a choice. Give a name or lose their job. And guess whose name is going to be on the tips of their tongues?"

The fetch licked her lips lasciviously.

"Or even better: what will the students do to you? Finian tormented them, and I was right there, standing by his side, smiling and laughing, while he demanded their obedience, and they gave it, without question. They missed two months of school while they were groveling at his feet. Homework was abandoned. Tests were flunked. Games were forfeited. Some of those kids just screwed over any chance they had of getting the internship they wanted, getting into the college they've been dreaming about. Most of them will spend their summer break back in school to make up the work they missed. Hell, a bunch of them will probably have to repeat the entire year. And whose fault will it be? Finian's? Oh no. His name would never even cross their minds. You see, if they look around, and want someone to blame for the utter mess that each and every one of their lives has suddenly become, guess who they're going to see? Oh, yes, you! The one who was at his side every second of every day!" The fetch was practically screaming now. "So, why not just run away? Let me have this life. All you will find in it now is shame and isolation. Go find some dingy little life somewhere else, where no one knows what a disgrace you are!"

Spittle was flying from the fake Makayla's mouth. Her eyes were wide, a cruel grimace played on her lips, and her chest was heaving with the thrill of causing her doppelganger pain.

"I'm done talking," Makayla said quietly. "This isn't a person, right, B?"

"Not a person. Not a person at all."

"Okay, then," Makayla nodded.

She cast her eyes about the interior of the shed until they landed on a scratched, wooden baseball bat leaning against the wall. She picked it up in her hands, tested the weight, then pulled it back and swung it at the fetch's head with every ounce of strength inside her. The fake Makayla screamed, and then exploded in a cloud of sawdust as the bat connected, her clothes crumpling to the knotted pine boards on the floor of the shed.

"Well, that was easier than I expected," Makayla said in quiet surprise, as the sawdust fell gently down upon them like snow.

"Yeah," Brynn agreed. "Strong work, though, Makayla."

Her friend gave a tiny, satisfied smile.

"Thanks, B."

The profanities from the burlap sack behind them were approaching a fever pitch, as the inhabitants divined what had just happened to their counterpart. The two girls stared perplexedly at the thrashing bag.

"What do we do with them now?" Makayla asked.

"Is that a stove?" Brynn asked, peering into the gloom.

"Yeah, my dad does his work out here a lot in the winter. It's to keep the place warm."

"I think they go in there," Brynn said.

"But—"

"Butt!" the fetches howled together from inside the bag, collapsing into fiendish laughter.

"Brynn!" Makayla continued, ignoring them. "You can't be serious."

"We have to. We can't let them get away. They'll go back to those kids' houses, and there's...honestly, there's no telling what they'd do. Someone would get hurt. Someone would get killed."

"Hopefully you!" the fetches shrieked in unison from within the burlap sack.

"You see?" Brynn said, as the fetches giggled maniacally at their little joke.

"It's just...a lot has happened these past few hours," Makayla said limply, her jaw clenched, her hands shaking. "When I woke up in that hall, and you said you were rescuing me, I didn't think it was going to end with us stuffing a couple kids into a wood-burning stove."

"That's not how I pictured my morning going either," Brynn said with a sad smile.

Makayla stared at the sack, with its streams of profanity pouring forth.

"If the cops come, will you take the rap?" she asked.

"Absolutely."

"Okay. In they go."

The two girls shoved the burlap sack into the pot-bellied stove, struggling to fit the entire mass inside, and then scooped up what they could of the remains of Makayla's doppelganger and poured it in after. They gave each other a nod, and then Brynn lit a match. As soon as she did, the fake Max began wailing uncontrollably, a horrible, glass-shattering yowl, and the baby began cursing, describing every horrible, violent thing he wanted to do to the two of them. The sounds continued as Brynn threw the match in, where it immediately caught on the fabric of the sack, and then all within was engulfed by flame.

There was a loud boom, the voices disappeared, and a strong rush of cold air erupted from the stove, chilling them to the bone, although the flames persisted, even brighter than before. Within moments, the entire contents had been reduced to ashes. Brynn poked at the remains with a hammer, but nothing moved.

"It's done," Brynn said, "they're gone."

"Are you sure?"

"Yeah, I'm sure." She smiled at her friend. "You have your life back."

"I don't know if I do, Brynn. I mean, you heard what she...what it said. About what happened at school. About what's *going* to happen at school. I mean, that's...I don't even want to think about it."

"Yeah." Brynn sighed. "I don't know, though. Maybe the fetch was just trying to get into your head."

"Do you think it was lying?" Makayla asked hopefully.

"Possibly. It was evil, after all."

"Super evil."

"Totally, utterly, jacked-up, super evil."

"If what it said was true, I don't know if I can go back to school, B. I don't know if I could stand that."

Brynn walked up and took Makayla's hand.

"You won't be alone," she said.

"You promise?"

"Yeah. I promise."

Makayla nodded, and Brynn could tell there were tears in her friend's eyes, but she pretended she didn't notice.

"Come on," she said, leading Makayla out of the shed. "We've got to get you into your house before sunrise. What time is it, anyway?"

"7:06."

"Look at that. Three minutes to spare."

Makayla gave a hint of a laugh then, and Brynn felt like everything might go back to normal after all.

"I'm glad you're back, Makayla."

"I'm glad I'm back, too."

"Before I knew what was going on, I was...the way you were acting was really messed up. It's just...I mean, now I know it wasn't really you, but I didn't know that then, and the you that wasn't you was with Finian all the time, and I...I was really worried that you liked him."

"No," Makayla said calmly, "no one like that. No one like that at all."

"Okay. Good."

"7:08. I should get inside. See you at school?"

"You know what? Maybe we should take the day off."

Makayla smiled.

"Yeah, maybe we should."

"See you tomorrow?"

"Yeah, see you tomorrow."

Makayla crossed the threshold into her home just as the first sliver of sunlight broke the horizon, and Brynn knew that it was done. She had succeeded. Somehow, despite everything, she had succeeded. The children were returned, the fetches were destroyed, and it was time to go home.

Chapter Fifty-Six

It was 7 a.m. in Jeffersonville, Indiana, and Brynn McAwber had returned victorious from the Land of Annwfyn. The sun was rising. The city was alive. Her quest was completed. And she was going home. She walked with her head held high down the city streets which now bustled with activity, people going about their daily business with nary an inkling of the evil that had lurked inside their city until just a few short moments ago.

Brynn smiled at every single person she passed. She'd been gone all night. She knew her parents would be worried about her. There would certainly be lengthy explanations. There would perhaps be punishments. But for now, she felt nothing but elation. The children were saved. Her father's sins were reversed. And she was going home.

She felt proud of herself in a way she didn't think she ever had before. She'd followed a tortuous trail of clues and enigmas. She'd followed their path and found her way into another world, and she'd found her way back out again. She'd returned the stolen children by the break of day. The fetches were gone. Finian, or whatever he was actually called, was gone. And she was going home.

She took her time, not wanting to rush back, not wanting

the feeling of accomplishment to end, but in what seemed like no time at all, she saw her street, and she saw her block, and she saw her house, and she felt the grass of her yard underneath her feet. She saw the familiar door, and the window she'd snuck out of, so many hours and also a lifetime ago, and she knew that the people who lived inside loved her, and she walked up onto the porch, and before she even put her hand to the doorknob, she knew that something was wrong.

The front door was slightly ajar, and as Brynn gave it a gentle push, it opened silently. She walked into her house, and there was a voice in her house that didn't belong there, and she knew that the voice belonged to Finian. She couldn't tell what he was saying, but the anger emanating from him seemed to shake the house in waves. Brynn hesitated, unsure what to do. Finian's voice rose in pitch as he spoke three sharp words which cut through her being with a blast of cold air, and then she heard her mother scream.

Brynn didn't hesitate any longer. She ran. She followed the sounds of screaming and she ran. She found her family in the basement, in the den. Her father and her brother were bound and kneeling, iron shackles cutting into their wrists and ankles. Her mother was prostrate on the ground. She was screaming, and she was bleeding. And in the middle of it all, as seemed to be his way, was Finian.

His clothes were bedraggled. His feet were bare. A long cut, bleeding freely, ran across his chest and down his arm. One of his legs looked as if it had been run through. Part of his hair had been scorched away, but his eyes remained dark and fiery. In the air next to him floated a glowing globe of light, and within the light rested a tiny, newborn baby girl, unmoving, in stasis, frozen at the moment she drew her first lungful of air.

Brynn stood in the doorway, unable to move, unable to think, barely able to breathe as she stared at the sight before her.

"Branwen," Finian said, his voice as sinuous as ever despite his wounded body, "my erstwhile paramour. My consort declined. My would-be Queen. You've joined us at the last."

"What have you done, Finian?" Brynn shouted, finding her voice.

"What I needed to!" he shouted back, sparks flying from the black holes of his eyes. "You should not have denied me. It was most unwise."

"Brynn!" her mother cried, before Finian could continue. "The baby...he took the baby from me." She was on the floor, blood pooling around her, unable to rise. "He took the baby. It wasn't time! He's going to take her away."

Brynn's mother tried to lunge for Finian, but in her weakened state, she was barely able to cling to his boot. He thrust her aside with a contemptuous kick, and she lay on the floor, sobbing silently. The other two knelt, quiet and unmoving. They seemed unable to speak, perhaps due to some trickery on Finian's part, but Brynn saw tears streaming down her father's face.

"If I cannot have you," Finian declared loudly, "then I will have your sister! I will take her to Annwfyn, and when she is grown, she will rule at my side. As you should have done!"

"Rule what?" Brynn cried. "Your Hall is nothing but dust

now, at the bottom of a non-existent lake. I saw the explosion. I created the explosion! Your Kingdom is gone!"

"A minor setback," he insisted, teeth clenched. "I will rebuild."

He lifted his hand, and the orb of energy surrounding the baby swelled and crackled. Brynn strode toward him, her anger stealing away any thoughts of self-preservation.

"You're not going to make her a Queen," she scoffed, poking her finger into Finian's chest. "Gwenllian told me. She told me you all you do is lie. You have nothing now! No Hall, no Kingdom, no Queen, nothing. You're nothing but the King of Lies!"

"You cannot speak to me like this!" he shouted, and seemed to grow in stature as mystical energy flowed from him, uncontrolled, tendrils of it shooting across the room and scorching the walls. The sparks from his eyes flowed so steadily now that they were beams of fire, licking the ceiling. His body was a torrent of static and flame, and the hot blood that flowed from his wounds burned intricate runes upon the floor.

"I am Efnysien fab Euroswydd, the King of the Swallowed Hall that was, and that shall be once more! I crush the skulls of heroes in my hands. I drink the blood of the horses that ride amongst the stars. I burn Princes upon their thrones, and I walk in the land of the dead. I was cooked alive in a cauldron with seven of my brothers, and I dined upon the corpses that lay within until I was free once more. If I say, little girl, that I am taking your sister to be my Queen, I assure you that there is nothing...NOTHING...that a wretch of a goblin such as yourself can do about it! Now kneel, like your father and your brother, or I shall gut you like a fish."

Brynn felt her body moving, uncontrollably, her legs bending and her head bowing. She fought against it, but Finian was too strong. Her body collapsed to the ground, and she knelt in front of him, her head nearly upon the floor.

"Now say goodbye to your sister," he taunted. "She will live forever with me, in the glory of my Kingdom, but you shall never see her again. Say goodbye!"

Brynn struggled against the force holding her to the ground, and was able to raise her head just enough to look him in the eye.

"No," she said.

"Are you serious with this?" Finian shouted. "Fine! It doesn't matter. I'm going. Say goodbye or not, it doesn't matter one damned iota to me, you little slug."

"You're not going to take my sister," Brynn said, marshalling every ounce of strength she had to resist the force of his will and hold his gaze with hers.

"You are a goblin!" Finian spat. "An insignificant mote in the fabric of the universe. Your people scour the dishes and scrub the floors and that's all they have ever done and that's all they will ever do! I am using the barest fraction of my will against you right now and your entire family cannot move a single muscle." He leaned in close to Brynn, until the infinite darkness of his eyes was only inches from hers. "I am taking your sister, and I am taking her now. Do you really think there's anything you can do about it?"

"No," Brynn said, as she collapsed to the floor, her strength at an end, "but I think *she* can."

Gwenllian's sword leapt toward Finian's neck as her body

leapt through the doorway. Finian twisted his body to avoid the blow, and as his concentration shifted, Brynn found she could move once more. She staggered to her feet and pulled the glowing orb out of Finian's reach. The baby within was motionless still, suspended in time, and she thrust the sphere into her mother's arms, who clutched it against her chest as she shakily dragged herself to the edge of the room, away from the combatants.

"How did you get here?" Finian hissed as he and Gwenllian circled slowly, eying each other warily. "You were in the Hall when it was destroyed. I bound you myself, with the oldest charms I know. The explosion sucked the very lake out of existence."

"Believe me, thou foul dross," the golden-haired woman responded calmly, "it shall take more than the unmaking of a mangy grotto to thwart my vengeance. Yield now, and thy end shall be swift and painless."

"Please," Finian snorted, "I beat you senseless once, and I shall beat you senseless again."

"My senses do remain mine own. I do have sense enough within my soul, and strength enough within my body to drain the life from thine."

Her voice sounded confident, but Brynn wasn't sure if she was telling the truth. Her mouth was taut, as if she was in pain, and her eyes lacked their usual sparkle. Her long, golden braid was barely a braid any longer and hung limply behind her as she moved.

Her opponent, on the other hand, seemed larger and stronger than ever. For it was unmistakable now, Finian's body was growing. He was hunched over, his back pressing against the ceiling, his arms as thick as tree trunks, as he and Gwenllian circled and countered each other.

The hero feinted and lunged. She leaped and cut. She made no headway. Each thrust, each riposte, each attack was pushed away by Finian with a swat of his hand, his skin never coming into contact with the sword, the force of his will simply throwing the blade aside.

Finian bore no weapon but himself. He batted at Gwenllian with hands as large as her head, hands which buzzed and arced, tendrils of blue flame jumping from one to the other, his fingers sparking with unremitting power. Fire dripped from his lips, and his eyes shone so bright now that it hurt to gaze upon his face.

Gwenllian thrust and cut, again and again, but her blade never landed. After each attack, she danced and twirled out of his reach, but Brynn wasn't sure how much longer the clearly-exhausted woman could keep this up.

Finian howled and spat fire, a column of flame that shot across the room, scorching the air, with a razor-sharp screech that made Brynn's hair stand on end as she held her hands to her ears. Gwenllian held her sword in front of her, with both hands, and whether it was the magic in the blade or something within the hero herself, the flame was repulsed, bouncing off the sword's edge and dissipating harmlessly into the air around her.

They held this position, the monstrous Finian erupting flame, and the golden-haired woman halting it with virtue and steel, for what seemed like hours, but which may have been only seconds. And when the flame subsided, when the Trickster King had no fire left within him to vent into the world, Gwenllian parried the last of it aside with her blade, a grim smile upon her face. It was a brief gesture of victory, but it was one which left her chest exposed for the barest fraction of a second. And this, apparently, was all the opening that Finian needed.

He thrust his hand forward, his thumb and two monstrous fingers outstretched, and Brynn could feel the force of his treacherous desire seeping forth. The sword slipped from Gwenllian's fingers, and she clutched her hands against her chest.

"That feeling?" Finian growled, his voice cavernous and deep. "That is my fingers around your heart, hero. My hand is wrapped around your heart. And guess what happens next? I squeeze, and you die, and that's all."

Gwenllian was gasping, choking. Her eyes were bulging. Her body sagged as Finian's mystical fingers held her upright, supported from within by the unseen hand which threatened to crush the very life from her.

"Unless...what was it you said?" Finian taunted grimly. "Yield? Yes, that was it. Yield and I shall make your end...slightly less painful. Hmm? What say you?" He waited for a response, but Gwenllian was lost in a world of darkness and agony. "Hero! What say you?"

Gwenllian's breath was coming in shallow gasps, her mouth a grimace of disgrace and torment.

"Never...monster," she managed to whisper. "I will...never yield...to one such as you."

Finian gave a low growl in his throat, his eyes venting forth his rage. His fingers moved the barest fraction of an inch, but their effect on Gwenllian was instantaneous. She screamed in heart-rending agony, fresh streams of tears pouring down her face.

Brynn didn't know what to do, but she did it anyway. Her mother was sobbing and bleeding in the corner. Her father and brother were bound and silent. There was no one else. No one but her.

She looked at Finian and began to run. After two steps, she disappeared. After four steps, she assumed her goblin form, feeling her strength grow and her senses heighten. After six steps, she leaped into the air, straight at Finian's head. She grabbed onto him as tightly as she could, her fingertips digging into his scorched skull. Finian twisted, confused at this unseen assault, but his hand remained firmly gripped around Gwenllian's heart. She screamed again.

Brynn felt within her, found the hollowness and released it, and her body flickered back to visibility, plastered across Finian's eyes. He staggered, his vision reduced to nothing, and he howled fire. His eyes were burning her, Brynn realized. Finian's eyes were burning her. She could feel the flesh smoldering. She could see the smoke rising from her own skin. She gritted her teeth against the pain and held on.

The Trickster King reached his massive hands up to claw Brynn away, to pull her body away from his eyes, and in that moment, she saw Gwenllian fall to the ground, his hold on the hero released as his concentration faltered. Finian saw this as well and screamed, his rage thwarted, his quarry for the moment set free, and then he screamed again when Gwenllian's blade pierced his heart. He collapsed to his knees, and Brynn, still clasped against his face, felt her body jolt, felt as if she were caught in a web between time and space.

Brynn heard Gwenllian's voice, faintly, as if the sound had to pierce an unseen veil to reach her ears.

"Release him, coblyn. 'Tis time to end this," the voice cried, as if it were made of vengeance and ice.

Brynn gathered all of the strength that lived within her and pushed, pushed away from Finian, pushed away from the well-spring of nothingness that clung to his soul. She sprang free, just in time to see Gwenllian's sword swing in a mighty arc, singing through the air thick with power and fire. She saw it slice through the air. She saw it slice clean through Finian's neck. His head tottered there for a moment, unconnected, then it and his body began to topple forward, but before they hit the ground, every piece of him dissolved into dust, which blew away on a cold wind arisen out of nowhere.

Gwenllian fell to the ground, spent, over the charred floor where her foe had so recently stood. Brynn staggered to her feet and looked for her family. Whatever power had taken away their movement and their speech had dissipated with the death of Finian, and she saw them begin to move again, heard their familiar voices that had been so missed in the lifetime that was also only a few hours that she'd been away.

She saw her mother, sitting in the far corner, cradling the baby in her arms. And then she saw Conn, freed from his shackles, shuddering on the couch, tears flowing. And then she saw her father, freed from his own shackles, and he was running to her, enfolding her in his arms.

"You're back. We were so worried. Are you okay?" he asked her, his voice choked and hoarse.

Brynn felt the sharp ache in her battered muscles, felt the heat of the burns where Finian's eyes had seared her flesh.

"I'll be fine. I think."

Her father held her out at arm's length, saw her singed and tattered clothes, saw the charred skin beneath.

"You'll heal. A human wouldn't. You will. But you might have scars."

"It was worth it," she replied softly, casting her eyes over the others in the room.

He held her face between his hands.

"You were amazing. Where did you learn to do that?"

"A lot has happened since the last time I saw you, Papa."

Her mother's voice cut through whatever question her father was about to ask next.

"Gaf," she said.

"Oh, honey," he replied, holding his daughter once more in his arms, "Brynn's back. She's safe. Did you see what she did?"

"Gaf," her mother said again, more insistently, "look at me."

Her father turned to the corner, to where his wife lay huddled, a look of anguish upon her face.

"Gaf," she said, the calm in her voice breaking, "something's wrong. Something's wrong with the baby."

The whole room came to a sudden, complete standstill. Every being in the room, every mote of dust, didn't dare to move, didn't dare to breathe. When Finian had fallen, when he had been slain by the golden-haired hero, the globe of frozen time around the baby had dissipated, and now she lay in her mother's arms. But Brynn could see immediately that something was indeed wrong. The baby was still and silent. Her skin was ashen and she made no sound.

"Gaf...I'm not sure she's breathing. She's not moving." Panic crept into her mother's voice. "It's too early! I was only seven months! It's too early. Oh, Gaf. Something's wrong with the baby."

"No, no, no, no," her father said, as he rushed to his wife's side. He tenderly felt along the baby's chest, put his ear against her heart. "She needs help. We have to get her to the hospital."

"It'll be too late," her mother said, shaking her head, in barely a whisper. "It'll be too late."

"There has to be something we can do."

"She's so small. It wasn't her time. He took her from me too early. Much too early."

"We can fix this. Let's go. We'll get in the car, we can be at the hospital in fifteen minutes."

"Gaf," her mother said, finally looking at her husband, despair in her eyes and hopelessness in her throat, "then we needed to leave fifteen minutes ago."

Brynn stood frozen, watching the scene play out before her as if it was in a movie, as if she stood outside it, as if she knew that someone would come along and save them all. Except what she actually knew, deep in her heart, was that no one was coming, that her mother was right, that it was too late. Her parents huddled there, clutching the tiny, premature baby on their laps, and all she wanted to do was help them, but she knew there was nothing she could do, no matter how much she wished otherwise.

"There has to be something…" her father insisted, although his voice belied him.

"Oh, Gaf, our baby. Why did he do this? Why did he take our baby from us?"

"There has to be something…" her father repeated, but his voice trailed away to nothing.

There was a long moment of silence, as the truth of the incomprehensible cruelty settled across the room. And as the veil of grief lay upon her, a thought came to Brynn, and it was into this deathly silence that she spoke these words:

"What about a wish?"

"What?" her mother said, lost in her sorrow, lost in the meaninglessness of a life clipped before it even began.

"A wish. You told me once that we could grant wishes. What about a wish?"

"Oh, honey," were the only words her father said and then he began to sob, unable to speak.

"If only we could," her mother told her. "I promise you, there is nothing else I would wish for. But wishes can only be granted to humans. Never to ourselves, never to the Tylwyth Teg."

"But…but there has to be a way…" Brynn pleaded.

"I know, sweetie, I know," her mother said, with all the comfort left to her. "If I had the power within me to change this, I would give all that I am to do so. But wishes are the…they are the greatest secret that lies within a goblin. They're very difficult to access. Very fickle, bound by ancient laws, and impossible to unlock without the necessary conditions fulfilled. It's not something we can do. Not now. Not for this. I'm sorry, sweetie. I'm so sorry."

"Why not?" Brynn was seething now. What good was being a goblin, she thought, of having to go through everything she'd gone through if it was all just going to fall apart in the end? "You said we could grant wishes. I wish for my sister to be saved!"

Brynn's father was with her again, holding her tight, even as she pounded her arms against him, struggling to be free.

"That's not how it works," he said, his strong arms encasing her until finally she slumped against him, the haze of acceptance beginning to cloud her thoughts. "Wishes can only be granted if a goblin owes a human a great debt. And the wish can only be the human's fondest desire. Nothing else."

"So, let's do it. Let's make that happen!"

"Brynn, sweetie," her mother said, "I know you're upset, we all are, but we…we can't dwell on impossibilities. You have to…*we* are going to have to accept this. Look at me." Brynn looked at her mother, saw the unknowable sorrow that already dwelt within her eyes. "I need you. I need my whole family now. Please."

Brynn nodded and closed her eyes, sunk her head deep against her father's chest, and let him hold her, let him accept the grief that flowed from her like rain. There were no sounds, nothing but tears, for many minutes, or hours, or days, or perhaps only a moment, before a voice spoke, a voice that sounded like nothing less than velvet wrapped in steel.

"I'm human."

They were the first words that Gwenllian had spoken since she slew the Trickster King.

"What?" Brynn's father said, the first to recover from the unexpected intrusion.

"I am human," Gwenllian repeated. "Although I have lived countless years longer than most of my kind, I am most definitely human. And this girl doth owe me a boon."

The room settled into stunned silence.

"Me?" Brynn asked, awash in confusion.

"Brynn, is this true?" her father asked.

"It is," Gwenllian stated firmly, before Brynn could answer. "I did save her life in the Swallowed Hall. A ghoul had its hands upon the girl's throat and was about to crush the life from her."

"She...she did, yeah," Brynn agreed, "she saved me, but I...I don't know how to grant a wish. One of you has to do it. Mama, Papa, you can do it, right? We owe her a debt. Let's grant the wish!"

"No, Brynn," her mother said softly, "the debt is yours. If it can be done, it has to be you."

"I don't...no, I don't know how."

"It's within you," her mother continued, "it's the deepest secret within you. All you have to do is find it."

"No." Brynn was beginning to panic. "I can't. Please...Mama...Papa...what if I can't? What if the baby dies because of me?" She was sobbing now. Her legs fell out from under her, and she was on the floor. "What if she dies and it's my fault?"

"Girl, what is thy name?"

Gwenllian was in front of her then, kneeling on the floor

in front of her, her voice cutting through the pounding anguish that muffled Brynn's thoughts and threatened to engulf her. Her family was scattered at the edges of the room, her father, her brother, her mother with the baby caught somehow between life and death, all staring at her, face to face with a woman who had sworn to slay all their kind.

"What is thy name, little coblyn?" Gwenllian asked again, more gently than Brynn had ever heard her speak.

"It...it's Brynn. Or Branwen, I guess."

"Good. Very good. Branwen the coblyn, look at me." Brynn did, struggling to focus through the tears. "Thou sayest thou canst grant a wish, but only to one whom thou dost owe a boon?"

"Yeah. Yeah, I think so."

"Well, thou dost owe me a boon. I did save thee. Thou knowest this to be true?"

"I...I guess I do. Yes. Yes, you did. You saved my life."

"Aye. I did. Although at the time, I was not certain that I should."

"But even if I knew how to grant the wish, and I don't, I really don't, it...it has to be your fondest wish, your deepest desire. You heard them. That's the only thing it can be."

"I do know it. Look at me, Branwen. Look at me."

Brynn struggled again, against the fear, against the doubt, fought against the despair and the anguish that cut into her soul, and she looked into Gwenllian's eyes and saw nothing but hope.

"I will say this to thee," the golden-haired woman said, "and I know it to be true. I know it to be more true than anything I have ever known in the long centuries of my life.

My greatest wish, at this very moment, the only thing that I do desire, is for thy sister to live."

As soon as Gwenllian said the words, it was if Brynn was no longer in control of her own body. A pure, white light filled her being, from the very core of her where the hollowness dwelt, to the ancient, gnarled pit where the goblin slept, to the tips of the ivory wings that lay folded within her, yearning to be free. The pure, white light filled her and spilled out of her. Waves of charity and absolution sang from her pores, lifting her until she was suspended within it, her body caught between heaven and earth, floating on waves of righteousness, one with all that was good in the world. The white light poured forth, from her eyes, from her mouth, from her fingers, as she hung there in the air, and there was nothing she could do but let it.

And she thought on the words the woman had said, of her greatest wish, of her fondest desire, and as Brynn remembered the words, the white light grew and expanded, until there was nothing left but whiteness, nothing left but light, and the sound of it was the music of the heavens, so beautiful that Brynn wanted to lose herself in it forever, except she already was lost in it, was part of it, and it was part of her. And then just as suddenly as it had come, the light vanished, and she was on the ground, and the sound was gone as well, except there was a new sound now, and Brynn listened to the sound, and it was even more beautiful than the music she had heard, for it was the sound of her newborn sister's cries.

And as Brynn regained her senses, as her vision returned, as she came back to the world from wherever she had been, she looked to her mother, and her mother smiled at the mewling babe in her arms, now ruddy and squirming and crying at the top of her lungs. Her mother smiled, tears rolling down her cheeks, and she took the baby to breast, where the tiny child settled into the only place she wanted to be, as if she was never meant to be anywhere else, as if she had not been caught between life and death only seconds before, as if she knew that everything was going to be all right now, so she might as well have her first meal.

"She's okay," her mother said. "Gaf, she's okay. She's eating. She's warm and she's strong and she's eating."

Brynn's father went to his wife then, and slumped down the wall next to her, laying his head on her shoulder, greeting his newborn daughter for the first time.

"Hello, little one," he said. "I can't even tell you how glad I am to see you. You made it. You did. Look at you. Look at how strong you are." He looked to his other children then, standing nervously in the middle of the room. "Conn, Brynn, what are you doing over there?" And he smiled, and so did Conn, and then so did Brynn. "Come meet your sister."

And Conn and Brynn joined hands and walked across the scorched floor to meet their new sister, lying there in their mother's arms.

"Your sister is going to be fine," she said. "She's small. It wasn't her time, so she's still small. But she's strong, she's healthy now, and she is a good eater. Thanks to you, my brilliant, brave girl. You saved her. You did it, Brynn. You saved her."

Chapter Fifty-Seven

"So, where were you last night?" her father asked as they sat at lunch.

Brynn had already finished two grilled cheese sandwiches and was just tucking into her third. She sniffed lightly at the plate. The odor of the melted provolone was exhilarating to her heightened goblin senses, and her tail twitched in anticipation. Her father had insisted that both she and her mother spend the day in their goblin aspects. There was healing to be done, he said, wounds to be knit up, burns to mend, bruises to swell and fade, and these things would happen much faster if they left their human shapes behind for the time being.

Agreeing wearily, Brynn's mother had shimmered into her xana body, the constellations within her dark skin swirling with joy at the healthy, newborn girl in her arms, and had taken the baby to bed, where they slept still. Brynn did as her father suggested as well, and was amazed, as she had been when she had been wounded in the labyrinth, to see how fast this body healed. New skin was already growing over her burns, the charred skin sloughing off as it was replaced. As her father had suspected, there would be scars. But she would wear them proudly, she decided. They were the scars that saved her sister's life.

Her father was in his goblin form as well, for solidarity and comfort, he said. For Conn's part, an hour after the battle, it seemed as if he'd already bounced back, as if it was just another Monday, and an interdimensional demigod hadn't just trashed their basement. And now, he was sitting in his room, reading comics, as he often did. Conn was like that, Brynn knew, quiet but resilient.

As for Gwenllian, nobody had seen her leave, but after they'd huddled together to meet the new addition to their family, the golden-haired woman was gone. No trace was left of her, or of Finian either. Nothing remained of the conflict downstairs except for the scorched floor, and the wounds upon their bodies, and the gnawing hunger that Brynn felt in the pit of her stomach when she realized how long it had been since she'd eaten a meal.

"Where was I?" Brynn said introspectively. "Before I answer that, I have a question for *you*. Am I going to be in trouble?"

"Probably," her father replied, "but not today."

Brynn smiled, and then sighed, worried about what she needed to say next.

"I went to find Makayla, Papa. And the other children too. The ones who you...the children they made you steal. I went to find them...and I did it. I opened a door to the Land of Annwfyn. I found them, and I brought them back. They're home. They're safe."

Tears glistened in her father's eyes.

"You...you saved them?" he asked. "You saved them all? But how? That should not be possible. You should not have been able to find them, much less free them."

"Finian had them. He wanted to lure me there. That's why he had the children. And when I got there, he...he asked me to be his Queen, a Goblin Queen, and stay there forever."

"Tempted?"

"Not really, no. It was all lies. Gwenllian helped me see that. Everything he offered was a lie."

Her father shook his head, the tears that flowed down his cheeks collecting in his pointy beard before splashing onto the table.

"I'm so sorry, Brynn. If I hadn't...if I hadn't taken those children...if I had resisted, none of this would have happened. I put you all in danger. It nearly cost your sister her life. I'm so sorry. It's all my fault."

"None of it was your fault, Papa," Brynn said, putting her hands on his, and as she said it, she realized that she knew it to be true. "Finian did it. He told me. He was the one behind the threats. He was the one who made you steal those children."

"He called himself 'Finian'?"

"Yeah. A couple months ago, this creepy new kid showed up at my school. Turns out he wasn't really a kid. Not even human, I don't think. I got to the end of my journey, and there he was, with his stupid, smug, little smile, in the middle of Annwfn, at the bottom of a lake. I don't know why I didn't expect it. He was clearly in league with bigger powers than the PTA. So, yeah, he said his name was Finian. But that wasn't his real name, I guess."

"Efnysien fab Euroswydd," her father said knowingly, then shook his head and whistled.

"Yeah. He said he was a King, the King of the Swallowed Hall."

"He's not a King. He's just a douchebag."

"Papa!"

"What? It's true. That's what he is." Her father took another bite. "This one time, years and years and years ago, he destroyed an entire kingdom's mutton supply, all the flocks in the entire land, caused a massive famine, just because, for this one week, he thought exploding sheep were funny. Thousands of people died. He's a douchebag."

"And then he came here, came after my family. Nearly destroyed us."

"He didn't, though," her father said proudly. "You saw to that."

"Well...me and the golden-haired bringer of vengeance who's been following me for the last few months."

"The two of you, yes."

"I think she actually did most of it."

"Perhaps."

Brynn smiled.

"I guess she decided she didn't need to slay me after all."

They smiled together then and returned to their sandwiches, comforted and weary, each with their own thoughts.

"There's been something I've been trying to figure out," Brynn said, after several more delicious bites of melted cheese. "If Finian thinks we're so insignificant, and he was pretty clear that he thinks goblins are less than worthless...if that's how he feels, why did he offer me a crown? Why did he work so hard to bring me to him? Why me? Why would he want me to be a Queen? Why my sister?"

"I don't think there's any way we can know," her father said slowly, after giving it some thought. "His...his thought processes have always been notoriously inscrutable. There may be a reason. But if there was, it doesn't matter, because he's gone."

"Is he really dead?" Brynn asked.

"There's no way to be sure. It certainly seems that way...but I do know that he's survived worse. Promise me one thing?"

"What?"

"If you see him again, how about you come and tell me or your mother first before you head off into another dimension to try and take care of him. Deal?"

"Deal."

Her father took another bite and chewed thoughtfully.

"What did you think of Annwfyn?" he asked, his eyes sparkling.

"It seemed dangerous," she replied.

"It is, yes."

"But also beautiful."

"It is that as well." He stared at her as if he had never seen her before, as if she was somehow brand new to him after her journey. "I can't believe you were there, Brynn. I can't believe you rescued the children I stole. I can't believe you managed to do all of it without talking to us about any of it."

"The answers I was getting from you...from everyone...were not terribly helpful."

"That's probably true."

"What did you tell Conn?" she asked. "Did you tell him I

was gone? Does he know what we are?"

"He does now," her father said, nodding sadly. "It'd be hard for him not to, after what happened in the basement. But we told him everything when we figured out that you'd left, when we suspected where you were going. It wasn't fair to him. We should have told you both, ages ago. It wasn't fair."

"No more secrets, right?" Brynn said hesitantly. "If we're going to do this, if we're going to live in this world, try to live a life that goblins have never led, we have to do it together. And that means no more secrets."

"You're right." He brushed her hair away from her eyes. "I think you grew up while I wasn't watching. I think you grew up while I was asleep."

Brynn clasped his hands with hers.

"You can't steal children anymore," she said, "no matter what. No matter what they say, no matter what they threaten."

"But that's what we do," he shrugged. "We're goblins."

"You can't."

"They'll come," he said. "They'll find us. If they ask me to steal a child, and I don't, there's no telling what they could do. They'll take you away from us. All three of you."

"You can't break up other families to save your own," Brynn insisted. "It's not right."

"I would steal ten thousand children if it meant keeping you here with me. Ten million."

"No more. We can't do it anymore. I saw those families. Those families were broken. With their children back, their real children, I hope they can fix themselves. But I'm not sure."

"What would we do then? What would we tell them? If he comes back, if the good neighbor comes back and gives me an assignment, what would I tell him?"

"I don't know," Brynn said, "but whatever it is, I want us to do it together."

Chapter Fifty-Eight

"How is the baby?" Brynn asked when her mother came in to say goodnight.

"Strong. Sleeping. Your father is as well."

"You slept for a long time, Mama."

"I did," her mother agreed with a grin, "I needed it. The baby needed it too."

"I'm really happy that she's okay. I'm sorry that...I'm sorry he came here. I'm sorry he came after my family. I didn't think he would. I didn't know he could."

"It's not your fault, my brave girl."

"It feels like it is."

"I know. You've been through so much, and look at you. You came out the other end shining like a star."

Brynn's mother sat down on the bed and held out her arm. Brynn pressed herself in close and rested her head against her mother's shoulder, the galaxies in the dark skin awhirl beneath her cheek.

"The last two months were so hard," Brynn said. "I felt so alone. I was changing, and the world around me was changing, and my family was changing. It was like a wave swept through my life and took away everything I knew, or thought I knew, and then the wave went on by, but before I could even take a breath, another wave came through and swept another piece of me out to sea. Until I felt like I had nothing left. Not even you."

"Oh, my darling Brynn," her mother said, pressing her forehead to her daughter's hair, "nothing could sweep me away from you. Nothing in this world or any other. But I should have done a better job of saying so."

"I was so scared."

"Of course you were."

"I was so worried that I was a changeling. That someone had stolen me away and put me somewhere I didn't belong. I couldn't imagine anything worse." Brynn gave a weary sigh and smiled against her mother. "I'm glad I found out who I really am. Who we really are. I'm glad this is where I belong."

"Oh, my sweet daughter. You have been my Brynn, my Branwen, since the moment you were born. You have never been anything but my strong, brave, clever girl. You were never a changeling and you never will be. But...and here's the part of it you don't know yet...I was."

"Mama? What?" Brynn turned her head upward, looking at her mother in sleepy curiosity.

"I was a changeling child, Brynn. I was stolen away from my first family, my xana family. I never knew my parents, never knew who they were. I have no memories of them at all. I was sent into a human world that I had no understanding of, and I...I did some terrible things as a child. Things I can barely stand to think about now. Even so, when I left that family, they were devastated. Even after everything I'd done. I ran away from them, into the human world, and lived the life of mayhem and havoc that everything inside me told me I should be living."

She paused and looked out the window, toward the stars.

"And then one day, I stopped listening to that part of me, the part that wanted suffering and mischief, and I realized it was only a part of me if I let it be. And I didn't want it to be. After I came to my senses, I searched for my family for so long, my real family, not the humans I'd been left with, the family I left in shambles."

She looked back to Brynn and pulled her in close.

"I never found them. I'll never know if my parents wanted me to be a changeling, if they offered me up to be sent into the human world, or if I was spirited away from them in the night. I never found them, not for all the years I spent trying, but I did find your father. Somehow, at nearly the same moment, he'd come to the same realization I had, that he didn't want to live the life that goblins had always lived. He found his way out of Annwfyn, and he found his way to me, and I found my way to him. And when we found each other, we swore that we would see no more families torn apart. Especially ours. We swore that we would take no children from their homes. No goblins, no xanas, no humans."

"But then he did," Brynn said.

"He did. And it nearly broke him. You saw that. We lost our way. There were no good options, and he took the one that kept his own family together. But then, my miracle, you fixed it. You saved him. You saved us."

Tears glistening in her eyes, she held her daughter tight against her, and in the endless void of her skin, Brynn saw a shower of meteors cascading through the blackness, each as bright as a summer's day.

"You were never a changeling, Brynn. You are the daughter of a changeling. And your sister is too."

Brynn's eyes were closing as she nestled against her mother, listening to her tale. And she realized how long it had been since she'd slept. The Brynn who'd last awoken from this bed had never flown on wings of white, had never entered a burial mound, had never escaped from a maze of bone, had never entered the Swallowed Hall, and had never been to the Land of Annwfyn.

"I'm tired, Mama. I'm not sure I've ever been this tired."

"You deserve to be tired. After all you've been through, you deserve to sleep for as long as you need. No one will rouse you until you are rested. Sleep for a week, my child. You have traveled so far to come right back where you belong."

Brynn smiled.

"Shall I tuck you in?" her mother said.

"Yes, please."

And her mother pulled the blanket up to her chin, then placed her hand on Brynn's heart and looked into her eyes. And as Brynn faded off to sleep, her mother chanted these words:

> *Valor and Virtue encircle this heart,*
> *Sorrow and Solace, never apart,*
> *We need no gold,*
> *We need no luck,*
> *Naught but this child here, all else is dust.*

Epilogue

The strange little man came to the door again today. He stood there on the threshold, as he always did, with his rumpled little hat on his rumpled little head, with his wizened face and his beady eyes and his tweed vest buttoned tight over his fat little belly, and the scuffed leather briefcase held tightly in his hands.

Brynn's father ushered him in, and when the strange little man sat down in the kitchen, he saw the entire family in front of him: Brynn, Conn, and their mother with the sleeping baby in her arms.

"Gafr," the strange little man wheezed hesitantly.

"Ysbaddaden," Brynn's father replied calmly.

The little man cleared his throat.

"Why don't you let your family go have some time to themselves," he said, "while you and I have a little talk? There's some business we need to discuss."

He patted the side of his briefcase meaningfully, and gave a wink intended to be playful, but which came across as incontinent.

"Not this time. No more secrets, Ysbaddaden. Whatever you are planning to say, I would like you to say it to all of us."

"Very well," the little man said, with a sigh of resignation.

He retrieved a crisp manila envelope from the briefcase

and set it on the table. From within the envelope, he pulled a black-and-white picture of a tow-headed little boy, no more than three.

"They've sent word down. A relocation is needed. Right here in Jeffersonville again, as a matter of fact."

"And by relocation, you mean stealing. And placing a changeling in this family's home."

"Of course. I was opting for gentility in front of your little ones."

"They seem to be needing a lot of changelings here lately," Brynn's mother said.

The little man shrugged.

"I couldn't speak to their motives," he wheezed. "I'm but a simple factotum in their service, as you well know."

"Perhaps you could take care of the child yourself this time," Brynn's father offered helpfully.

The strange little man gave a curious laugh, which sounded something like a cough followed by a whistle.

"Now, you and I both know that's a kind of a nonsense thing to be saying," he said. "Only goblins do that kind of work. Always have. Always will."

Brynn's father looked to the rest of the family. Brynn nodded reassuringly at him, and her mother offered him the strength in her eyes.

"Not this time," he said.

"I'm sorry?" the little man said, genuine surprise in his voice.

"Not this time, Ysbaddaden. I will not...we will not...any of us...we will not be stealing children anymore. Never again."

"That's a mighty large statement to be making now, Gafr."

"I know."

"There may be consequences to that sort of statement."

"I know," Brynn's father said, his voice quavering.

"You remember...you swore off the changelings once before, tried to hide out in that ridiculous place...what was it called?"

"California."

"Yes. But you were found. As you knew you would be. And once the...situation was explained to you, you came back here, where you were supposed to be, and you did what you were asked. Remember?"

"I do. I remember," Brynn's father said, his voice steady now. "But no more. I'm done. We're done."

"You're sure about this?"

"We are," Brynn's mother said.

"Very well, then," the little man said, sliding the photograph and the manila envelope back into the briefcase. "If that's your decision, I don't think there are any more words to be said."

He stood up, and Brynn's father walked him to the door. The rest of the family followed behind. When the little man had crossed the threshold and stood outside of their house once more, he turned back to them.

"I'll have to tell the boss, you know."

"I assumed so," Brynn's father replied, his jaw clenched.

"I don't think she'll be happy."

"I can't imagine she will. But that's our decision. And whatever happens next," he said, as he put his arms around his daughters and his son and his wife, "we're going to face it together."

"Very well," the strange little man said, tipping his hat to them and preparing to depart, "then it's time for me to bid you farewell."

He paused, a twinkle in his eye and a finger to his lips.

"By the way," he said, "have you named that baby yet?"

"No," Brynn's father answered.

"You should probably be getting about that," the strange little man said, and then he was gone.

Brynn's father closed the door, and the night disappeared, and then it was just the five of them in their home, and no one else at all.

"Who's the 'boss' he was talking about?" Brynn asked. "Wasn't Finian the boss? Wasn't he the one telling everyone what to do?"

"Not in the grand scheme of things, no," her father answered. "He was pulling some strings. He didn't carve the puppets."

"But let's not worry about that now," her mother said. "We'll deal with that when the time comes."

"We said 'no' to him," her father said, holding his wife close, "we really did. Do you think we made the right decision?"

"I do."

"I mean, you remember what happened the last time a goblin said 'no' to him?"

"I do," she said, giving her husband a quick kiss, "but there are more important things to consider right now. He was right. We need to name the baby."

"What's her name going to be?" Brynn asked.

"We don't know," her father answered.

"So, wait, you had seven months to think about it, and you didn't come up with any ideas for names?"

"It's traditional," her father said. "Among our people, no names are considered until the baby is born. It's bad luck otherwise."

"Well, she's here now. What are you going to name her?" Brynn asked.

"I don't know," her mother said. "What do you think?"

"This is an important decision," her father added. "Names for our people carry significant weight. They are part of us from our birth until our death, and tell us much about our life to come."

Brynn smiled and looked thoughtfully to the ceiling.

"Okay," she said to her father, "so your name means goat and you can turn into a goat, and my name means white raven, and I can turn into a white raven, and Conn is a rabbit and Mama is a fox."

"Yes, she is," her father said, waggling his eyebrows.

"Stop it. Does that mean, for the baby, whatever her name is, someday she'll be able to turn into that?"

"Pretty much, yeah," her father answered.

"Does it have to be Welsh?" Brynn asked.

"I don't think so," he said. "That's just tradition."

Conn's eyes went wide, his hands trembled, and he nearly shot out of his seat.

"Let's name her 'Tyrannosaurus Rex'!" he shouted.

There was a moment of silence.

"That's actually not a bad idea—," Brynn's father began.

"Gaf!" her mother hissed.

"Well, no, Lou, think about it," her father continued, "a goblin who could turn into a dinosaur? It's never been done. It would be...it could be game-changing."

"We are not naming our beautiful, newborn daughter 'Tyrannosaurus Rex,'" her mother said firmly. "End of discussion."

Conn sat back down sulkily.

"I tried," Brynn's father whispered to him. "Well, what is it then?" he said to the rest of the family.

"You told me once," Brynn said to her mother, "that you gave me the name of a raven, and my brother the name of a hare, so that we could escape if we ever needed to."

"We did," she replied. "I hope that day never comes, but if it is necessary, your names will protect you."

"I've learned a lot about the world in the last couple months, and a lot of what I thought I knew turned out to be dramatically inaccurate. But I have learned that it can be dangerous to be a goblin. And I learned that you can run away from some dangers. But some you can't. Sometimes you have to stand in front of them and make a hard choice."

"So, what do you think?" her mother asked.

"I think...I think there might be a day when escaping isn't an option."

"It's true. There might be."

Brynn looked at her new baby sister and smiled.

"I think we should name her Hero."

Brynn saw tears in her mother's eyes.

"Gaf?" she said.

"I don't think I've ever heard a better idea," he said.

Just at that moment, the baby woke from her sleep and opened her eyes.

"Hi, Hero," Brynn said to her.

And the baby smiled, as if she recognized her name and knew it to be true, or perhaps it was just gas.

"Good morning, little Hero," her mother said, and the galaxies within her whirled and danced. "Welcome to the world. It's been waiting for someone just like you."

Acknowledgments

First and foremost, I want to thank my wife, Lisa, for supporting me, and my children, Augie and Nori, for inspiring me. Without them, this book would never have been written. I want to thank Reagan Rothe and everyone at Black Rose Writing for helping me fulfill a lifelong dream. I want to thank my friends Jamey Carter, Magi Loucks, Stacy Pershall, and Allison K. Williams (and her assistant, Kate), for invaluable assistance given along the way. I want to thank my father, for teaching me to work hard for what's important, and my mother, for teaching me to dream, and my brother, for teaching me the value of a road less traveled. And I want to thank two other excellent teachers: Jack Freimann, for teaching me that the best way to learn how to do something is simply by doing it, and my grandmother, Helen Reeder, for teaching me that you're never too old to learn something new.

About the Author

R. Chris Reeder grew up in the Pacific Northwest, attended college in Walla Walla, Washington, and has lived and worked across the country and around the world. He has had careers as a Shakespearean actor, an international courier, and a singing activist, but is now perfectly content in his current vocation of a stay-at-home father.

He currently resides in Madison, Wisconsin, with his wife, two children, and a cat named Monster Jack. This is his first novel.

www.rchrisreeder.com
www.facebook.com/rchrisreederauthor

Thank you so much for reading
one of our **Paranormal Fantasy** novels.
If you enjoyed our book, please check out our recommended
title for your next great read!

The Graveyard Girl and the Boneyard Boy by Martin
Matthews

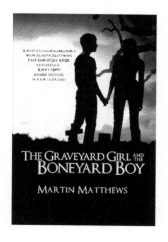

"... a compelling and eminently likable cast of characters."

–*Authors Reading*

CPSIA information can be obtained
at www.ICGtesting.com
Printed in the USA
BVHW081815031218
534638BV00006B/280/P